Thick as Blood

Wynter Cannatelli

First Edition, 2017

ISBN: 978-1-977-71640-8 (paperback)

Most animals sense their time is up when they feel me coming. Even though I resemble them, they know better. Some try to run; need the threat of my teeth in their flesh, my desperation. Others cling to life until I'm right inside their chests, tugging at their heartstrings.

But in the end they all give in, one way or another.

One

Our family portrait was the first thing Mom hung in the house when we moved in. She made sure to put it in the hallway, right where you could see it no matter where you had to go. The three faces smiling out of it have followed me every day for the past six years. Dad stands behind Mom and me, a good couple heads taller than both of us, with a hand on our shoulders. His hazel eyes, the ones we share, penetrate even the darkest gloom. I can still feel Mom's hand pressed into the small of my back as she poses next to me, her small mouth tilted just a little, waiting to share a secret. Nine-year-old me tries to stand tall. My grin is crooked from the missing front tooth, which matches the bangs I insisted I could cut myself. My blonde hair used to curl around my face in tight rings, but over the years it slowly gave way.

I used to run my fingers along the frame when I passed, but I don't do that anymore. For the longest time I couldn't even look at us.

The front door opens, rattles the house as it bangs against the wooden bench we stuck behind it for a stopper, and I look up from *Frankenstein* to watch Mom's petite form struggle down the hallway into the kitchen.

"I'm sorry," she says breathlessly, dumping her purse and a take-out bag on the table in front of me.

"I waited for you because you told me we'd go out for a fly." I make sure she sees me glance at the analog clock propped up on the stove.

She tucks a soft brunette curl behind one ear and kicks off her heels. "Damien's coming home."

I only pause for a second.

"Ray came in tonight," she continues, too excited. She pulls out a couple styrofoam boxes from the plastic bag, and my mouth waters at the steam of bar burgers filling the kitchen. "I haven't seen him so excited in months. He just kept cheering 'My boy's coming home!' with every round, and bought drinks for everyone, even the townies."

"Really?" I slide my feet off the table and toss the book on top of a stack of her magazines. Damien disappeared close to six months ago, right after his twenty-first birthday. Just up and left. "His homecoming is a good thing?"

"Of course it is. Now everyone can get back on with their lives." She pops open one of the styrofoam containers and slides

2

it over to me. A massive bacon burger peeks out.

"But, won't he be, you know, punished or something?" The guy took off. Ditched his family. Ray, our Clan Leader, sunk so low into his depression you'd have thought Damien died. It scared people. Damien is his only son, the only one next in line to take over, and Ray is such a powerhead in the town that without him pointing in any direction, everyone just kinda wandered. Mona, his wife, stopped going out. Camping plans were cancelled. The clan hadn't hit that kind of wall since…

I make eye contact with Dad's portrait in the hall.

"We're just happy he's safe. I can't imagine what Ray and Mona went through, losing him like that."

Her words shoot up my spine, making me squeeze the greasy bun filling my hands. "Damien left without telling anyone, without a goodbye or anything."

"Right, and you wouldn't be doing the same thing if you picked up and left me after graduation, would you?" There's that edge to her voice.

"I'd be going to college," I protest. "Not vanishing off the planet. And I wouldn't ignore you."

She pauses at the sink with her hands on the edge of the counter, fingers curled around the lip. Quiet seeps into the room and covers the floor, and as her heartbeat slows to a simple rhythm, one that's too familiar to me, I wish I could take whatever images she's seeing in her head. When she stops like this, not necessarily on purpose, she goes somewhere. It's a deep place, and I imagine Dad is alive there. Though over the years I've

3

learned not to ask, not to push her about how her features smooth or how her eyes close, how she sometimes sways and her breath gets shaky, it still makes this little hole in my chest tear.

"It will be different," I say as steady as I can.

She raises her head to look out of the window above the sink.

"When is he coming?" I ask, not because I really care, but because I want her to come back to me.

"In a few days. That's what the letter said."

Who writes letters? "Did he say where he went?"

"Ray didn't say."

"Maybe why he took off?"

"I don't know."

Pause. "Will he be okay?"

She turns. I don't even know where it came from. I hardly know Damien; we've talked a handful of times, and once he bought me a Mountain Dew, but he runs with a whole different crowd. Besides being part of the same clan, there's only one thing to link us together, one that might make me ask if he's going to be okay. The same thing that makes it hard to look at him, the thing that might get my hopes up for his homecoming.

The house shook with every one of Dad's syllables. "Kid, get down here!"

"What?" I hollered back, upheaving a box of clothes on my

4

bed.

"Char, we've got company, come down," Mom answered, her voice not nearly carrying as far.

I turned immediately at the unfamiliar phrase, picked past boxes in my room and the ones towering in the narrow hallway, and hopped down the creaky steps. The front door, our new front door, was open, Dad standing just outside on the porch. I stepped out, the hard wood warm on my bare feet. Beyond Dad was Mom and two other adults, and a boy older than me.

Dad and the man were laughing, and Mom and the woman were rolling their eyes. Mom was picking her nails behind her back.

"Char," Dad began when he saw me. He pulled me out farther when I hesitated. "This is Ray, Mona, and Damien Portman. They're the owners of the house, remember? They're like us."

"Ah," the man said, and his dark eyes lit up. He came up to Dad's chin, the stubble on his cheeks were dark and mixed with gray, and he had more around his middle. But his smile was wide and it made me want to smile, too. "Charlotte Reed, we meet in the flesh!" He thrusted out a hand for me to shake.

I gripped it as firm as I could muster. I'm not sure what I was expecting, meeting other skinwalkers for the first time, but Ray and his family weren't it. They seemed too normal, I guess, like us. There should've been a distinguishing factor that set them apart, a reason why they stayed in a clan.

"What beautiful hair," the woman, Mona, said to Mom.

Mom smiled and touched her own. "She gets it from my

mother——" She stopped short, giving dad a quick look like she sometimes did.

Dad didn't notice. "Damien's fifteen, only a few years older than you," he said brightly.

The boy, who had wandered off the porch into the yard, glanced at us when his name was heard. He was tall and thin, his wild black hair matched his even wilder and blacker eyes. They found mine and held me, ready for some sort of secret kid code letting him know I was cool.

Knowing I would let him down, I looked away.

"Oh, yeah," Ray agreed. "I believe we've got a kid in the middle school, and a few in the high school."

"What grade are you going into?" Mona asked.

I cleared my throat. "Seventh."

"You'll have no problem making friends, then," Ray confirmed, like he remembered being in the seventh grade.

I glanced at Dad, who had a goofy grin on his face. *Get used to these people,* it said. *You're gonna be dealing with them on the regular.*

"Your pop's been telling us you're pretty fast." Ray winked.

Damien's head jerked toward us at his father's words, and blood rushed up my neck. I looked down at Ray's sandaled feet.

"Faster than me on a good day." Dad said, bringing his heavy hand down on my shoulder.

Fuck it. I'll deal with the exhaustion in the morning; it's not the first time I've survived a school day running on three hours of sleep. I dig in my closet under the haphazard pile of clothes for my old oak box. A pair of worn jeans fall on my head as I get a grip on the slippery wood and pull it out.

I run my fingers over the clumps of fur, and their whispers greet me like little imaginary friends. Each small soul asks to be taken for a walk. I lift the bit of speckled owl pelt and tie it around my wrist. She flutters a bit, sending a ripple over my skin. It's been awhile since we went out for a fly. I bury the box again and dart out of the room, down the stairs, through the dark kitchen, and out the back door before Mom can dish out a threat.

The air is reluctant to warm from the winter, but the forest is coming alive. Our tangled backyard looks like a monster ready to swallow someone whole. My worn path withstood the months of snow, now open again and waiting at the edge of the forest.

The aspen trees sway overhead as I quicken my pace through them, their branches and budding leaves blocking out the moon. My eyes are quick to adjust, and so are my ears. Chittering bats occasionally swoop through the thick, crickets call to one another, twigs break and limbs bow with perching nighttime predators. Above all I like the night air more than any other; the staleness of the sun disappears, gets replaced by the dark.

My skin is tingling, almost itchy, by the time I get to the little creek. Water bubbles and tumbles over rocks as I stop by its edge. A break in the trees upstream gives me a little light. I kick off my sandals, and pull the too-thin dress over my head.

The strip of owl pelt, tied tight around my wrist, sends goosebumps up my arm, over my chest, down my belly, and through my knees to my feet. Her whims, urges, promises fill my ears.

The burning sensation comes next, and soon turns to a raging fire through my veins. My bones bend, dropping me to the ground, the ability to stand on two legs gone. Vision blurs into a haze and I can't hear past the flood in my ears. The blood is the worst part; as my heart contorts it needs to find new routes to get into the muscle, to pump through it.

I breathe.

She moves fast, sweeping through me, changing me. I shed my skin, mold into a version of her. She's been a part of me for years, so it doesn't take long. The whimpers become screeches when she's taken hold and I'm left in the dirt stretching out my new wingspan.

I double her in size when she was alive. My color is a painting of hers, and only someone who's never seen an owl before would mistake me for one. I'm just her copy—she lends me her soul and skin, but I only mimic her.

The last joints pop into place as I stretch and let out a hoot. My vision is bright, illuminating the dark, hearing more sensitive.

There's not much wind tonight so I cruise through the air with ease. The earth lets me go for this moment but the universe won't take me. The owl hums, glad for the night out, at peace in the middle of the air.

We fly together over the miles and miles of forest, the

mountains in the distance all around us and the little town dipped in the valley, like God himself poured it into this basin to settle in the middle.

Trillions of stars twinkle at us overhead, beckoning us towards them as gravity keeps us down.

Two

I wake up a few minutes before my alarm signals six o'clock, and stretch my back until it pops. A few school assignments roll through my mind: the Calculus (shudder) project, the History summary on good ole Teddy R., reading chapter 10 of *Frankenstein*.

I roll out of bed, and my toes curl on the cool wood. It's still dark outside but I open the blinds anyway. The peach tree out front sways in the early morning chill. My room faces the rocky, potholed driveway that snakes through the woods a half mile before meeting the street. This was Damien's old house, when he was a kid. Ray bought it for Mona right after they married, but once his father died they moved into the manor across town. They rent it to us for practically nothing, which is good since Mom doesn't make a lot at the bar and she won't let me work during the school year.

I flip on the lamp in the corner and pull Dad's old shirt over my head. Looking in the mirror, I inspect a bruise on my leg, and one on my side. The faint scar across my ribs and the more prominent one running down my spine. Shifting can be dangerous and almost always leaves traces, especially for kids. It's hard work, changing a body. Making things break and regrow.

I look at myself in the mirror for a little longer than necessary, and out of habit cup my hands around my boobs to see whether they've been growing or not—

They haven't.

I give myself a cold shower to wake up, not bothering to shave or wash my hair. Then I quietly check on Mom. She's buried in blankets on her bed, snoring softly. Even though she's almost always home in the mornings, I can't help but breathe a little sigh of relief when I see her. Just knowing that she's here, safe, with me, is the only thing I can hold onto sometimes.

Following every Thursday routine, I skip the bra and throw on a loose shirt and jeans. On my way out the door I grab *Frankenstein* from the kitchen table and a cereal bar.

My tan Ford truck roars to life, thankfully, and I'm off for school. She's older than I am but still kicking, even if the passenger door doesn't close all the way and the right tail light hasn't worked in years. She rattles on through the trees, putting up a fight as the sky slowly lightens. I play music from my phone, since the radio only recognizes two stations.

The parking lot is a little more than half full when I pull in, and I take my usual spot near the back. Also, as usual, eyes divert themselves when I walk into the multi-story brick building. Clusters of teenagers and a few teachers look away from me, lowering their voices just a little when I pass through the main lobby to the courtyard off of the cafeteria.

We make people uneasy. They can't quite figure out why. A little voice in the back of their head tells them to not engage, to ignore us, and they subconsciously push us out. It's worse, with a group of us in an area like this. When Mom, Dad, and me lived on our own, people could hardly tell. Their instinct was nothing more than a fly in their ear. I mean, there was nothing wrong with a little family that kept to themselves. But a big one that disappears every few weeks for a weekend, one that sticks together even though they're not all related, one with roots at every angle in the town—that's weird. It doesn't help that we have to be careful, too. Not just because of the whole getting exposed thing, or being spotted while we're transformed (which would probably give a body a heart attack before they could attempt to explain their sighting of a deformed, steroid-stuffed Bambi), but because of a more subtle giveaway; we're physically stronger. More resilient. Our muscles hold more tension, our bodies more evolved. After all, we need to tear our skin, break our bones, and shift our muscles to hold the souls we take.

Some people, mostly guys, can get away with a show of their power, at least some of it, but not-particularly impressive teenage girls like me have to hold back. Of course, I'd give anything to finish The Mile in under six minutes forty-nine seconds just to get the stupid thing over with, but even that's pushing it.

I spread out on a stone bench, using my bag as a pillow, and try to soak up some sun before wasting the day in florescent lights. My ears prick at the sounds of cranky high schoolers. Music blaring from phones, girls' high-pitched whines, guys' loud voices that carry too far all set the perfect foundation for a day-long headache.

He sneaks up on me, and before I can open my eyes Freddie hops onto the bench by my head.

"Got a surprise for me, babe?" He bends down, sending his sickly scent over me, his cold gray eyes hungry. Freddie's always hungry for something, even if it's not food.

"Maybe." I go for his bare ankle but he's too quick, jumping off and dropping his backpack to the ground.

Freddie flashes a smile, revealing white, perfect teeth, and pushes his unnaturally blond hair from his face. "I love your surprises."

I pull myself into a sitting position to make room for him and dig in my bag for the cereal bar.

"Better not be a Cheerios one." He falls into place next to me.

"It's Cinnamon Toast Crunch," I assure him, opening the wrapper.

He gives me a small smile, the closest he can get to a thank you. "Now I remember why I keep you around."

I break off half the bar and hand it to him.

Freddie bumps his leg into mine as he eats, gazing around the courtyard. His skin looks almost translucent in the morning light.

"Like you can't afford a new shirt?" I say, poking him in the ribs. His white shirt has a giant gash in the side, revealing a storm of a bruise he asked for two days ago at the Sadie Hawkins Dance, where he groped a football player in a drunken daze and then later went up his girlfriend's dress.

"This is a reminder."

"Of?"

"Of why you should ask me to dances. And not let me get blackout drunk. And keep me out of trouble."

"You couldn't stay out of trouble even if you did listen to me." Unlike me, Freddie's so peculiar enough that people are actually interested in him. We've been the same height since I can remember, but he's thin and pale like a poltergeist, with an attitude to match. And where I'd rather scoot through any social engagement, he makes a point to be at every one. From parties to clan meetings to Walmart parking lots, he's always around. He supplies the drugs and alcohol, pretends to act friendly, but I know better.

He's a leech for information, obsessed with knowing things about others, things to make them tick, make them squirm. It's scary, some of the secrets Freddie knows, and scarier to think of how he discovers them.

He was a weak baby, born premature and always struggling to keep up. His parents didn't know what to do when his skills didn't improve like his older brother Ro's, who practically burst from the womb ready to kill something. I guess keeping him in the background gave him the tools he needed to stay there, to do it better than anyone else.

Freddie throws his cereal bar wrapper on the ground and reaches for his bag to hunt for a prescription bottle. *The* prescription bottle; it might as well be a trademark at this point. "Want one? You're looking especially uptight today."

"I don't need your Xanax, and neither do you."

"I have horrible anxiety." He struggles with the child proof lid. "So? What's stressing my baby bird today? Is it *Frankenstein?* I bet it's *Frankenstein*—you're too attached to the monster, I swear."

"Damien's on his way home," I say, even though the monster *was* at the forefront of my mind last night, before Mom broke the news. In his time away from Frankenstein, the monster learned to be almost human.

Almost human.

"Yeah." He pops a white pill and leans an elbow on my shoulder. "Going to Ray's tonight?"

"What for?"

"He wants to announce it. Officially."

I pick at a loose thread on my shirt. "Bet Ro's happy."

"My brother couldn't be happier if he figured out how to suck his own dick."

"Mom said everyone's freaking out."

He sighs, knowing where my mind is. "Not everyone."

"It's not that I'm *not* happy, it's just like, oh hey son, back after abandoning us for six months? Thank God, here's a drink. Are they just going to forget everything he did to them?"

"Big bad Damien can do no wrong." He eyes a group of freshmen girls huddled under a dogwood tree. They keep throwing him looks and giggling.

"And Ellie? She's just going to jump back into it, isn't she?"

"Don't you worry about Ellie."

Damien's girlfriend, or ex, or whatever she is, is as unstable as they come. She strolled off the deep end when he disappeared, and Freddie, being her go-to for drugs, knows more about her than he'll ever tell me. "I'm worried that nothing will change."

"I didn't realize you cared so much." He traces circles on my shoulder.

I lean forward, out of his grasp. "If he were my kid I'd beat him, that's all I'm saying."

"Well he's not your kid, but I'd like to see you take your proposal to Ray." He stretches his arms above his head, letting the T-shirt rise to show his stomach.

The girls erupt in squeals.

"Do you have to do that now, Freddie?"

He laughs. It's a light, hollow sound. "You *are* in a bad mood. I'm not believing it's just out of concern for Ellie and the precious clan."

I scratch my wrist and pull my leg up to rest my chin on my knee.

He waits.

"It's just—him coming back reminds me of…"

"Sam."

16

I squint in the sun. "Yeah."

"Why?"

"We've talked about this before."

"Ray and Damien told you what happened." He pauses. "And their story seemed alright."

He doesn't understand. No one can. Damien and his father were the last people to see Dad alive, and they're the ones who know what really happened when he fell. When he died. Away from me, away from Mom, in the middle of nowhere, on a camping trip he wasn't supposed to be on.

Alone, he died alone.

And after the funeral it was like he didn't exist anymore and no one talked about it. I was thirteen and I was scared. Too scared to ask what I wanted to ask and demand a real explanation. Mom knew better than to badger Ray, who seemed really torn up by it, and even Damien wasn't seen for days. I could never ask Ray; as far as he's concerned it's over with. We said our goodbyes.

But since then I've pictured myself talking to Damien about it, rehearsing what I would say, but never quite working up the courage or finding the right time. And then he left. Just dropped off the earth, taking his memory with him.

It's been eating me up inside. Late at night, just before sleep, it crawls out of its dark hole to gnaw on my heart.

Freddie's hand slides up my back as he moves closer to me. "Why do you need to know so bad?"

"I don't know."

"You obsess over this."

17

"Wouldn't you?"

He grunts. "No. Because he's dead."

I know. I also know the way his absence ripped my soul in two. The way it tore a chunk of my life right out of my heart, how that chunk formed a hole, how that hole swells and tries to repair itself only to be torn open every time I see our picture in the hallway, every time his birthday passes, every time Mom gets that blank stare on her face and her eyes lock up right before they close. I know he's dead.

And as much as the little details make me sick to my stomach, I want to know them. I need to know how the strongest skinwalker I've ever known just went out, never came home.

Freddie drops his voice so it's almost soft. "I'm just saying it's not worth it to stress over something that won't change anything."

"I don't expect anything to change. I just want to know."

"Yeah? Going to walk up to Damien at his welcome-home party and ask?"

"Maybe I will." In front of the clan, in front of Ray, holding a clear plastic cup of lemonade in one hand and a napkin piled high with cookies in the other. I pinch Freddie's cheek before he can grab my hand.

"You're so full of shit." He grins. It's a real smile, just for me; not reserved for his family or the clan or the freshmen girls who don't have enough common sense to stay away from him.

I laugh. "I know. But give me a Xanax and I might be able to."

"That's all you're missing from your life, babe, trust me. Pop

18

one of these and smoke a blunt and you'll be set."

"Remind me to thank whoever corrupted you, they did a good job."

He leans into me. "Don't act innocent. Who was it again that found her mother's weed and made me smoke it?"

"Who showed me how to pack the bowl?"

"Miss Reed? Still with us?"

Here we go. I slowly close *Frankenstein* and focus on Greer standing behind his ridiculous podium. What kind of high school math teacher teaching twenty-four kids at a time needs a podium? "Yes?"

A few heads swivel to look back at me, ready to enjoy the show.

Greer's bald head shines under the lights and his button-up is just a little too crisp for him to have done it himself. "Number four. What would be the x-intercept?"

I watch the vein in his neck a beat before glancing at my paper. "Eight point three seven."

"And you think that's fair?"

The air is still. I stare into his wire-brimmed glasses for another beat. "Yes."

"And if I were to say that you were wrong?"

A snort from the back of the class.

This is a fun game Greer and I play. "If you told me I was wrong then I'd have to show you how I got my answer, wouldn't I?"

His mouth gets really small as we lock eyes in our western shootout. "You'd have to show me how you got your answer either way. Why don't you come up to the board and do so?"

I rise slowly from my seat and get a sort of sick satisfaction when I tie my hair up to let the class get a view of the healed-over scar carved down my spine. I pass by Greer, a little too close for his comfort. His heartbeat stammers, letting me know I'm winning this time. I uncap a marker and ponder for a moment before scribbling the equation over the smooth white surface.

Three

Ray and his family live deeper into the bowl of forest than anyone who's not a forester will go. Their large white manor was built several generations back by Ray's great-great-great grandad, when the town was nothing more than a few shops and houses. Many townies refuse to acknowledge this, because it's easier for them to pretend we're outsiders rather than people who've had roots here since the beginnings of Ruhn Roads.

Freddie told me that Ray's family even outnumbered the townsfolk when they first settled. They chose the secluded area in the mountains as a clear statement to be left alone. But the numbers grew and dwindled throughout the years. Some Leaders sought out fresh blood in other clans, while others, Ray included, thought it best not to stir the pot unless someone actively wanted to be with someone from another clan. As I drive through the squat town, with crumbling roads and blinking yellow streetlights, it's a wonder how any previous Leaders got anyone to come here at all, let alone how it gets tourists to pass through during summer on their way to the Rockies.

It's nearly eight when I pull into their winding driveway. Moonlight won't even penetrate the tall pine trees lining the rocky road. It's impossible to see around the bends, but even before the house comes into view I can feel them. There's maybe seventy of us in all, and it seems that most have come tonight.

The driveway opens to a large clearing, mostly dirt, the house sitting center. Cars and trucks litter the lawn and I manage a spot near the side of the house by the tree line. Light pours from the house and the air smells like smoke. A few people are mingling around outside but most are gravitating toward the backyard. Mom isn't here yet. As I get closer to the large covered porch I spot three familiar silhouettes sitting on the railings. I haven't been around to the Portmans' in a long time, but of course nothing's changed. Mona's stone duck peeps out from beneath the front steps, the paint's still peeling from that weird spot by the front door, all the upstairs curtains are drawn shut like the rooms inside will never see the light of day.

Ro's the first one to spot me, and waves the beer in his hand. "What's up, girl?"

Freddie's brother is big. Big chest, big hands, big smile, big laugh. Ro's presence is big and even though he doesn't demand it (most of the time) he's almost always the center of attention.

A few heads swivel at his deafening words. I smile.

Bass, his best friend, turns also and nearly falls off the railing. He's smaller than Ro, but just as solid. He also drinks too much and can't hold his liquor. "Hey. Haven't seen you in a while."

"Yeah, been busy with school. Some of us plan to graduate."

"Ouch." He got halfway through his Senior year before his grades slipped and they cut him from the football team. After that there really was no point in continuing.

Ro nods, wagging his head like I won't believe what he's about to say. "Dude just got himself suspended from work. Tell her what you did, Bass, tell her."

He looks me dead in the eye. "I took Ellie in a mulcher because she wanted to see how it worked—"

"Yeah, that's what she wanted," Freddie butts in, detaching from the wall to stand by me.

"Damien's Ellie?" I question.

"Know another?" Ro asks, taking a gulp of beer. He lowers his voice, which is still loud enough for anyone in earshot to hear. "You saw how much of a wreck that girl was when he left. We were in the same class, she ran around with us, we party. It was my duty to tell her she just needs to get back on the horse. It's what a friend would do."

"And she's been back on the horse," Bass says, too defensively. "So I don't see the big deal. The keys weren't in the ignition or anything. Nothing would've happened."

Ro throws up his hands. "Go for it, she's hot, but during the workday, Bass, really? What did you think was gonna happen?"

"Leanna's just out to get me, I fucking swear."

I'm sure Leanna, Ray's sister and owner of the logging company, has bigger fish to fry than Bass. "You're lucky you didn't get fired."

"I didn't get lucky at all," he shoots back, finishing the beer. There's an edge to his voice that should've been long gone by now with the way he's drinking, but Bass is only my best friend's brother's friend, so I can't ask him if he's okay.

"I need a drink," Freddie says. He gives me a hard look and nudges me towards the front door.

I let him lead us into the house. "What? Don't you want to stay outside with your drunk brother and his horny Bass?"

He shakes his shoulders like something slimy is sliding down his back. "Barbarians."

The arches are high in the entryway and the air swirls with baking sweets and dozens of familiar heartbeats coming together. The old home is well-lit and clean and I've never seen it otherwise, or void of people. Its main function is a meeting place or parties (or in this case the announcement of the second coming of Christ) and people live here only as an afterthought.

We pass through the drawing room and living room, and Freddie gives me a nudge when I pause by family photos taking up the mantle of the fireplace. Most are older, holding people I've never met, members of the clan who've moved on, but the few on the end are of Ray, Mona, and Damien. They're the ones I can linger at; one is a shot right after Damien was born. Mona holds her little red potato-boy close to her, while Ray leans against the

24

stuffed lounge chair that now sits only a few feet away, filling his eyes with the both of them. The next is a photo of the three of them, Damien right around the age when we came to Ruhn Roads. It's a proper photograph, each of them in their Sunday best and posed by a photographer. Damien's Senior portrait, wallet-sized, is stuck into the corner of the frame. The third one, my favorite, was taken at his twenty-first birthday party, the last time any of us saw him. Ray and Mona stand with Damien between them by the fire pit in their backyard. It's just their backs, whoever took the photo snuck up behind them with it, but they look like a perfect trio, a single unit. Mom, Dad, kid.

Freddie swipes a couple beers from Mona's shiny, stainless steel fridge with a TV built into it; supposedly a Christmas gift from Ray, but we all know better.

"Was Bass actually with Ellie?" I ask as we step onto the deck.

"Ro swears he was."

"What would she want with him?" Bass isn't a bad-looking guy... but he's Bass. The fucked-up Ro clone that someone stuck in the dryer too long—Freddie's words, not mine.

Freddie lights a cigarette between his chapped lips. "He was right about her losing her shit."

"Do you think Damien broke up with her before he left?" I try to keep my voice light.

"He didn't bother."

The fire pit's going on the lawn and the barbecue is spitting out burgers and dogs. We stop at the corner of the deck.

"Ellie's the type to like to occupy her time. I don't think she

25

cares who she's with." His face is unreadable, but something tells me he knows exactly who she cares to be with.

"Are you close with her?"

He leans against the chipped railing and won't look at me. The cigarette lingers in his fingers, almost completely unsmoked. "She likes to get fucked up, Char. She likes my Xanax."

I poke him in the ribs, on the bruise. "Sorry if we can't all appreciate you the way *Ellie* can."

He doesn't wince, and only the corner of his mouth lifts. "She's not that hot, by the way, like everyone says."

I shrug. She's got boobs and a small waist. Aren't those the ingredients for a hot girl? I don't normally get too close to her, so I can't know what the real damage is from her drinking and drugs, but she caught the attention of Damien, a guy who could get whoever he wanted.

A log cracks when someone drops it into the fire, and I look up into the sky. The stars are bright tonight. They wink.

Freddie's eyes are on me but he doesn't say anything.

We wait on the deck, watching the yard fill up. There's a lot of drinking and laughing, and my ears prick every time I hear Ray's voice above the others. Mona buzzes past us several times, setting up food on the picnic tables and supervising what goes on the grill. She's lean and tall with no soft edges, and wears her wild black hair down so it billows behind her when she walks. Or hustles; she really only has one speed. It's good to see her with a purpose again. Efficient, and taking care of everything and everyone, all at once.

Mom finds us loitering. "You two up to no good?" she asks, squeezing me around the shoulders. Jessica, her best friend and the only other person I'd ever take any orders from, stops beside her.

"I'm always up to no good, Jule," Freddie says, cracking open his second beer.

"Who gives you these?" Jessica says, snatching the bottle from his lips. "God, it's worse than being at the bar."

Freddie coughs. "No one tells you to babysit, Jess."

"Well, you need a babysitter." Her plump lips frown and she flicks her dyed red hair behind a shoulder.

"What do you think Charlotte's for?"

"Or your own mother, maybe," Mom says, pushing the bangs from his face like she does to me.

He moves out of her fingers, acting insulted, but he loves it. On the rare occasion he's on speaking terms with Nicole, they're usually arguing. I think he gets his fix of motherly love from mine.

"No more of this." Jessica shakes the bottle in front of him before taking a swig of it. "You're only a child."

"You are a pretty big baby," I whisper.

"Fuck all of you," he says, pointing at each of us.

Jessica moves to smack him, giving him what he wants, but Ray hollers from inside the house, telling everyone to move it outside. His voice is deep and raspy. We shuffle to accommodate him, huddling around the fire pit. The flames are as tall as I am and their sparks mingle with the voices.

The lot is kind of raggedy, and I don't have anything for

comparison, so that's saying something. Most of them are in the logging business, working under Leanna, or have stakes in town. Garages, grocery stores, bars, the school system. Freddie's Dad is a realtor. For the most part they're beat up and hardy, a few missing limbs or stolen chunks of skin and muscle here and there, but tonight their faces show a childlike giddiness. A gaggle of elementary kids gathering outside the bus about to go on a fieldtrip.

I can't see Ray from where I'm standing, but I catch sight of Ellie not too far from the circle, with a couple of her friends and older guys Damien hangs around. She *is* pretty. Her thick brunette hair is long and frames her round face. Her cleavage makes me sigh.

"Alright, alright," Ray booms. "Settle it down. I'll make this quick, I promise."

I lean into Freddie so I can see Ray's smile. His weathered face is red from drinking, but his eyes are bright, reflecting the flames. For a second I see the same man I met six years ago.

He throws his hands up. "Damien's coming home!"

Roars of approval.

"When?" someone shouts.

"Within the next week. I was thinking we ought to celebrate with a camping trip."

More cheers.

"Two weeks from now. Clear your schedules."

"Where's he been?" Another person. I don't catch who speaks because he's probably hiding behind someone in case Ray blows his top, as he sometimes does.

But the Clan Leader only rubs the back of his neck, casting a quick glance at his wife. Mona returns his gaze, her expression set in a small smile. "The letter was brief," Ray admits. "He's been travelling."

Silence, then a few whispers.

Before they can grow, Ray cuts, "He always planned on coming back. His heart his here, his soul is with us. His loyalty has never wavered. He's coming back a good man, and very well a competent leader."

Man.

"And no one's going to flood him with questions," Ray continues. "Let him get settled in."

Freddie nudges my side with his elbow.

"I'll do what I want," I hiss.

"You won't," he promises in my ear.

He's not going to be right this time.

"But more about the future when he's home—for now we're going to play it by ear. Get prepared for the camping trip, though, we'll settle on details next week. Now get some food, I don't want leftovers." Ray adjourns the meeting with a flick of his wrist, already bringing the bottle to his lips.

I watch him just long enough to take a shot of beer and kiss Mona on the cheek. So Damien really can do no wrong. I know Ray wouldn't be throwing a party for a disgraced son crawling home to Mommy and Daddy, and I didn't honestly expect anyone in the clan to voice their resentment openly, but I hoped to see some sort of flicker of acidity in Ray. Or Mona. Anyone but me.

And all I see is relief.

"You want a wiener?" Freddie asks.

"No, I'm getting a burger," I say, trying to understand my disappointment. Why would I expect anything different from the clan who looks at the Portman family as gods? As the law? There was almost a riot the last time Ray got arrested for fighting in the streets. And the time Damien drove into a ditch. Ellie broke her arm and he walked away with a bloody nose, but who was out there in the early dawn to tow his Jeep from the side of the road? Whose garage fixed that Jeep in days, good as new? Who made sure Damien didn't get busted and who didn't stop Ellie from hopping back in his passenger seat?

Mom disappears behind Jessica, in search of more drinks, and as we near a picnic table laden with smoky grilled meat, Ellie appears next to Freddie.

"Hey, youngblood." She reveals her teeth and throws a thin arm around his neck.

I try not to stare. Her eyes are red from crying and she's got a smile plastered on her face. Her two girlfriends follow a couple steps behind.

"Hey yourself," Freddie says, not breaking his stride.

She leans around him to see who he's with and after brief eye contact doesn't say hello. "We're going for a walk in a few. Want to come?"

"No, I'm tapped out."

"You must have something."

"Nothing hard enough for you at this point."

She laughs, unaware of the jab, and holds him back. "C'mon, Freddie. You must have *something* for me."

I stop for a second, but when he doesn't shut her down I start walking again. Ellie's always been one of those train wrecks you couldn't look away from. She got a teacher fired her Freshman year for sexual harassment, and tons of naked photos of her got spread around. She's been arrested a few times for drunk driving, or just high-out-of-her-mind driving. Her parents probably would've sent her away by now if they could. The closest rehab center is hours away, even if it was an option. Damien dulled her, some, the times they were together. She still did the things that made her Ellie, but wasn't found nearly as much passed out on someone's lawn. Her plunge after he disappeared wasn't surprising, but this time she's acting out with a vengeance, and I don't want to think a boy could make any girl act like that.

Of course, I don't have firsthand experience, so I wouldn't really know.

Four

I wait in the parking lot for Freddie before school, but he doesn't show. Ignoring the pang in the back of my head telling me his absence has something to do with Ellie, I meander the halls, my sandals squeaking on the freshly mopped vinyl tiles. Freddie might be dumb enough to do something stupid for Ellie's sake, since he loves doing stupid things regardless, but he should know better. Maybe Damien and Bass know better, too, but they're just willing to do anything for a feel of her perfect boobs.

I'm coming up on my locker, and a shiver runs down my arms. It's way too quiet for a Friday. Kids hush as I pass, which is nothing new, but their gaze lingers on my back. Their hearts quicken, and a couple of them actually follow me.

As I turn the last corner I see why. There's an ugly black

32

silhouette of a wolf spray-painted on the metal door of my locker. Its eyes are crude, teeth giant fangs looking for something to rip apart. Wet paint drips onto the floor.

A slurry of wolf howls erupt from behind me and I turn. A pack of boys crowd the hallway. They cup their hands around their mouths to imitate the hollow sound. One of them, a stout junior, stands in front of the herd, laughing. Joey Mahone.

It could have been avoidable. I could have been more careful. A few weeks ago, in a haze of waking up late for school, I somehow rationalized packing my wolf pelt into my bag. I'm not sure what possessed me to do it; maybe it was her voice, her comfort. She's usually louder than the rest, and that morning she pounded at my eardrums. With one slip, after I rushed into class and was pulling out my notebook, the pelt fell to the floor.

Joey, whose family has been here for generations, has always had a problem with us. His family (Freddie suspects riddled with incest) used to own a competing logging company. After Ray's dad died, Leanna took over the logging business, and it became her baby. Her obsession. She turned it into a raging monster that devoured several incompetent companies, and Joey's family was forced to hand theirs over or face bankruptcy. I think she did them a favor, but they don't see it that way.

Joey is short and thick like the rest of them, with a pudgy face and buzz-cut hair. Since his Freshman year he's picked at me, jeering at me when I walk by, starting up little rumors about Mom, heckled his dead-dad jokes to anyone who would listen, but lately he's gotten brave enough to spit harsh words to my face,

33

get girls to bump me in the halls, even had a freshman slap a food tray out of my hands. Of course, he only grows the balls when he has his friends with him. His heart still races, though, when I look at him.

I can never tell if it's out of fear or infatuation.

The crowd's already formed, mostly seniors, unsure yet if it's bullying or some prank—waiting for me to react. I level my gaze with Joey's, keeping my face straight.

He can't hold eye contact and forces himself to keep laughing.

Freddie's messy head pops out from behind the group of boys. "Throwing parties without me again, Charlotte?"

Their laughs cut off short, and Joey flinches. He falters when Freddie squeezes by him, brushing his neck with a knuckle. Obviously, he didn't think Freddie was coming to school, either.

"I think it looks nice." Joey's voice cracks, and one of his friends jabs him in the back. "Better than carrying around dead animals."

Freddie loves getting into it with Joey. He comes to stand by me. "At least she doesn't set fire to them in her backyard."

Joey pauses just long enough for me to know it's true. "Yeah, well, at least I don't have a fag for a friend."

"You're sure?" Freddie says to one of the boys behind Joey, a tall lanky one.

Joey glances behind him and the boy goes red. The rest of the world may not bat an eye at a gay teenage boy, but in a town like this, for a family like Joey's, where you put your dick determines your worth. I mean, how else would you breed cousins?

"And besides," Freddie says, kicking the locker. Several people jump from the metallic shot. "If you're gonna howl like a wolf, you'd better do it right." And then Freddie's howling, the sound coming deep from his belly and rattling out of his throat. His voice rings in our ears and sends a chill up my spine.

"Whatever," Joey spits to cut him off. He's shaking, from rage or terror it's hard to tell, but he's not alone. Several of the kids around us exchange looks and are already shuffling backwards. He sneers. "Have fun with your wolf girl."

Joey takes his friends down the hall without looking back.

My mouth hasn't started working again, but Freddie's never stops.

"What?" he says to those still lingering. "You wanna help clean this up?"

Eyes dart away and suddenly everyone has somewhere to be.

I turn back to my locker. The lock is sticky and I have to rub it clean to see the numbers. My stomach bubbles and my fingers shake. This is the first time he's made a statement. Joey's always singled me out, maybe because I'm a girl or because he has repressed sexual desires for Freddie, or maybe because even he knows I'm different from the clan, but he's never gone so far as to do any dirty work or leave physical evidence.

"Hey," Freddie says, leaning against the wall beside me. "You're not letting that little bitch get to you."

I nod, almost annoyed, still fiddling with the lock.

"He's really nothing without his brother-cousins around."

"They're always around."

"He's alone sometimes."

The locker finally springs open. I have to change the subject before I vibrate out of my skin. "Coming for a run with me tonight?"

He tugs on an ear and sort of slumps over. "Nah, today's gonna be a long day."

"Out of weed?"

He nods.

"Mom has some. We can smoke after." Sometimes, to get Freddie's attention, you have to beg—or bribe.

"Not tonight, Char."

The bell signals five minutes until class starts. I slide my math book from the top shelf and shut the locker. Freddie doesn't mind talking about a lot of things—he enjoys subjects that make other people squirm—but a few topics are almost always off limits. This is one of them. "I know you've been going at it hard lately," I start. The bruises go deeper than the skin, the little tears in his flesh are proof he's being reckless in his shifting.

He pushes himself from the wall, prepared to slip away.

I hook my arm in his, keep my voice higher than usual. "We need to start practicing more, taking it easy."

"You don't need the practice."

"Everyone needs practice."

"And I am, don't worry."

I drop my voice. "What you're doing isn't practicing, Freddie. You're forcing it and hurting yourself. You were doing really good during the winter."

He's quiet for a moment, and his pulse is even. "I was so full of Valium this winter you could've thrown me off a roof and I wouldn't have noticed." He pulls his arm out of mine. "If I need your advice on breathing, I'll ask."

I watch his retreating figure stroll towards the Junior hall. "Breathing is key! Cells need oxygen!"

He ignores me, turning the corner and out of sight.

"Do you even try, Charlotte?" Dad asked me, squatting in the dirt to study a snake. He ushered me off the path a few paces back. We were supposed to be searching for a swift fox.

"Of course," I replied quietly, a few feet away.

He handled the snake with care, felt her weight in his hands.

"What kind is it?" I asked.

The snake went still, trying to get a read on Dad. She was wary.

"She's a northern Garter," he said in his gravelly voice. "Pretty docile."

From my vantage point I made out the cool tones of her. There was a white stripe traveling up the length of her, and she gleamed. Dad looked like he was handling a worm in his massive hands. He'd been letting his hair grow out so he looked more like a Viking than ever. All he needed was some furs and a wooden shield.

"We moved here for you, Char," Dad said, twisting her to get a better look at her head. The snake complied and moved slowly over his wrists. "So you could get to know your people, not just dear old Mom and Dad."

I watched him as he watched the snake.

"We just want you to be happy. That's what any parent wants."

"I am happy."

"You don't act happy."

"I am, I have Freddie. There's enough happiness him for five people."

He straightened up, and the snake, free of his grasp and strong gaze, slithered back into the underbrush. "Her spirit wasn't strong enough. Reptiles don't have that strong of souls, but I was hoping we'd get lucky."

I followed him back to the path.

"Is your heart open?" he asked lightly.

I rolled my eyes. "Yes."

"Your ears?"

"Yes."

"How's your soul? How's she doing?"

"She's fine," I huffed.

He stopped and I bumped into him. With a great laugh, he turned and squatted in front of me. "You have to keep everything open out here. One heartbeat and you could be on the right path."

"If she wants me, I'll hear her," I quoted him.

His grin spread and his eyes twinkled. "Smartass."

I kept my smile to myself when he stood and continued down the soft brown trail.

"I have nothing against Freddie," he said in his shallow tone. A tone he used when he was trying to say something without actually saying it. "But he's younger than you."

"You and Mom have a bigger age gap."

"He's smaller."

"You think everyone's smaller."

"He's not as strong."

"His parents don't take him out that much. They have work."

"Ro is strong, and so is Damien. They could really teach you something."

"Nothing I don't already know, plus they're boring. And mean."

"Mean?"

That stopped me short, right when I felt like I was going to win. "Well, Ro is nice enough, but all he cares about is sports. Damien's just a jerk."

"How so?"

I sighed. I didn't want to have to talk about boys with my father. "To girls." My face burned and I was thankful he didn't turn around. "He bites at them and swears to look cool."

"He does sound like a jerk," he agreed, but I heard the smile on his lips. "I mean, it's not like *you* show off or anything."

I jabbed him in his solid back. "I don't." Especially for boys like Damien.

Dad threw me a look over his shoulder. "If you say so, kid."

The shift back is always harder. It's sad, saying goodbye to a skin. Living together twists souls into knots and changing onto two legs is like cutting through them. The swift fox whispers seductively into my ear, asking for more, but dusk is steadily coming and I've got to walk back home.

The forest buzzes quietly, giving a pause for me to shed the copper skin and I find myself on all fours next to the small creek. My hair falls in a curtain around me, jumbled. I crawl lazily to a flat stone and lean forward to dip my hand into the running water. The current is cool against my raw skin and sends pins up my arm.

A breeze sweeps through the trees and I fall back on my knees, letting it wash over me. Smells like rain. I look down at the red patches on my skin, running my fingers over my arms and up my thighs. Trace the little scars, and the big one across my ribs. I poke my nipples and goosebumps spread across my arms.

A branch cracks, and I feel it. Over my own thundering pulse I couldn't before, but now that it slows the other heartbeat vibrates like thunder. It's coming from across the creek, somewhat irregular, but strong. My head snaps forward and I scan the trees. The heart picks up right before my eyes find him and he reveals himself.

Damien's more broad in the shoulders. His dark hair is longer, coming down to his jaw in windswept locks, but the sides are trimmed. Two little shadows make up his eyes. His jaw is set with stubble sprawled across it and a new scar runs down his neck.

All I can do is stare when he steps forward and hops across the stream. His black shirt has holes in it and his beaten jeans are rolled up just past his ankles. He smiles.

My heart stops and the blood drops into my feet. "W-what are you doing here?"

His lips move before the words form and he tilts his head to the side. "Hello to you, too."

I blink, his two little shadows move in the dim, roaming over my body.

Like I've just been struck by lightning (if I could only be so lucky) I jump and try to cover myself with my hands as I search the ground for my dress. I can't force my brain to work. It's rolling around in my head like mush. "H-hello."

He laughs—it's a nice sound, I notice through the electricity coursing through my veins. "I was just passing through on my way home. Felt you out here, thought I'd see who was bumbling around the forest."

I find the white sundress and turn my back to him, throwing it on and yanking it down. I spin when his boots hit the rock I was just leaning on. "You were coming back home through the woods?" I try to sound angry and fail.

He searches my face and stares at my mouth while I speak, even bigger up close.

I know I'm burning up, but his eyes are watching me too close and I was so, so naked. How long had he been lurking in the trees?

41

He only stepped forward when he realized he'd been caught, like a kid who didn't want to face the terror of being found while playing hide-and-seek. He probably would've spied on me until I left, not letting himself be seen at all. That would have at least spared me some embarrassment.

He's not fazed by my sudden increase in heartrate. "Kind of ran out of gas on my way into town. The truck's somewhere on Seminole."

I nod stiffly. We're feet apart, but there's a heat coming off him I've never felt from another person. Like he's a wild animal trapped in a boy's—man's—body. His hands are dirty and there's a scabbing gash on his forearm.

He openly watches me, at complete ease.

I clear my throat and glance down the trail. "Do—you need a ride? Or gas?"

He grins at me, revealing a chipped front tooth I've never noticed before. "No, thanks. It's a nice night out, I'll probably walk."

"Your house is across town."

He sighs, squinting up into the sky. "Doesn't seem far enough, does it?"

I try to keep my face neutral. "Are you alright?"

His eyes find mine again and hold them there. They're so dark, just a shade away from coal. But they sparkle. "Yeah. It's so strange to be back. To be around…" He trails off, looking me up and down. He lingers on the fox fur tied around my arm, even though he doesn't seem to be focusing on it.

What the hell happened to him out there? I nod like I understand. He's treating me like we're old buddies, catching up at our five-year high school reunion over the spiked punch, when we've had maybe two real conversations in the past. Plus the Mountain Dew. "Well, it's getting dark. I should probably head home."

"Yeah," he agrees, gazing into the sky again.

I take a step back. "Alrighty, then, I'll just see you around."

He smiles again. The chipped tooth gleams in the moonlight. "I'm glad your face was the first I saw, Charlotte. Thanks."

My face. Right. I grimace, hoping to pass it for a smile. "Take it easy."

I move backwards a couple steps before realizing he's going to stare at me walk away. With a final nod I turn and quickly stumble down the path, forcing myself not to run. Or look back.

My heart's in my throat and my hands are shaking from the adrenaline. If anyone else had been watching me shift I would have ripped their insides out. It's just about the most personal, humbling thing a skinwalker can undergo. The process is intimate and there's only two people in the world I trust to be around when I do. And I still don't give them a show.

But Damien is not a normal person. He's the Clan Leader's son. Attacking him would mean certain death—even though I've never known Ray to execute someone, but still. I'm sure Damien could kill me with one hand. And a look.

Those eyes could probably kill me.

The blood rushes to my head again. How could I ever face

43

Damien after tonight? And what if he tells people—Ro or Bass? Or any one of the guys he used to hang around? Ellie's laugh when he describes my small boobs reverberates through my skull.

As soon as I'm inside I lock all the doors and shut the windows. A storm is coming. I find my phone and already have Freddie's number on the screen before I pause. It's liberating knowing something before he does—

But is it my news to give? Maybe Damien doesn't want anyone to know he's back yet. I mean, he opted for a fifteen-mile hike instead of getting a ride or calling someone. Maybe he's not ready to be home.

I lower the phone. Creepy or not, it wouldn't be right for me to tell. He's obviously gone through something out there, something that's making him hesitant to come back. And what if he changes his mind? What if he never makes it home—just turns around and goes back the way he came? I wouldn't want to get anyone's hopes up, especially a dad waiting for his son. No, I won't say anything. It's not my business anyway. Even if he was ogling *my* business.

I slip the fox pelt from my arm and put her back in my box. She goes without any objection. My skin is still tingling when I get into the shower, and I can't tell if it's from the shift or the encounter. I sink to my knees in the tub, cupping my hands to my chest.

For the first time in my life I'm glad my boobs aren't bigger.

Five

She has the courtesy to wait until I wake up before pouncing.

Mom's head pokes out of her room as soon as I open my door. "Damien's back."

I return her smile and edge into her open doorway. At least it wasn't my secret for long.

She props her foot on her bed and ties the worn laces of her work shoes—nurse shoes, we call them. "Jessica just texted me saying he got in this morning. Everyone's gonna try to meet up at the bar for lunch, just to get a look at him."

"Yeah, cool."

"You should really come," she adds, springing from the bed. "Ralph's gonna open early today just for us."

Ralph, her boss and the second of her best friends, is the owner and the only guy professionally trained to cook at a licensed establishment. His dark skin is covered in even darker tattoos and he mixes a mean Long Island Iced Tea, and even though he doesn't serve to anyone under 21, that's the drink that somehow always ends up in front of me when I go in. He and Jessica have been on and off since I've known them. After their fourth cancelled wedding (they actually managed to make it to the altar that time), Ralph threatened to fire Jessica. She set fire to the bar.

"That's nice of him," I say.

"The bar's been hurting since Damien left, just like everything else. People are less inclined to go when Ray's not there, and when he does come a fight always breaks out."

She leans over her dresser to get closer to the mirror to brush on her mascara. "He'll definitely be in a better mood today," I say. I pull at the hem of my pajama shorts, last night's rendezvous stinging my brain. I couldn't figure out if I should be more embarrassed or angry, but as I watch Mom fumble with her purse, scrunch her soft waves in the mirror, and check out her butt, the anger intensifies.

"What do you think he looks like?" Mom asks, applying a second coat of mascara, her final touch. "Hope the poor boy isn't all skin and bone. Or worse."

No, not skin and bone. He's stronger than when he left. Bigger. His face, the little nick on his chin, his chipped tooth, those dark, dark eyes, hold no trace of the boy who disappeared. Will they even recognize him? "I don't know. I mean, he always

46

liked camping."

She shakes her head. "It's different when we're alone, Char. Our kind has to stick together."

I lean against the warped dresser. "That's what Dad thought." It comes out more as a statement than the question I intended.

She caps the thin black tube, letting out a small sigh.

Good one, Char. The familiar cloud of doom washes over her face and I know what's coming next, but instead of turning away from me she tears her eyes to mine. "That's what we both thought," she says gently. "You'll see it, when you're grown and have a kid of your own."

A kid of my own. At this rate probably not likely, and she knows it, but instead of pointing out the obvious I play along and nod.

"You are so strong. Just like Sam. You're turning into him more and more every day."

"Does that scare you?"

"It's fucking terrifying."

I walk into her and lean my head on her shoulder. "Scares me, too."

Her arms slide around me and I concentrate on her familiar heartbeat. "Colorado State isn't *that* close to here. A good few hours. You'd have your distance from us."

"From you guys, yeah, but what about Kenny and Monica and Jamie who go up there? You know everyone's going to expect me to move into the house."

"No one expects you to do anything. You can live on campus

if you want, or get your own apartment. I'm not going to force you to live in the Beta Kappa Skinwalker house."

I laugh. "That's comforting."

"I mean it." She squeezes me. "We've got you a workable savings account, and you've already applied for financial aid. You've got a good start."

I look at her. Her soft brown eyes and straight nose. The way her lips curl into a smile. "Thanks, Mom."

"Just don't leave me yet, okay?"

For the first time in a long while, I stand in front of my closet just staring in. It's really hard to find something that says I actually care what I look like, or at least gives the impression I do. Towards the back, between the big winter coats I vowed to not touch for another five months, my fingers brush against one of my eighteenth birthday presents from Mom (which until now was way less practical than Freddie's red and white striped pipe shaped like a candy cane). It's a short ivory summer dress that's a little too nice to lounge around in, and as soon as I saw it I knew I'd wear it for graduation; but it could be my savior tonight.

First I try it on without a bra, then a bralette, and finally realize I have to wear a real bra with it because the fitted top just doesn't sit right on my B-cups. It's a hassle to get adjusted and I almost give up, but eventually I'm left standing in front of my mirror to admire my attempt at conforming. I detangle my hair with my fingers and dab on some stolen makeup, sure to apply two coats of mascara, and say a silent prayer to the Boob God.

I don't want to admit that I'm doing this for Damien—but I am. He has to know that I'm a person, not just some scraggly naked girl in the forest. Plus, when everyone's attention turns on me after he tells them about catching me nude, I want to look halfway decent. Have a shield to hide behind.

At the bar, I adjust my bra again before getting out of the truck. The straps are already digging into my shoulders but I can't loosen them without taking the whole thing off.

The parking lot behind Ralph's is nearly full, and it's only four. My sandals crunch on the gravel lot as I make my way around to the front. My stomach bubbles. It's gloomy out; the storm has retreated from last night and is gearing up again. Ray's truck is already in the lot, so Damien has to be here. I'm feeling way less confident, but I try to grasp onto the anger to give me something to hold onto.

The squat brick building is one of quite a few bars and pubs on Second Street, which runs parallel to Main Street, but this one typically sees more traffic in the off-season. Hotels, commercial businesses, restaurants, and the wandering tourists stick to Main, but the locals and hard drinkers use this road more often. Though, at four in the afternoon, Main Street is a little livelier.

I actually can't remember the last time I saw the bar in the partial-daylight. The bricks are weathered and most of the windows are boarded. The front door is made of heavy wood and there's nothing indicating this place is a bar except the vomit and blood-stained concrete sidewalk out front.

I adjust a final time, and start to push open the heavy oak door, but a bell across the street stops me. Joey and an older guy are coming out of the Army Surplus store. The man could be his grandfather.

Joey's left eye is busted and bruised and his lip is split. He hunches his shoulders and his gaze slides over the street to me. Cheeks going dark, he mutters something to the older man, who immediately looks up from the work boots that are too heavy for him.

He coughs and waves me away with his hand, like I'm a bad thought he wants to shake.

I trip up the single step through the doorway and I plunge into the bar.

It's slightly dimmer inside with the Old English style lamps hanging from the ceiling. Nearly every piece of furniture is made of dark, worn wood. Heavy tables take up the floor and high backed booths line the walls, on which hundreds of framed photos hang. The bar takes up half the wall on the left, and in the back corner a stage sits, even though Ralph's never had a live band. He enjoys his small collection of jukeboxes, which are huddled together on the stage instead. The space is pretty full and the few drunk townies who caught the early open are sulking by the bar, determined not to make eye contact. Ray's voice roars over the rest, and I catch a glimpse of him at one of the center tables, his arm slung over a smiling Damien's shoulders. The grin seems a little crooked, not like the one he plastered on for me last night. But that could just be because he hasn't seen any naked girls in the last few minutes.

It only takes one sweep to spot Freddie taking up a booth by himself. I make a beeline.

I land hard on my knees on the upholstered seat across from him. "What the fuck did you do?"

The drink nearly slips from his fingers and his eyes take me in. "Damn, babe."

I take the glass. "To Joey."

"Are you wearing a bra?" The smile is too big, and he can't fool me. His knuckles are raw.

"It would've been over with," I say, and take a gulp of his drink. My Long Island Iced Tea.

His head lolls back and he wipes the smirk from his face. His gray eyes glint like two little pools of steel. "I just happened to be walking by the Shell where his dad works and wow, there he was. I couldn't believe my luck."

"Freddie." I can almost accept his fights, which he gladly jumps into any chance he gets, but I hate when he jumps in for me. Exchanging death-threats on my behalf are one thing, but seeking out brawls, any excuse to bring himself pain, sets me off. Last summer, at Ray's, a bunch of us were huddled around the campfire close to the end of the night. We'd all had too much alcohol, too much weed, and Freddie had been itching all day. By that point, all it took was Ro to stumble into me and grab my ass for him to pounce. Freddie's favorite person to fight with is his

51

brother, since he always comes back for more. And because Ro always wins.

Freddie leans over and cups his hand around mine. "It was just a love tap, babe."

"That love tap left evidence and now his whole family wants me dead. You can't mess with the Mahones'."

He blinks. "What happened?"

"Outside, Joey pointed me out to Grandpa. Pointed. Me. Out. Like it was my fault."

He squints, not really following, and nods. "Well do you want me to beat up Gramps, too, 'cause I will."

I finish the rest of the drink. It's no use, talking sense into Freddie. His brain may absorb it, but he processes remorse at a different level than other people.

"No, but you could get me another."

He flicks the tip of my nose and stands. "That's my girl."

It makes me sneeze, which is not a pretty sound, and when I look back up Damien's staring at me.

He's shaved his face, and the new scar on his jaw gleams against his near-bronze skin. I search for his heartbeat in the throng. That weird irregular beating, almost like two hearts merged into one. I can't pick it up. Ray's beside him, face red from the alcohol and toasting to something, and Ellie's on his other side, arm looped through his. The way she looks at him plucks my heart chords. Like nothing happened.

His eyes trap me and slowly a small smile crosses his features. Not a weird one, but a friendly one. One that says he didn't tell anyone about last night, that maybe he's not going to.

I return his smile.

Mom zips behind their table, carrying a mountain of plates, and catches my attention. She points not-so-discreetly to Damien, an eyebrow raised. Everyone's got a drink and energy fills every nook and cranny. It's crazy how one person can affect an entire clan. Even Dad had an effect on them, and he had to work to get them to accept us in the first place. He spent months here before we officially moved, living with Ray, Mona, and Damien. He left us in Virginia and only came home every few weeks. Each time he felt more certain that they'd let us into the clan, and each time, my excitement grew. I didn't know what I was excited for, but Mom and Dad were happy, and that made me happy.

But then we got here. Dad had made friends with Ray and his boys, and Mom got the job at the bar where she met Jessica and finally had some women to gossip with. But I couldn't find anyone. "They treat you different because you are different," Dad would say. It's because I was stronger and faster than them, and that their parents weren't as diligent as he was when it came to skinwalking. He told me not to worry about it, don't let them bully me, and just leave them alone if they want to play it that way. Besides, they just thought I was showing off.

Maybe I was. Freddie was the only one to listen to me when I talked, tried to help him, but he's so set in his own ways and his attention span is so short I don't think I've ever made a difference.

They let Dad teach them, though. I think he made a real difference in the clan. He got Ray into doing regular camping trips, showed the clan that what we are isn't so much a burden as it is a gift. He built them up, like he'd been doing to me my whole life. Before him, most of the clan were in the groove of living their lives as regular people, stressing about work, money, acceptance into society. But he taught them how to *enjoy* skinwalking, make it an ability they can be proud of, make it a skill that they can improve on.

I admire him for that.

"You look thirsty."

I jump, snapping out of the past, and focus on Damien in front of me with a drink in each hand. He's like Freddie's level of stealthy.

Damien smiles—not the crooked one he's been pulling— before setting the smaller glass on the table.

"Thanks," I say, vaguely aware half of the bar has gone silent. "What is it?"

"Rum and Coke. You don't like beer, do you?" He lifts the other drink slightly, offering it to me.

I shake my head. "No, this is great, thanks."

"Want to go for a walk?"

"A walk?"

He nods, eyes focused on me, lucid, exploring my expression. "Yeah. Real quick."

It's not like I can refuse. "Okay, sure."

I stand, and when I follow him I can't help but admire the looks of horror from the clan. Ellie is openly confused and staring. Ro and Bass are grinning like idiots, ready for a show. Ray and

Mom look like they're about to have an aneurysm. I'm scared to try to pick out Freddie's face. Damien holds the door for me and lets it close behind us with a *thunk*.

It's lightly raining, but Damien doesn't seem to notice. We fall into step, side by side.

"You look nice," he says, taking a drink of beer, like it's legal to walk around with a pint.

"Yeah, with clothes on."

He coughs into his drink. "I wanted to say sorry. You caught me by surprise last night."

"That makes sense, me being in my own backyard and all at eleven o'clock at night."

"You really did. I've never seen you shift before, it was nice."

Nice?

"And I was a little out of it. It hadn't fully hit me I was home, and by the time I came back down I was halfway to the house when I realized what it must have looked like."

"It did look like something," I agree, downing half my drink. The rum warms my mouth and coats my insides. Who is this guy?

He looks at me sideways. "It was beautiful."

Oh God. Is this real life? "Did you drug this?"

He laughs, loud. "No, Jesus, I'm serious little one, I've never seen anything like it."

"Little one?" I repeat like an idiot.

His sharp eyes snap to me. "Even you must know the story."

"Of course I know the story," I lie. Well, kind of lie. Dad wasn't one for the legends, so I've only gotten bits and pieces of the tale.

Damien calls my bluff and begins talking like he's recapping an episode of *Buffy*. "The Little One was the first skinwalker, a small medicine woman surviving on the edges of civilization. Legend says she lived in one of the tallest caves, on the most rugged of mountains. A group of hunters determined to get rich from furs of the animals who lived there set up camp at the foot of her mountain. Every day they would try to make it to her cave in search of her advice for killing the most savage of beasts, since she survived unscathed for all those years, but they could never reach the top."

He's walking slowly now, the drinks catching up with him, and his words are heavy. But I like it.

"Then one night, a lookout caught sight of a massive mountain lion making its way to the cave. Instead of hunting it and killing it, he followed it step for step up the rocky face until they both reached the top. The mountain lion transformed into the little woman, and as a reward for showing restraint she taught him how to skin animals and take their souls. The man took this knowledge back to the hunters, and they became the First Clan. They were the fast, strong, and impossibly skilled because they were half beasts themselves. Before long they returned to their village with as many pelts as they could carry.

"But they weren't counting on the villagers to be frightened of them and their new abilities. Their families and friends banished them, and the hunters had no choice but to return to the Little One and beg for her guidance. She agreed to take them and guide them in her ways, and now the term is one of respect and strength, reserved for especially gifted female skinwalkers."

No one has ever called me little one before, not even Dad. I've heard the term thrown around here and there, but, like the Legend of the Skinwalkers, Dad never acknowledged it. Or Mom, for that matter.

"Have any plans tomorrow?" he asks, stopping.

I nearly bump into him. "Huh? No, I don't think so."

"Mind if I stop by? It's been awhile since I've seen the old house." He watches my mouth, then brings his eyes up to mine.

"Yeah, of course," I say, like he has to ask. Like I can even refuse.

His lips break into a smile, and I get a flash of his chipped tooth again. "Perfect. And take a breath, Charlotte, I'm not going to bite you."

Six

My nose wakes me from a dreamless sleep. Last night, after the walk with Damien, I could only endure the bar for another hour (long enough to drink the Rum and Coke from Damien and the Long Island Iced Tea from Freddie) before I had to leave. Freddie's hissing and Mom's not-so-subtle "Did I miss something?" looks and Ray's questionable glares became too much, mostly because the only answer I could come up with for anything was "I don't know."

And I really, really, don't.

The covers are wrapped around my bare legs and I open an eye to the odd scent traveling up the stairs and through my open door.

Sizzle. Pop.

I kick the blanket off. Dad's old shirt drops to my thighs as I stumble into the hallway. Mom's in a better mood than I thought; cooking breakfast after a late night out, especially since we hardly use the stove because it heats up the house better than the twenty-year-old furnace, means she must be super, duper happy. And what's better: she's making bacon.

I half fall, half hop down the stairs in my frenzy. A few of the windows are open, their curtains hanging in the breeze that sweeps through the house making the greasy aroma of frying meat even more intoxicating.

"Hope you're frying up the whole package because I think I have a hangover," I say, tapping the family portrait before I cross the threshold into the kitchen.

He's standing with his back to me in Mom's frilly pink apron.

Damien turns around.

"Jesus Christ!" I yank the ratty hem of the T-shirt down further over my legs. "What are you doing?"

He gives a half shrug, eyes wandering down my body. "Bacon, then eggs if you want."

"In my kitchen, in Mom's apron, this early in the morning?" Dad bought it for her as a joke one year for Mother's Day and tried to pin it on me.

He looks down at the flower print. "I thought it was cute. I can take it off."

I open my mouth but no words come out.

"You said I could come over," he reminds me, turning to briefly tend to the bacon.

"How did you get in?" The shirt is too thin. Too many holes. I should've stopped sleeping in it a long time ago.

"Ray has a key. And you can calm down, it's nothing I haven't seen before."

I can't stop the squeal that escapes my lips before retreating out of the kitchen. "Too fucking soon!"

"Wait, Charlotte, I'm sorry. That was supposed to be a joke." His words come out mangled through this choked-back laughter.

I don't reply, charging up the stairs. My legs wobble. Damien's in the kitchen, making bacon (then eggs, if I want), like he does that sort of thing all the time for girls he hardly knows.

His voice carries up the stairs behind me, completely calm. "I'll get started on the eggs, then?"

I ignore him and stomp down the hall to Mom's room. I crack open her door and listen to her soft snoring, tempted to wake her. No matter how happy everyone is to see him, he can't get away with breaking and entering. How dare he make me breakfast?

Then again, the apron does look cute on him.

I take a breath and close her door. I pull myself together and start in the bathroom. There's mascara running down my face because I forgot I had on makeup last night. I scrub my teeth and shove myself into a bra again. If I keep the blushing to a minimum, this might turn out okay.

There's some scraping against a pan when I return to the kitchen. He's finishing up the scrambled eggs. The open carton is next to him on the counter, as well as the empty plastic from the bacon—the whole package, like I requested. He's got a spread around him of cheese, milk, and spices. The apron hangs untied on his body, way too small for him, and his shirt shows off his tanned arms. I can just make out a few light scars and nicks.

"I didn't know we had bacon," I say, stepping up to the kitchen table.

"You didn't. Or eggs. Picked some up on the way over."

"Why?"

He shuts the stove off and turns. "Mind getting some plates?"

I do as he asks, and stand by him while he piles food onto each one. He's clean, like he just showered, and there's a brush of deodorant, but his own scent hovers underneath, earthy and soft.

My heartrate is hard to keep down when his hand brushes against mine when he hands me a plate. "Sit," he says, gesturing to the table.

I take my usual spot and let the hot food waft into my nostrils, but I can't stop staring at him as he wraps up the other plate in tin foil.

"We'll leave some for Jule," he says, licking a finger sliding it into the fridge. He stops when he realizes I'm staring. "What's wrong? Eat."

I tear my gaze away from him and pick up a strip of bacon. "When you said you were coming over I was sort of expecting a warning."

He finds the silverware drawer and plucks out a couple forks. "I don't have your number. Didn't really realize the time, either. Been used to getting up early." He hands me a fork and eats the remaining eggs straight from the pan.

"Ray has the home phone number," I say, trying not to shove the whole strip of bacon into my mouth.

"He was still sleeping when I left. Old man had a long night."

"Did you?" I can't keep the image of Ellie from my mind, sitting next to him with a hand in his, determined to keep his attention once we came back inside.

He shakes his head, letting his mane fall into his face as he scoops up the last of the eggs. "I took off right after you did. Everyone just kept staring, making me drink." He grins up at me.

That stupid, broken tooth.

He moves to the strips of bacon.

"Where'd you learn to cook?" I ask, shoveling some eggs down my throat when he's not looking.

"Mona, of course. She cooks for an army and bugging her was the only escape I *ever* got from Ray."

Not so much anymore. She hardly left the house at all while he was gone, and they rarely had people in it. Does he know the damage he caused when he left? Will anyone tell him? When I glance at him he's watching me, taking in my expression. His gaze is just as intense as last night, and the night before that. I hold back a shiver.

He steps to the table, the remaining pieces of bacon in his hand. "But what about you, how have you been?"

Like he knew anything about me from before. I could probably say I won homecoming queen, that despite Trisha Morris stuffing the ballad box and dumping pig's blood on my head, it was a great night. "I've been fine."

"Graduating this year?"

"Yeah."

"Have good grades?"

"Good enough." No need for him to know I'm top ten of my class.

"That Ford hasn't died on you yet?"

"She's holding strong."

"College?"

I stop short.

"Alright." He grins, pulling a chair and plopping across from me. "Now we're getting somewhere. Out with it, little one."

"I'm going to college," I affirm, trying to act more annoyed than shocked at his interest.

"But." He leans towards me, bacon grease still on his fingers. His eyes are so dark, almost black. The only things that separate his irises from the color are the light brown, almost yellow, almost gold flecks in them.

My mouth is dry. I try to focus on the thin scar on his jaw. "But I just don't know where, yet."

"Thinking about leaving?" The light, joking tone is gone. He doesn't seem angry, but he doesn't seem concerned, either. I can't tell what he's feeling.

All I know is I can't look him in the eye, so I shrug. "No, not leave. I wouldn't do that to Mom." Maybe a little lie?

I know my heart is giving me away, but he just nods, not pressing it further.

I watch him watch me while I finish my eggs. He could have

called me out, but who is he to talk? "What do you think of the house?"

"Glad you let me come by." He leans back in the chair and takes in the little kitchen.

"Not much has changed."

"No," he disagrees, eyes returning to me. "A lot has changed."

Oh, boy.

He stands, taking my empty plate. "You've made it a home," he says, turning on the sink faucet. "Ray was never comfortable here. He couldn't wait for his old man to die and to kick Grandma out of the manor."

Ouch. "He talked about that?"

"Not to me. I was only a kid, but I can remember him and Mona arguing about it all the time."

I can't picture Mom and Dad arguing. They bickered like crazy, but never actually fought. If they did, I wasn't around for it. I rise and take the pan from the stove, and try not to get too close as I hand it to him.

He looks sideways at me. "Wanna go for a run?"

"With you?"

"Yes," he answers, plucking the pan from my grasp and dropping it in the sink.

Seven

Damien's Jeep isn't as old as my Ford, but it's definitely more beat up. With its grime, dried mud and dents, it looks like it *belongs* in my driveway in front of the crumbling little house. We climb in, the pronghorn pelt humming in my pocket. She's a funny-looking antelope with a black muzzle—one of my fastest.

He rolls down the windows and turns up the volume of the radio before we pull out. "Still only two good stations, huh?"

"Sometimes the Christian rock channel comes through from Chandlerville," I say brightly.

He smiles sideways at me to make sure I'm joking before glancing in the backseat. "Grab something from back there."

I reach around, twisting my torso to search the back. He's got blankets, clothes, trash and empty bottles, both alcohol and water. "Never knew it was actually possible to live out of a car," I mumble, throwing some boy-smelling pants aside to hunt through the CD cases on the floor.

"It's harder than it looks."

I pick up the first CD case I find and push the disk into the CD player. The bacon in my stomach bubbles. I would have been totally fine jumping into the woods behind the house, but as soon as Damien slipped his keys from his back pocket I realized he already knew where we'd be running.

"This was my favorite ground to run," he says, wind whipping through his hair. He throws an arm out the window as we get onto the highway, going South.

It's times like this that I wish I had more experience with boys. Experience that would prepare me for when I came face-to-face with them. Thankfully, the alternative spilling out of the busted speakers and the wind gushing around us distracts from my thundering pulse. "So you really have nothing to do today?" I say stupidly.

He bites back a grin, bringing his arm into the truck and replacing it with the one on the wheel. He leans toward me just a little. "Sick of me already? After I made breakfast for you? Why, Charlotte?"

"No, that's not it, your bacon was amazing." The way my name rolls off his tongue.

"Then what, little one? Scared?"

"Scared?"

He looks at me, and my heart drops into my deep-fried stomach. "Scared that I'm faster than you?"

"You're definitely not faster than me." The guy on the CD's voice cracks while he sings about a girl who broke his heart.

"Is that so?"

"I just figured... you probably have a lot to do, being back and all."

He straightens in his seat and we turn off the highway. "Plenty of time to do everything."

All the time in the world. Enough to cook me breakfast, at least.

In the pause that comes next I turn up the music. The song lulls like the ocean; the singer's voice a lonely ship lost on the waves.

"You like the band?"

"Yeah. The singer sounds like he's in pain, doesn't he?"

"Oh, he is. I met them over on the East Coast. They're skinwalkers."

The way he so casually talks about other skinwalkers, like he wasn't shielded from them his whole life. "Did you get an autograph?"

His mouth twitches as he recalls a memory. "I got more than that."

We're between towns, Damien driving a little too fast down back roads. But he avoids all potholes and slows for blind curves. Did he think about this a lot, while he was gone? How did his secret running spot measure to the wilderness outside of

Colorado?

The road becomes more decrepit the farther we go, and when I think it might run out, Damien plunges off of it all together, into the trees. Instead of driving headfirst into a spruce, his tires find a dirt path.

He turns the stereo down and drives slowly on the snaking, one way drive. My anxiety temporarily forgotten, I lean forward to peer out the windshield. The pines here are tall and each turn brings more of them.

We roll up to a large gate and he cuts the engine.

"It's a driveway," I say, glancing at him, silence engulfing us.

He's already looking at me. "Ready?"

"I mean, I'm here."

He hops out of the truck, and I follow. The claps of the doors slamming closed echo through the trees and birds fall silent for a moment. The gate is of the wrought iron kind, once black but now encrusted in red. It's tall and hooked onto brick walls that disappear into the forest on either side. Our feet crunch on some lingering gravel and dead leaves. He slips through the ajar gate, a few paces ahead of me.

"Why don't you drive all the way through?" I say, sliding through behind him. My fingers brush against the cool metal and its cracked surface catches a few of my hairs.

"This is an old place. Someone used to live here," he answers. "Never felt it was right to drive on in."

The trees on this side are planted with a purpose. Crabapples, just starting to bloom, their reds and whites already showing.

Tricolor beeches, with their pink edges. And winter kings, not yet bloomed. Their flowers are the whitest white. In summer, this road must look like it's on fire with all the warm hues. My footsteps become even with his and we make our way down the overgrown dirt road. The sun shines more freely and the bugs buzz louder. It's a place out of a book, not belonging in our time.

We round the final bend and are met with an enormous house. A mansion. It's mostly red brick, four stories high with wooden balconies and railings bending to termites and moisture. The porch sits as a welcome and the chimneys and turrets flag us down. Roofs are peaked and wooden, their shingles a dull gray from years of rain. Its many little windows peek out through the ivy, while the giant ones on the ground floor stand agape. The heavy front door is closed, like it won't ever open again. I find it difficult to step forward into the circular drive.

Damien turns when he hears me stop.

"How'd you find this place?" I whisper, not able to move.

"One of the older guys told me about it when I was younger, but I didn't start looking for it until I got the Jeep. Wanted it to be a secret if I found it."

I meet his gaze. He stands at the dried-up fountain in the middle of the gravel circle. A woman in a flowing gown with a bird perched on her outstretched arm poses at its center. "You were able to keep *this* a secret?"

"Yeah." He smiles. Those eyes.

"Ever go in?" I step up next to him. The sun is high but the shadows from the pointy roofs slowly creep toward us.

He gives a shrug. "Nah. I tried a few times to find out who lived here, but..."

"Maybe they never left," I murmur, taking in the heavy black door with metal bolts.

His finger brushes against my cheek, and it sends a fire over my skin. "Bug," he says, fingertips lingering just below my eye.

I blink, willing him to come closer.

But he just smiles again, tilting his head so his eyes can escape the sun. "Still have the best part. Follow me."

My heart withers when he strides away from me, towards the side of the house. It takes a few moments before my feet listen to my brain and I take his path through the wild grass. I keep my eyes on the house as we round it, past its towers and odd angles. A large glass extension juts out of the side just before we reach the back. The sun room has vines poking between panes of glass and ivy creeping through shattered windows. I'm tempted to get a peek inside but a flash of red stops me.

Just beyond a small row of overgrown hedges that serve as a barrier, I make out stone fixtures rising above my line of sight. Damien plunges through the green wall and I slide through behind him.

A garden spreads out before us, wild and unkempt. Obviously once laid in a grid and well thought out, years of being left to its own devices let it breathe. Sunflowers stand proudly in tall clumps and creepers take over narrow stone paths. Fountains and statues struggle to be seen through the wildflowers and weeds. Rose bushes tumble over round hedges and there's little towers of pink and blue and yellow flowers poking through the thick mat of green. Alliums, with their big round purple heads cluster in cliques. Indian blanket flowers with their burning petals sway in the wind, attracting the bees. Butterflies and dragonflies float just close enough to check us out. Birds rise from heaps of bushes, leaving their nests.

"How...?" The fragrance of the garden—all the sweet, floral scents—steal my breath.

"Almost magic," Damien says quietly, taking me in. "We came at just the right time, everything is waking up."

I walk slowly into the thick, trying to stick to the path and not disturb a single flower. Damien keeps in step behind me, his gaze on my back. The sun is warm on my head and the low buzzing of flying critters hum against my heart. My fingers tickle petals and thorns and remind me this isn't a dream. The thick tree line begins at the edge of the garden, but to our left sits an immense field with tall grass.

The path ends before it hits the trees, stones broken, like it once continued into the forest. Damien stops behind me and I turn.

"Ready?" He slips his shirt over his head, revealing the most beautiful torso I've ever seen. His chest is smooth, every line defined with only a trail of hair running down his belly button into his jeans. His body ripples with anticipation, and I realize mine is, too.

Oh, boy.

He drops his shirt to the ground and takes a step toward me.

"You *are* ready, aren't you?"

His eyes are fire and his mouth is open just a little and I realize he's breathing me in, taking in my flavor. He takes another step toward me.

I nod, not trusting my voice. It's different letting your guard down with a single person rather than a group. When we camp, gaggles of us run or hunt out of convenience and rank. Because shifting with another person can be like squeezing into a bath with them. Taking a long car ride with a broken radio. Getting stuck together on an elevator with the power out.

Damien's the picture of ease when he comes closer and slowly reaches into my pocket. The pressure of his fingers sliding out the pronghorn pelt makes my whole leg tingle. He doesn't break eye contact when he ties it around my wrist.

"I've never brought anyone here," he says softly.

The pronghorn hums quietly to me at the sound of his voice. "Why am I so lucky?"

"I'm *really* sorry about the other night." The corner of his mouth lifts just a little.

"So this is a bribe?"

"Pretty much." He nods, reaching into his back pocket. "I also wanted to see what you've got."

The pronghorn jumps, growing warm.

He cocks his head to the side, smile growing, and holds out a dark matted fur with gray spots.

I can't tell what it is. But, following his lead, I take the ends and tie it around his forearm. His skin starts searing and his pulse thunders. I hold back a gasp, looking up into his face.

The smile fades and he flips the hair out of his eyes. They're glazed over, dark and wet, pupils dilated. He steps back from me, out of reach, and turns into the woods.

He has a thick scar running the length of his spine.

The pronghorn jumps again, impatient, and my chest bursts. As quick as I can, I kick off my shoes and pull off my top. Stumbling into the cover of the trees, I strip the rest of my clothes. Blood rushes to my head and before I know it I'm on all fours. The pronghorn fur melts, consuming me. I feel myself thin out and stretch, my back breaks and reforms. The change blinds me.

It's a dream, being an animal. I swim through the air, running on new legs. Every little sound of the forest pulses through me like angry waves, demanding to me heard. I gallop hard, slicing through the forest. The sun spreads its rays through the trees overhead and it soon I lose sight of the overflowing garden.

I almost forget about Damien until I feel him.

He's low to the ground. My skin tingles again, fur standing on end. A small twinge of fear trickles across my shoulders, but it's overpowered by excitement. I follow his breath, the only thing giving him away.

He's crouched behind a fallen tree, leering at me through its branches. A mass of stone gray fur, the bobcat straightens when I approach, golden eyes glinting in the sun. He's larger than any bobcat there ever was. His features are gaunt, shoulder blades protrude, and under his massive head I spot the bullet hole that killed the original. I know only an idiot would mistake me for a real pronghorn, but he looks like a science experiment gone wrong.

A beautiful experiment gone horribly, horribly wrong.

My heart thumps in my chest when he hops on the log, head cocked and eyes unblinking. His heartbeat wants to be familiar. He takes me in, head level, his only movement coming from his breathing belly. He makes a small noise in the back of his throat, resonating like a stroke of thunder, and I propel myself away from him.

In a dozen leaps, he's right behind me. Damien's snapping at my heels but I haven't been this calm in days. He lets me lead, deeper and deeper into the forgotten land, every so often coming level with me long enough to throw a wink with one of his golden eyes. Part of me expects him to pounce and sink his large pointed teeth into my hot flesh, and while the girl in me isn't sure that's such a problem, the antelope is nervous.

She presses me, threatening me to run faster, and when I do I get ahead of him.

The sound of rushing water catches my attention and I veer from our course towards it. He disappears from behind me, but I don't slow until I come to the water's edge.

The inky pool before me is so dark I can't see the bottom. Trees overhead almost completely block out the sun and only the wall of rocks on the opposite side offer a waterfall to break the surface. I pause on a smooth piece of rock; its charcoal surface untainted, except for a perfect crack running right through its middle.

I step off it into the pond, stopping at my wobbly knees. The water is frigid against my overheated body.

A figure comes hurtling from the top of the waterfall. Damien, the person, completely naked, falls into the black water, sending a splash through the forest. After a couple seconds he resurfaces, grinning up at me.

"Up for a swim, little one?" He throws his head back and grins up at the sky.

Get naked in front of him again? I huff in his direction and turn.

"Charlotte," he calls, and there's a splash as he flings water towards me.

I turn to glare at him.

He bites his bottom lip. "I've never felt so threatened by a woodland creature before."

I stand still, and huff at him again.

"Please?" He smiles, pushing his wet hair back.

Has anyone done anything more beautiful? I puff out my chest.

"I won't look, I promise," he says, and makes a point to swim away from me, to the waterfall.

I wait a few seconds, watching him with his back turned, and shuffle a little to let the soft mud settle around my joints. My heartbeat slows, and my skin tingles, begging for a break. I huff one more time, loud enough for him to hear me, and let my human form take shape. It's satisfying to regrow my bones and limbs, shed the fur. The water makes it more bearable when my muscles regroup, and I allow myself a few seconds of crouching

75

on the bank before looking at Damien.

His back is still to me, and he's playing where the waterfall meets the water. Trying to keep myself covered, I wade into the pond and make sure the water is well above my chest before I swim towards him. My feet leave the muddy bottom closer to the waterfall, and my skin chills with every stroke. I let the cold seep into my muscles.

"If you want to get even," he starts, spinning toward me when I get closer, "now's your chance."

I keep a good distance. "And how's that?"

His dark eyes are even more intense when his hair is wet. He dips down just below the surface and pops up again with a smile. "You could check me out if you wanted to. I wouldn't mind."

"I bet you wouldn't." I laugh, splashing water at him. I dunk my head to wet my hair and get rid of the last of the pronghorn. Even though I feel naked—really naked—I don't feel so vulnerable.

Damien laughs with me.

"How'd you know it was deep enough to jump?"

"Didn't take me long to find the pond. It's a nice little break in the run." He floats closer to me.

The water level stays just above my shoulders. He looks up into the trees and I let myself watch his throat.

"Your heartbeat's so slow," he says softly, bringing his head back down to look at me straight on.

I glide closer to the waterfall, not able to meet his eyes. "I'm comfortable," I say, reaching to let the water hit my skin.

"This is the first time I've felt it so slow."

I risk a glance at him. "You haven't been around me long."

His eyes wander my face and he has an unreadable expression. "I always knew I'd come back."

"Ray betted on it."

"Old man thinks he knows everything."

"Doesn't every dad?"

"Did Sam?"

My heart skips at his name, a defensive tick popping in the back of my brain. My name rolls off Damien's tongue, but my father's sounds like butter sliding over his gums. "Sometimes I think he did know everything."

Damien smiles. Not in a sympathetic sort of way but in a way that makes me think he understands.

"So why'd you come back?" I'm feeling bold. Could this be my chance?

His smile widens. "Ray and Mona keep asking me why I left and everyone else attempts to steer me toward the topic, but no one seems to care why I'm home."

He squints at me through his wet lashes. It doesn't matter why he's home because he's *home*. The good people just want to know what set him off so they can remember to never do it again.

"But maybe it's obvious." He moves towards me, floating closer and closer until he's a breath away and his dark eyes look like marbles.

Rogue drops of water plunk on our heads and I don't dare back away from him. Even though the water's cooled us down there's heat warming my chest.

"I came to take the clan." His eyes glint and his voice is low.

"Take the clan?"

His mouth lifts again, but it doesn't reach his eyes. He uses his arms to propel him backward. "It's about that time, isn't it?"

I can't help but pull myself towards him, wanting to feel his heartbeat through the flow of the water.

He's peering into the trees overhead, partially on his back. "Think you're ready for me?"

"The clan is," I say quietly. It *is* about time he was taking this seriously, for their sake. But his tone, his odd smile, the way he keeps looking at me, like I should be in on some joke, sets me on edge.

He tilts his head. "Are you?"

That makes me laugh. "Does that matter?"

"You're part of the clan, aren't you?"

"One vote won't put you out." I laugh again. I can't help it. I've always shared a gray area with them. I'd want to fit in, so badly sometimes, but Dad just told me to not worry about being different. It's not bad to be different, but wanting to be normal shouldn't be bad, either.

Damien straightens up and I find the ledge to get a footing. The water ripples around me as he floats closer.

When he speaks, he's right behind me. "Your vote could." His fingers press into my back, between my shoulder blades.

My breath gets caught. I have no idea what he means, but my mind's already leaped—

"Can I ask you something?" I whisper.

His fingers trail slowly up my spine, tracing my scar. "Sure."

I open my mouth but the question leaves me. This could very well be the only time I can ask him about what happened on that camping trip years ago, but a part of me doesn't want him to lie, get angry, ruin this oddly perfect moment. And a part is still terrified of the truth.

"How'd you get that scar on your back?"

Eight

I catch sight of Freddie by the buses on the other side of the parking lot when I pull in, and before I can even put the truck in park he's on his way over.

My palms are sweaty. I got home late yesterday. Not like past-curfew late (even if I did have a curfew), but late enough for Mom to give me the third degree while scarfing down Damien's breakfast. I didn't realize what it must've looked like until she used the word *date,* and now there's a pit sitting in my stomach. It wasn't a date. It couldn't have been. I mean just because he made me bacon and drove me to a secret spot and we swam naked together doesn't mean it was a date. I pointed out to her that he'll probably get back together with Ellie (right?) and we just hung out. Clan Leader's son or not, she wouldn't let him live if I told her why he took me out.

I try to escape before Freddie opens the door and slithers in, but I'm not fast enough. He slams the chunk of metal hard, sticking it so it won't pop open into the Chevy next to me. His jeans are torn but at least he's covered up his green bruises with a real shirt. He throws his backpack on the dash. "Gonna explain yourself, little girl?"

I can see it all over his face; his features are squinty and tense just like Mom's were. "It wasn't a date."

"What the fuck, Charlotte? Damien, really?"

I glare out the front windshield. It's cloudy outside and the rain is going to make a comeback but I keep the windows down. "We just hung out."

He's quiet for a beat. "Why?"

"He wanted to check on the house. I don't know, okay? What was I supposed to do?"

His seat groans, leaning back into the worn fabric. "Why did I have to hear it from Ellie and not you?"

"I was going to tell you."

"Damien told her." His voice stings.

I look at him fast but his expression is set. How much does she know? Even though we didn't agree it would be a secret or anything, a cloud of betrayal looms overhead.

"And of course she ran right to Ray."

Lightening erupts from Betrayal Cloud. "Wonderful."

He peers at me through narrowed eyes. "What does he want

81

with you?"

Good question. I make myself stare blankly back at him, trying to decide if I should just tell him. After all, yesterday was just one big apology, wasn't it? To make up for being a pervert. It was easy to use the excuse he wanted to check out his old house to Mom, but Freddie obviously doesn't buy it. And if Damien did tell Ellie everything, everyone would know soon enough, anyway. I put my hands on the steering wheel. "He wanted to apologize."

Freddie leans in so his elbow is in my side. "For what?"

I glance at him. "Freddie, if this leaves this truck I'll fucking strangle you."

He inches closer, biting his bottom lip and watching my mouth. "Tell me."

"The night he came home he saw me, shifting, in the woods."

His lip twitches and his heart skips a beat. "Saw you?"

I tilt away from him. "He caught me shifting back. Naked."

He laughs, loud. "Oh, no."

I find my mouth pulling a smile. At least he's not raging. "So he felt bad about it and made me breakfast, okay? We drove around after that and that's all."

"That's all?" he wheezes. "Babe, there's no such thing."

"Stop." The back of my neck burns. "This is bad enough without you trying to add to the story."

The wheezing subsides and he scans my face with blunt curiosity. Then he rips open his backpack and digs around, blood pumping with an odd tension that I block out. "This is bad."

"Thanks," I nod, looking out the window. I'm expecting the

clan to drop out of the clouds with torches and pitchforks. Forget about taking up some of Damien's precious time—if they knew we shifted together they would lose it. It's just not something you do with a near stranger, a girl who isn't your girlfriend.

Freddie flicks his lighter. "Ellie is not happy. Damien made it clear he's done with her."

"That had nothing to do with me."

He lights the joint salvaged from his backpack, ignoring me. "Apparently, he ended things a while ago." This isn't news to him. "The fact seemed to slip Ellie's mind. Last night at the bar they had it out."

I cringe. "They fought?"

He inhales the joint nice and slow, eyeing me. "She tried. He really wasn't taking her on. Until..."

I wait for him to finish but I know he's waiting for me to bite. I look out of the windshield again. "Until?"

I see the grin out of the corner of my eye. "She brought you into it. Because a guy like Damien can't buy a girl like you a drink. Not that he even paid, but it's the thought, right?"

"How is it my fault? He doesn't even know me."

"Oh, I think he knows you plenty well."

I hit him, making sure to land my knuckles on a bruise.

Unphased, he winks. "And that was before she found out about your date."

"Before everyone found out about it," I hedge.

"No. He got her to go outside and talk with him, but she torpedoed back in a little while later and beelined it to Ray to deliver the news. She just wanted Damien to get some heat. Then she drank all night and made Bass drive her home."

I take the joint from his fingers and inhale, deep. This is too much. I can't process what it means—if it means anything. What did Damien think was going to happen when he told her? She was never really stable to begin with, but she's been hanging on threads lately and he must have seen that. "What exactly did she tell Ray?"

Freddie leans back in the protesting seat again, throwing an arm behind his headrest. "That he spent the day with you. Basically what you told me."

Suspicion and disappointment coat his voice. He knows I'm not telling the whole truth.

But that's all he's going to get, and it's more than Damien told Ellie. "Was Ray mad?"

His gray eyes are glazed but steady. He shrugs. "I think they all are. *You're* not part of the plan."

"I'm *not* part of the plan," I agree.

We sit a few minutes, taking in the brewing storm. I'm waiting for the familiar wave to hit me. A good buzz will settle my heart. Bringing Ellie into it is one thing, but Ray? He's a good guy, at least by Dad's standards, but I am *not* part of the plan, and it doesn't take much to rile him up. What's he going to do? Maybe this'll push him over the edge and he'll just banish me forever. Or eat me alive.

"They're just scared," Freddie says.

He's been looking at me. "Of what?"

84

His mouth twitches. "Losing him again."

By math my high is wearing off and I just want to get home before Ray has a chance to assassinate me. I keep checking my phone even though Damien doesn't have my number. I should have given it to him. Slumped in my middle-row seat I watch the rain beat the windows. The fluorescent lights are especially bad today because of the darkness seeping inside and I can't stop myself from yawning. Does the mansion flood when it rains really hard? There were holes in the roof so rain definitely gets in, but does it have a basement? What furniture is left inside? Maybe, in the parlor, there's a framed portrait of the family that used to live there.

I rub my fingers along my notebook, remembering the feeling of flower petals and thorns. Damien's naked torso. The nicks on his arms. That wide smile. His hand pressed into my back on our matching scar. *How'd you get yours?* He shot right back when I asked.

"Miss Reed? Still with us?"

And it's only Monday. I don't answer.

He knows I'm not sharp and smiles brightly. "Question fifteen? From the homework?"

Several pairs of eyes turn to me, waiting.

I break eye contact with Greer to look at my peers. The kid to my left and one row up has wet hair from sneaking outside to smoke between classes and blinks at me when I meet his gaze. The girl in front of me with a too thick layer of foundation quickly turns around when I focus on her, and after I make the boy on my right squirm, Greer clears his throat.

"Number fifteen, Charlotte," he says, and the murmur in his chest increases. This might be his chance.

I glance at my paper briefly. "Negative one-twenty-one."

His jaw tightens. "And would you like to show us how you got to that answer?"

Every time. It never bothered me until right this moment. I know it's his sick way of picking me out to try to appeal to the mouth breathers in the class and so far I've happily obliged, but I can't care enough to day to move.

Greer's beady eyes bear into me, waiting for me to question him before walking too close to him to get to the white board.

"No, I don't think that'd be necessary today," I say, making sure to shrug.

Over half the class visibly stops breathing and turns to me. The rain pelts the window panes and a flash of lightening crosses the sky. Greer waits for the thunder to pass before speaking.

"Excuse me?"

I sit a little straighter in my seat, an unfamiliar tingle spreading over my back. All this time I didn't think it was worth it—calling Greer out. It didn't matter. He was just a math teacher, and I was just a student with one more year between me and absolute freedom. Who was he in the grand scheme of things? After a couple months I'll never see him again as long as I live. Twenty years from now I probably won't even remember his name, his stupid bald head and his too-crisp button-down shirts. His trembling pulse.

But it does matter, right now. To me, in this moment, *he* matters. So who cares if in twenty years I won't be able to remember the way he grips his podium? The way his pulse quickens when he calls on me? I'm dealing with his ridiculous treatment right now. And I don't want to.

"My answers are right," I say. "If anyone disagrees then they can work it out on the board."

His face turns a slight shade of plum and I bite back a smile. "Well, Miss Reed, I'm not asking anyone else to show their work. I'm asking you."

I lean forward a little. The tingle bursts into an all-out inferno. "And I'm declining."

A choke comes from the back, a laugh mingled with a cough, and the class stirs.

Greer takes a step forward. "This is my classroom, Miss Reed. Part of being in my class is showing your work when it's requested from you."

I nod in agreement. "Why don't you request it from Jackson? Anne? Sarah, Seth, Aaron?" Each kid jerks at the sound of their name coming from my lips—each one guilty of jeering at me when Greer calls me out. "I can tell you right now that Taylor behind me didn't even do her work, so this could be a great teaching exercise."

His face darkens and he lays a hand on his podium to give him strength. "If you don't come up here and show your work then you're going to have to leave, Charlotte. I won't be disrespected in my classroom."

I stand, making Seth to my right flinch, and grab my bag and notebook. "Alrighty, then I guess we're done here."

Greer has stopped breathing.

I point to his desk phone as I walk out. "Be sure to ring up the office and tell them I'm on my way, okay?"

He doesn't work up the breath to say any more until the door is closed behind me and his words are only a murky drum.

Dad urged me from the safety of the ground. "You've got to jump, Char, come on!"

The speckled owl purred inside me and tried to tell me it was going to be okay, and I had to remember that she did that sort of thing all the time. But the earth was just so far away. The branch shook from my weight and my eyes kept darting from the ground to the trees to the clear sky and back down again.

Dad stood at the base of the tree, his face tilted up, arms outstretched. I could hardly make him out through the dense green leaves, but the owl's eyes knew right where he was. I glanced into the bright sky at the other birds giving me a wide berth.

I'd never flown before. The owl was my first winged animal.

It wasn't planned; Dad and me were just walking through the woods like we sometimes did when I felt her. It was twilight. She had just dropped from a branch and before I could even think Dad had grabbed me by the shirt and threw me toward her like he was tossing me from a burning building. I latched on at once and now I was gripping onto her for dear life.

"She'll know what to do, Char!" Dad shouted up at me. "It's a lot like learning to run on four legs. The animal already knows how, so you just have to do half the work."

Like jumping from the topmost branch of a very tall tree.

"You've got to trust her," He said, softer. "You've got to trust yourself. I won't let you fall."

Except that's exactly what I had to do. A choked hoot escaped me. He'd said that so many times before. When I was sad or angry or in pain. When he let me cry into his shoulder after skinning my first animal, when I realized I'd have to start running on my own, when I told him how scared I was to move, when he needed me to dive off a tree.

When I had to fall.

Nine

I don't see Damien for the rest of the week as a result of lightly avoiding him. Though I feel like I should maybe thank him because I haven't heard any more details about our outing through the grapevine. He stuck to our unofficial story that neither of us agreed on.

Only after my write-up and meeting the principal for the first time did that reality sink in. It's not exactly guilt, but I can't help but think the confrontation was unnecessary. I riled up my math teacher because I knew I could. I've always considered our shootouts a game, but something this time set me off. You'd think that my only friend might somehow rub off on me through the years, but Freddie has almost never influenced me to act like that.

No, it was Damien. He ploughed through the earth of my brain, poked a hole with his pinky, and dropped a seed in. All anyone had to do was harvest it.

But it felt good. The satisfaction comes in waves, drowning out any regret. Greer hardly looks at me now. He's taken to singling out the kids who fall asleep in the back of the class, or the ones who sneak in Hot Cheetos.

Everyone gathered in the bar last night as a pre-game for the camping trip this weekend, but I faked having essential homework. Mom called me twice to try to get me to come, but I couldn't.

The problem is that I *want* to see Damien.

I want to tell him about Greer, I want him to smile at me, I want to drive around in his Jeep with the windows down. I want things I've never wanted with someone else.

And I don't know why.

I'm picking at my steering wheel, stuck in the parking lot gridlock after school, when Freddie practically comes flying through my passenger window.

"Give me a ride?" he says, already yanking the door open. He's wired. His jaw is hard.

"I guess."

"I'm riding with you and Jule to the campground." It only takes one slam for the door to stick and it rattles the cab.

"You mean you're going?"

"Nicole and Liam are noosing me into it because Ro couldn't keep his goddamn mouth shut."

Freddie hates camping. Despises sleeping in the woods. Can't stand the quiet of the great outdoors. Up until this second I was contemplating not going, visualizing his relief when I told him we'd have the entire weekend to ourselves...

"What did he say?" I ask, treading lightly.

He scowls out the window. "Told them I was going to have a party at our house. Like I'd waste the energy trying to hide it from Nicole." There's an angry gash on his shoulder, right on top of the blade. His blood pressure is making it pulse and I resist the urge to clamp my hand over it. He challenged some guys from my class at lunch, and coaxed them into the parking lot. Twenty minutes later Freddie returned with an extra wound, and minus two boys. Even though I couldn't be a part of it, it was inevitable. They'd taken to howling at us—me in particular—and after several threats Freddie had enough. One by one he's been squashing out Joey's followers, and I'd be touched if he didn't enjoy it so much.

"Were you going to have a party?" Because I wasn't invited.

He glances at me with his cold eyes. "No."

We break free of the parking lot and I start speeding. The engine cries at me. "You need to stop at your place to pack?"

"Fuck, no. Ro can do it for me since he wants me to go so bad."

Here we go.

"That asshole," he sneers, digging in his backpack for a bottle of pills. "I thought that when Damien came home he'd stick himself up his ass and leave mine alone—but no. Worse than ever."

"You know he cares."

"He looks at me like they all do. He doesn't care."

"He doesn't want you to hurt yourself." Neither do I, but it would be a death wish to go behind Freddie's back to Nicole and Liam like Ro can.

He stops his search of Xanax to look at me. "Hurt myself?"

I don't return his gaze and keep my tone from turning accusatory. "You push yourself too hard."

"Don't start this shit again," he says, not as harsh.

"I'm not starting anything. Just saying he's not out to get you." Before he can object I add, "But your parents definitely are."

He shuts his mouth to acknowledge I'm right and starts chewing on a Xanax.

Nicole and Liam are their own breed. They're the most cookie-cutter out of all of us and I don't understand how they do it. Liam's a dentist and goes for a two-legged run every morning. Nicole is Homemaker of the Year and head of their neighborhood watch. Both blonde and tall and perfect. Even though Ro drinks too much and never amounted to anything more than an average at-least-he-hasn't-cut-his-arm-off-yet logger, he's still Mr. Popular.

Then there's Freddie.

He fiddles with the radio as we bump along to my house, slowly lightening up. He knows I'm on his side, even if I sometimes don't know which side that is.

I pull up behind Mom's small white Honda in the driveway and as soon as we step inside the house Freddie goes for the kitchen.

"Got any pizza rolls?" he whines, throwing his backpack on the ground, anger dissolved into self-pity; I'd take that over his wrath any day.

"Yeah, do the whole bag," I tell him, stepping over Mom's duffel and our tent in the hallway. I guess I need to pack.

"Hey, Char!" Mom hollers from upstairs. "Is that Freddie with you?"

"Hi, Jule," Freddie answers, slamming the freezer shut.

I take the stairs two at a time and stop just inside her room. "He's riding with us," I say, watching her shove clothes into her old wooden dresser. "Whatcha doing?"

"Finishing laundry," she says, breathless and trying to close her top drawer. She's got a bandana tied around her head and one of her flowery sun dresses on. "Are you all packed up?"

"Yeah," I lie, leaning against her doorframe.

"How was your last day of detention?"

The school counselor called Mom once the principal had a sit-down with me, as if they expected some home discipline. My punishment was Chinese for dinner. "It's just free period in the library."

"Same thing." With one last heave, she shuts the drawer.

"It was peaceful."

She peeks at me out of the corner of her eye. "Damien called."

"Oh?" My voice is a little too high.

"Mhmm." She pretends to fix her hair in the mirror sitting on her dresser.

"What did he want?"

She purses her lips to hold back a smile. "To make sure you were going on the trip."

"You're screwing with me."

"Well you skipped out on the bar and the meeting at Ray's on Wednesday. Poor boy doesn't get the hint."

"Did you just call Damien a poor boy?"

"Honey, every boy is a poor boy. Especially when a girl is involved."

I let her hug me, but keep my hands by my sides. She's trying to get a read on my heartbeat, like she's being sneaky. "There's no hint to not get. No hint at all."

"He just wants to see you," she says.

"I don't know why."

She pulls back to cup my face with her soft hands. "You have an amazing personality."

"Okay." I lean out of her grasp.

She laughs and turns back to her mirror. "You're an amazing person, Char, everyone should want to spend time with you."

She has to say that. "What did you tell him?"

"I told him you wouldn't miss the trip for the world."

"Way to make me sound eager." I leave before my face can get too hot. He wants to see me. I hunt for my sleeping bag in the abyss of my closet and start contemplating what skins to bring when Freddie makes a racket hopping up the stairs.

He gives Mom a quick hello before sliding into my room. "Ten more minutes."

"Damien called my house," I say, low.

He takes my pillow and falls onto the bed. "That's what you get for avoiding him."

"It's weird, though, isn't it?"

"No weirder than you." He inhales my pillow.

"I'm going to ask him."

Freddie sits up so fast the pillow goes flying. "This weekend?"

I nod, heart stammering as I take *Frankenstein* from my school bag. I have to know, before this can get more out of hand than it already is. He wasn't supposed to catch me naked in the woods, wasn't supposed to apologize, wasn't supposed to get me to like him. In all my years wondering what I'd say, how the story could come out, us in a position of friendship wasn't a factor I squeezed in. We were supposed to be near-strangers, and were going to be near-strangers after I got the truth. "He wants to see me? Get to know me? Then I deserve a real answer first."

The side of Freddie's mouth pulls up. "We'll see."

He doesn't think I'll demand a real explanation about Dad, and I'm not so confident it'll work out, either, but the right time might not come. I thought I'd be uncomfortable around Damien, but I'm not, and that's scary. What's worse, he's comfortable around me.

"What are you bringing?" Freddie asks, eyeing me while I pull out my oak box.

The wolf howls at me as soon as I lift the lid.

"'Cause she better be fast. You might have to run for your life."

"Shut up," I snap. I wrap up the wolf and owl pelts in a cloth

96

before sliding them deep into my duffel. "Don't you have pizza rolls to check on?"

He jumps up and hops to the door. "Right-O."

It doesn't take long to finish packing, smoke a bowl with Freddie, and eat an entire bag of pizza rolls before we load up the truck and get on the road. Our campsite is smack in the middle of Arapaho & Roosevelt National Forest, about two hours farther into the middle of nowhere than our town already is. The clan's been going there for longer than Ray's been alive, taking the scenic path down ranger service roads to an obscure pull off where we have to hike another thirty minutes to the clearing. I normally like the little adventure. The buildup gets me in the spirit of camping and being secluded. Today it's making me anxious.

Most of the clan are sure to turn out for the weekend because of Damien. I didn't need to go to the meeting at their house to know the pressure Mona and Ray are going to put on him. Everyone's watching.

"Think there's gonna be fights?" Freddie muses hopefully on my right, bumping his leg against mine.

Through my haze I blink at him. He's got an arm out the open window, soaking some of the sun into his pale skin. I managed to pour some alcohol on his wound before we left but he wouldn't let me cover it.

"Just some tumbles," Mom predicts on my left. She's flying in the left-hand lane down the highway and I don't think the truck's going to make it.

"Why?" If anyone's going to start a fight it'll be Freddie, like always.

"Lots of testosterone."

"And serotonin." Freddie winks for me to see.

"Everyone's going to want a piece of him," Mom adds.

Freddie shoots me a look that I ignore. "What did you bring, Mom?"

"Just the fox. She hasn't spread her legs in a while."

She would, if the woman took a day off to go running. I turn to Freddie. "And you?"

He leans his head out of the window. "I guess whatever Nicole and Liam packed."

Bullshit.

"Stop calling your parents by their first names, Freddie," Mom says.

"They like it."

"It's weird."

I snort, giving in to the fit of laughter that follows. The day is warm and my brain is just as fuzzy. Mom makes Freddie pick out one of her cassettes from the 80s to stick in the ancient slot under the radio. She brings them on every car trip since her Honda only plays CDs and her cassette player broke. We jam to bands that aren't together anymore or dead, or a combination of both, until we get off the highway and reach the first of the service roads. It starts to get rocky and dense with tall trees.

It was around here that I caught the wolf. Maybe two years ago. It's common knowledge that wild wolves haven't been a thing in Colorado for years, and that introducing them back into the state was a real battle. They had laws and protocols for getting them relocated into certain areas. I never expected to see any in my lifetime.

I came out here alone around the third anniversary of Dad's death. Just got my license and was still shuffling around in Mom's Honda. Thought myself grown up for daring a small road trip by myself. I brought a few skins with me, hungry for these mountain ranges. I didn't dare go all the way up to our campsite. It just seemed off-limits to me, so I found a pull-off on a cliff face. It was hot, the end of summer, and for the briefest of moments I contemplated lunging over the barrier on the rocky shoulder to see if I could fly in my skin alone. The wind breezed by me, keeping me back while the thousands of miles of wilderness beckoned. I felt that Dad was out there, wandering on his own through streams and up mountains, sleeping in trees and reaching out to touch whatever animals passed.

I don't remember much of what I did before I found her. At the time things were livid and sharp, a lone excursion I was sure would stick with me forever, but all I remember was running as far as I could outward, away from all the roads. I remember the pronghorn, whose thin legs let me glide through the ferns. She was with me when we heard it. She felt it first, heart fluttering like a butterfly after someone ripped one of its wings off, willing me to run away. But we were miles and miles from Mom's car, from anyone.

I followed the noise. It almost sounded like a broken whistle;

air being blown down a pipe that's given up. The closer we got, the quieter the noise became. The strange animal's heartbeat was irregular, dulling, and even when I heard her howl catch in her throat, I still didn't believe what it was.

When we caught sight of the gray fur in the dip of the land, the pronghorn let go. She tore herself from me out of pure fright and instinct. Left without her, naked body hot and shaking, I heaved myself from the ground, determined. The rocks and boulders sloped into a small crevice like a dried riverbed, trees clear of the spot and leaving the surrounding vegetation thirsty.

The wolf was half concealed behind a cracked, fallen tree. At first I thought she was hiding, or maybe asleep, but her heartbeat said otherwise. Her broken whistle of a howl ceased when she caught my scent and grew into a low growl when she saw me.

For a second, I thought the tree had fallen on her, until I saw the rusted bear trap snaring her back leg. It looked to be years old, forgotten. How long had it waited for this moment? How much weight was needed to snap it? She must have walked directly on top of its jaws.

She eyed me as best she could and soon got tired of growling. Her fur, nearly white on her belly and growing darker on her back stood on end, her legs tensed as she gave a final struggle to stand.

I dropped the pronghorn pelt and got down on all fours, crawling over the jagged earth closer to her. Her breathing became ragged and labored, and I had to make a choice. I could take her in, if she wanted me, or I could let her go. She had a fight in her until the very end. She wasn't ready to let go of this world, even if she did split my back open, right down the middle.

Over half the clan's already made it out, judging by the clumps of cars in the rough clearing.

"Nicole and Liam here, yet?" I ask, escaping the truck. It's making ticking noises and definitely over-heated.

"Doesn't look like it," Freddie answers, not too broken up. He hops into the bed of the truck to hand off our stuff.

There's several families pulling things out of their vehicles, and in the small chaos I spot Ray's truck. The path leading out of the clearing has been beaten back by now and I'm itching to hike up it.

Loud rock music fills the air before Ralph's Firebird arrives, kicking up a cloud of dust as he makes himself a spot near us.

"Hope he brought food," I mumble.

Freddie grins, handing me my duffel.

Jessica and Ralph both emerge from his car and Mom makes a beeline towards them.

"Never fails," Freddie sighs, handing me Mom's bag next. He's got a hand on his side.

I open my mouth to tell him he's being an idiot, but the Cormack family pulls up next to us in their silver minivan and I swear instead. First comes the oldest out of the side door, followed by the twins and the fourth boy. The look of disgust on

Freddie's face when the boys bump into me to get out in the open makes me want to kiss him. A house with five boys all under the age of ten is a great one to live next door to. When we were younger, Freddie would indulge them without ever getting too close because there was only one or two. Now with five and possibly another on the way, he's dropped the charade and openly talks about his fantasies of burning down their house.

I glance at the driver's side window to see the Mr. and Mrs. arguing again.

Freddie hands me the tent and the identical seven-year-olds jump up on my truck, yelling Freddie's name and going wild to make the bed shake under their weight. The younger one can't get up on his own and starts to cry. The oldest disappears.

"Get down, you fucking gremlins." Freddie shakes one off when he clings to his legs.

Mr. Cormack escapes the van, slamming the door behind him and running a hand through his Dad Haircut. "Let's go, boys," he grunts.

They ignore him.

"Leave the baby home?" I ask to make him look our way.

Mr. Cormack blinks in my general direction before nodding and popping the hatchback.

"Zack's at home with Gram," the little one says, poking me in my stomach. He's got a Spider-Man shirt on with something sticky running down the front.

"Boys!" Mrs. Cormack shrieks, emerging behind her husband. "Get over here."

They contemplate ignoring her, too, but Freddie shoves one of the twins by the head and they get down.

"Where's your brother?" she continues loudly.

Freddie jumps down and hoists our tent over a shoulder. He does his best not to wince and turns his back before I can say anything. By the time Ralph and Jessica have gotten their things from his trunk and we're ready for the hike, the Cormack crew has already left. We catch up to them in minutes and most the trip up the trail is filled with a lot of yelling.

Both from Mrs. Cormack and Freddie.

Our field is overgrown and grassy; even the fire pits have sprouted weeds. Several large canopies have already been erected on the slight incline in the middle. Tents are jumping up around the edges, some closer to others, everyone claiming their favorite spots. Ray's voice comes from somewhere but I can't make him out in the pack. As we pass a few groups I sense a shift in conversation. If Mom feels it she doesn't let on, too preoccupied with babbling to Jessica and Ralph. Eyes are on me and I will the heat not to creep onto my neck. Freddie acts as a barrier as we head for a spot by the tree line.

"Off to a great start," I say.

"I'm having so much fun," he confesses, jabbing me in the side.

Mom and Jessica bring our cooler of ice to the collection in the middle while Ralph, Freddie and I set up the tents.

"You'd think by now you'd have figured how to pitch a tent," Ralph chides at Freddie, hammering his last stake into place with a final swing.

"Oh, I know how to pitch a tent," Freddie answers, pushing his hair from his face while we struggle to hoist the tent up between us.

"I try to follow the directions, but Freddie just picks up and starts wherever the hell he pleases," I snap.

"It *always* gets up one way or another."

Ralph straightens up, grinning, and helps lift the tent into place. Then he tells us what to hold and where to move and we're done in the next four minutes.

"Alright, I gotta get started on the grill. Hammer down those stakes some more and you're all set," Ralph instructs. "Don't forget to tighten the guylines for the fly."

"Yeah," Freddie agrees when Ralph's out of earshot. "Get to it, Char." He ducks into the tent, bringing our bags with him.

I'm about to tell him I forgot the weed when Damien's laugh echoes through the clearing, right into my brain. The hairs on my arms stand on end and I lean around the tent to see him, Ro, and Bass enter the clearing.

Freddie groans. "And the day's getting better still."

I keep my smile to myself as the voices draw closer. Ro calls Freddie's name and I come around front. The trio spots me and head my way, knowing Freddie's got to be within a ten-foot radius of me. I avoid Damien's stare. His beating heart stands stronger above the rest, like my ears are already tuned to it.

"I don't think Ro thinks he did anything wrong," I say in a low voice to Freddie, trying to keep him calm.

He births himself from the tent, face flushed.

"He probably heard what you did to John and Toby and didn't want to leave you alone to finish the job," I add.

He stares at me hard. "I did that for you."

"No, you did that for *you*."

"What's up, baby brother? Hey, Char," Ro says. He's ripped the sleeves off his shirt and his bulky arms glisten in the sun. He slides Freddie's Pepto Pink duffel bag over his shoulder and tosses it at him. Bass looks like a miniature version of Ro, with their matching logging company snapbacks.

Damien stops next to me, too close. His eyes roll over me but I still don't look. I can almost taste his sweat.

Freddie drops the duffel.

"You two all set up for the night, then?" Bass says, pointing between Freddie and me.

Damien's finger taps my wrist, sending a jolt up my bones. He prods my arm, almost kneading me, like a cat. It takes a lot not to shiver, not to laugh, even when his mouth twitches in my peripheral.

"Nah, baby brother is bunking with you and me." Ro laughs, clapping Freddie on his good shoulder.

I take a small step back, not only to get away from Damien but also in case Freddie starts swinging.

Freddie slaps his hand away. "Shut the fuck up, Sasquatch. You're sleeping in the dirt."

Bass nudges Ro in the side. "I mean you might not be doing any sleeping at all, so."

They both start guffawing.

This time Damien's fingers wrap around my wrist, and I can't stop myself from looking up at him. His onyx eyes seep into mine, looking for an answer to why I ignored him all week.

But all I can think of is him letting the whole clan know we spent time together. The walk outside the bar. Ray's rage. Ellie and Bass hooking up. Rose thorns. His big, comforting hand on my back in that pool of dark water. Who is he to look at me like that?

I tear myself from him and he releases my arm.

"I wonder, Robert, how hard it would be for you to learn to stop talking out of your ass." Freddie's spitting in his brother's face.

The smile's gone from Ro at this point. "Leave you to yourself for a weekend? Like I don't know what you'd do?"

"Wouldn't throw a fucking party."

Ro gets close and slouches down to look at him better. "Telling them you were going to have a party was better than telling them the truth."

Freddie stutters. "Oh really?"

Ro jabs him in the ribs and he almost doubles over. "Because if I told them what you really do, you'd never leave the house again."

Freddie straightens up and shoves him away.

Enough. I step forward, scoop up Freddie's bag and toss it in our tent. Freddie spins on me and Ro clenches his fist. "Freddie, you're bunking with us for the weekend," I say flatly, staring at them both. "We're not going through this bullshit again."

Freddie bites the inside of his cheek but Ro opens his mouth.

"Don't start," Damien cuts in, and several heads around us turn at the sound of his voice.

Ro clamps his jaw and Bass stares wide-eyed.

"Go find some beer," Damien adds with a lesser tone of authority. "Freddie, Liam's looking for you. They should be halfway up the trail by now. You should go meet them."

After a beat Ro and Bass sulk away. Freddie lingers, harsh words still rolling around in his mouth. He looks to me, but Damien blocks his path.

"Go, Freddie. You need to talk to your parents. And your shoulder's looking infected. Nicole brought some bandages."

"Why would she do that?" he asks.

"Why do you think?" The back of Damien's head tilts toward the direction of Ro's retreating figure.

Freddie hesitates another couple seconds. He was never really good at picking his battles, and part of me hopes he'll stay to argue some more, but instead he turns and strides toward the trail, head held high.

Without an order, I stand in place and try to ignore the few shameless people openly staring. Like we're separated by a TV screen and they can't wait for the commercial break to end.

Damien rounds on me, stepping close. His eyes squint a little in the sun. "And don't think you're off the hook, either."

I open my mouth but no words come out.

He puts his hands on his hips. "You've been avoiding me, little one. I'm offended."

"I thanked you a thousand times for breakfast. We're even."

He plucks up a smile. "I don't think so. I still owe you."

"For what? Blabbing to Ellie?" There's the anger.

That stops him short. "I didn't mean to blow it up. And the conversation wasn't about you."

I keep my gaze with his, letting the anger wash over my heart to silence it. My brain needs to do the talking now.

"I mentioned visiting your house and she took it and ran with it to Ray, hoping he'd do something, I don't know what." He tilts his head, then leans down to whisper in my ear. "The mansion is my secret, remember? If I haven't told her about that by now, it's safe to say I'm never going to."

His breath tickles my neck.

More people have peered over, disappointed that they missed another Randall Showdown. Their eyes are so much more penetrating than regular people's. The thing is, I know exactly what the kids at school are thinking. The teachers, old guys at the bar, the pimply super-senior who rips my ticket in two at the movie theater. Curious, envious, lustful, sometimes a little fearful—not full of scrutiny and judgement. Being an outsider among outsiders is the worst kind of rejection.

And they watch Damien in the strangest way; holding their breaths, waiting for reassurance that everything is fine with him and he's not going anywhere. Talking to me doesn't do anything in the way of putting them at ease. I don't think they fully believed Ellie's claim that Damien spent the day with me. Until now.

He's too close, too hot. Ray's laugh from across the clearing sends a jolt through me.

Damien sees my concern, and reaches out to me.

"Don't," I say, harsher than I need to. I step away and lower my voice. "Can we talk later?"

His eyes reveal nothing, but I can tell he wants to look behind him again, maybe tell a few people to mind their own fucking business. But he doesn't. He just nods and turns, letting the clan swallow him up.

Face burning and wanting to make it look like I have something to do, I grab *Frankenstein* out of the tent and head into the woods. I just want their eyes off me. Need their little prying marbles off my skin. I only slow my pace when I can't hear the camp anymore, and my body cools when the trees' whispers fill my ears. I want to go for a fly, but the first night is always something special, and we can't go out before then. Even though everyone runs in groups out here, people look the other way when I string off by myself. I only ever run with Freddie or Mom, far away from camp.

When Dad was alive, he'd let me tag along with him and some of the other guys, and I know it freaked them out having to run with me, having to struggle to keep up with me. I was a show-off, a freaky little girl.

So now I only show myself to Freddie and Mom. And Damien, apparently.

Giant boulders and fallen bits of mountain congest the ground and I pick over them, finding a nice crevice to stick myself in. But I can't focus on the book; only half of what I read registers and I stop before I can ruin the ending.

"You have to do it, Char," I say out loud, to the trees. "You have to ask him." His smile flashes before my eyes, that chipped tooth and those gleaming pupils. I like that he likes me, if he likes me. *Frankenstein* falls closed. Once I demand he tells me about Dad it'll ruin everything, any crazy feelings he might be developing. I'll be letting him down, bringing up the past, something I know he doesn't want to relive. Who would want to remember having to make a two-hour drive with a dead guy in the same car as you? Who would want to walk into a forest with two companions and only come out with one?

He won't smile at me anymore. He won't want to make me breakfast in Mom's apron. Won't buy me drinks at the bar. Won't help me break up Randall Showdowns. He'll still make my skin tingle, make me want to pick out his heartbeat in a crowd, but he won't give me those eyes.

But knowing the truth is more important than Damien's feelings. My feelings.

This weekend, for sure.

Tonight.

Maybe.

Ten

Several fires light up the black sky and cast dangerous shadows into the trees, making the tall pines look like a wall. My empty stomach tells me to eat, but my appetite is gone. I duck into the tent to throw *Frankenstein* by my bag, still unfinished.

Everyone's gathered around the main campfire, and Ray's voice drifts over. "Glad so many of you were able to make it out, at least if it's only for tonight. Now more than ever it's essential that we come together and stay together."

They linger on his every word; eating up his thoughts. I skirt around the fringes, searching for the shorty with the blond hair. Freddie's fiddling with his lighter, a cigarette dangling from his lips.

"There's a change coming—I know you all feel it." Ray's voice cuts through the still air like a crack through marble.

Agreements.

I bump into Freddie, flicking the cancer stick from his mouth.

His steel eyes are nearly warm in the firelight as he pockets the lighter. "C'mere," he mumbles, wrapping an arm around my neck and pulling me into a hug.

A real hug.

"Liam must've given you a stern talking-to." My fingers brush against his bandaged shoulder. He smells like cigarettes, liquor, and something too sweet.

He doesn't say anything, just buries his head into my hair.

"You're taller than me," I say. I can feel his ribs, every disk of his spine, but there's new meat packed between his bones. "You're stronger."

"You make me want to be stronger."

He must be a happy-drunk tonight; a rare occurrence that I'm willing to take full advantage of. "That's the most romantic thing you've ever said to me."

He pulls away and searches my eyes, trying to get under them. He doesn't sway, holds me steady. "I mean it, babe. I know I'm a shit friend and I don't tell you enough—but thanks for being there."

"I'll always be there," I whisper. "Whether you listen to me or not."

"I do listen. I just ignore you."

We watch each other. Our friendship is a dance, back and forth and side to side, occasionally coming into step with one another long enough to see that it's worth it. We've fine-tuned ourselves over the years, me building him up and him bringing me down. Out of our own minds and into this real world.

Ray repeats a familiar line, an inside joke no one's ever explained to me, and there's laughs from around us.

I mess Freddie's hair and he pinches my cheek. We turn into the others, and from across the fire, through the bodies, my eyes meet Damien's. He stands next to Ray, Mona on his other side, watching me, lips pressed together. I glance at Freddie, who's biting his bottom lip to keep his smile under control.

"Who'd of thought I'd ever be here, in this spot, quoting my old man?" Ray says. "A few of you can remember me puking my guts out after going after that elk for the first time. Most of you were with me, growing up. Growing up together."

Ray looks skyward, scrutinizing the stars above for a glimpse of his father. "That change is almost here again." His eyes drop to his people, wander over every intimate face, and land on Damien. "Tonight's the first step to your right of passage, son."

Damien's face is set, attention serious, but his mouth betrays him. There's a lift in one corner, an eagerness trying to escape.

In the few passing seconds before he can control himself I see it. He's never doubted his ability, willingness, to take the clan. He's been waiting for this his whole life. He didn't leave because he was scared or felt trapped. He left for another reason.

My stomach bubbles and my brain clicks. I want him to meet my gaze again, I want to see what's inside him.

But Ray pulls Damien out of my view and I straighten up to

stare into the smoke.

"And, hopefully, you'll be here to quote me someday." Ray chuckles, and the clan follows suit, lifting their drinks to them.

"Alright," Ray goes on, like he's in front of the Board and about to deliver his multi-million-dollar pitch. "Damien's going to be leading his generation tonight in the first run. Those following him can step forward now."

Most people shuffle back, letting their kids and nephews and nieces get closer to the inner circle. My view is opened to Damien straight across the flames. Ray and Mona position themselves behind him to let room for Ro and Bass, and Ellie and her girls. Even a few shaking middle schoolers step forward after prods from their parents.

My heart shrivels like a plant begging for water as the crowd stirs up, exciting mumblings spreading through it like weeds. My heart pumps my blood too fast and I can't move until Freddie nudges me.

"We're up, babe," he whispers. He doesn't seem especially pleased, either. I know he shouldn't be shifting tonight with his shoulder and even though he's going to act like it doesn't bother him, he knows it, too.

I bring one foot in front of the other, the licking flames promising me all sorts of things as long as I come forward. Out of the corner of my eye I catch one of the younger kids look back at his parents when I approach, ready to bolt. It's a mixture of excitement and fear when I reach the center; some people haven't forgotten the freaky little show-off, and the rest haven't let the rumors die.

There's a leap of a heartbeat in the bodies, and maybe because I really am tuning myself to him, my eyes instinctively go to Damien.

His dark irises reflect the scarlet and gold of the fire, giving him suns in his sockets. It's haunting. His mouth lifts into a smirk.

I'm a leap away from lifting into the sky. The wolf remembers these woods, she's at home here. Her joy propels me forward in the darkness. Only two bodies surround me, ahead of the group. Ro's crashing through the brush, more bull than buck. One of his shoulders is knotted and bulging, misshapen from the bullet he'd used to take it down. Ellie keeps leaping into my field of vision, a near black fox that more resembles a shadow. Her back legs can't stretch as far as they need to match the stride of the fox. The younger kids quickly fell behind, clumsy on their four legs. Freddie made sure to get lost early, a mass of scraggly gray coyote. Bass is on our heels, Ro's twin of a buck sprinting to keep the pace. He'll drop back soon. The others just don't have the stamina or a keen enough mindset to navigate for themselves. They think like people, not animals.

At first they gave me a wide berth when we all converged together, startled at the wolf I inhibited. But now sheer determination, even a little rage, follows me by Ro and Ellie.

We're out to find Damien. The one who finds him first gets a few precious moments alone with him before he rounds up the group.

Ellie comes up to my side again and doesn't dodge away. I know what she's going to do before she veers in front of me to knock me off my feet. In one step, I go far enough right to avoid her and nearly knock Ro off his course. With a grunt, he nearly collides into a tree. I stifle a heckle and lunge ahead of them, widening my stride. They fall behind me in seconds, their harsh breaths and struggling pulses no match for me.

The wolf breathes steadily, on alert for another heartbeat. She and I race forward, her mind pulsing through mine, our blood mixing, her wish for one more night the only thought. I've never taken her back here, not since I found her. I've been too afraid, worried that being in these woods would be too painful for her.

But she loves it—she feels alive. I could laugh.

Damien's thrum hits me and I take to following it even when the wolf gives a little tug in a different direction. She resists as we move closer and closer to Damien. My own heart pounds in anticipation, but hers strikes with something else.

He lets me find him, and I come to a dead stop when I see the large wolf perched on the far end of a little valley. How could he have known what I would bring? The spruces are light here in the dip of mostly flat land and his dark figure is blunt in the moonlight, like a hole ripped through the air. I can't see his eyes—only the gangly bulk of coal colored fur.

I take one step forward, two, and then he leaps forward at a run, coming toward me.

The wolf stirs, beckoning me to run away from him, and I indulge her. I turn, throwing one last look at his approaching figure before darting back into the woods. Instinct tells her to get away, and her howl escapes my throat.

I ignore her, keeping a steady pace for him to catch up, and soon he's at my heels.

The wolf growls. His presence sparks something—his ragged breath almost on me and the sound of him padding behind us flips a switch and she pushes me forward, out of his grasp.

It gets hard to see. We're going so fast. Damien tries to keep up. There's a desperate urge radiating off him, seeping through every forged pore. The sky gets darker, moonlight disappearing. I run faster, propelled by something I can't focus on. A fire starts in my chest and moves through my veins, latching onto bones and burning up my neck. The wolf rips through me, clawing to get out.

I choke. I can't breathe. She grabs hold of my legs, moving them mechanically away from him, away from me. She twists in my belly and pounds at my brain. Pulls at my heart and tries to split my soul.

My vision goes in and out, cloudy, like I'm looking through someone else's eyes. My breathing is different, unfamiliar. I can only hear the blood rushing, feel my breath coming back at me.

And things go entirely black.

The world goes quiet. I don't feel anything.

I press against her. Into the dark. But there's nothing.

Then I'm screaming into the silence. It's cold—I can't see the moon. The light.

Any sign of life.

I'm small, shrinking.

Whatever's keeping me alive is pouring out of me and into her; a leaky pipe in the basement decided to flood. I howl, straining for the natural beat of my heart and the sweet tension of running legs.

The dull sound of breathing starts to build.

Her breathing. Her lungs, her heartbeat, her skin, her bones, her blood, her eyes, her ears, her mind. Hers, hers, hers.

But what about me? Where's my blood?

Like running into a wall, the wolf and I collide.

We fall, bouncing off a tree and then the ground. The world comes onto me all at once. It ignites the change. My bones bend before they crack. Blood bursts from my veins and soon the wolf's howls are replaced with my own. We split—

Our souls separate.

My will floods back like a limb that's fallen asleep. Vision pours into my eyes and I can smell the earth again. I'm flat on my back, staring into the bold face of the moon. The light. Each gasp helps inflate my lungs. I'm on fire, the only relief coming from the cool ground and the breeze that flutters my hair and makes my nipples hard.

Everything throbs.

It's quiet except for the whispering of the trees.

Damien is close. He might have always been here, waiting for me to come back.

His breath comes out in little clouds and he comes up on my left. He's panting, even though he's probably had plenty of time to calm his heart rate. I watch from the corner of my eyes, half blurred with tears, as the massive black wolf stalks silently toward me.

I roll onto my side, away from him, face wet.

A low rumble comes from his chest and his nose touches the back of my neck. He breathes me in deeply, moving up to my head and nuzzling my hair.

The small action of smelling me, drinking in my skin in full animal form, while I lay vulnerable and weak, is the most empathetic thing anyone's ever done.

"Go," I whisper, voice hoarse. The others are looking for him. If they find me they might eat me.

He lingers, waiting for me to move, but I don't. This time, seeing me naked, is different. The wolf molded into me, and I don't know for how long. We both inhibited a body, and she took over. I felt what it was like to be the second soul, incapable of thinking for myself and stripped of senses. Truly alone and naked.

He gives a soft, reassuring lick on my shoulder and then he's gone.

The wolf wasn't angry or hateful. She was desperate for something she once had. She saw a chance and seized it—the last night she was robbed of. For some reason, tonight, rather than the hundreds of other nights we've run together, she decided she wanted out. My heart aches to think about her desperation so I wipe it from my mind on my long limp back to camp. She's quiet. Damien did a good job of leading everyone away, and I don't feel anyone on my trek through the forest. I find the spot where I left my clothes with little difficulty. My right side, where I hit the tree, pulls at my skin when I slide my shirt on. Legs are wobbly as I step into my shorts. I have to sit on the ground to get my breath back. To cool down. Camp isn't too far—laughs reach my ears every so often. The others are already back.

A rustling comes from somewhere in the dark.

"Bring any of that Xanax?" I ask, expecting Freddie, and for once dead serious. There's a probing in the back of my brain that's starting to seep forward.

"Whoa, didn't know you did that kind of stuff," a female voice answers, and Ellie's form appears in the dim.

I tense, the giant muscle in the middle of my chest hardening. I move, starting to stand, but think better of it and stay on the ground.

She's fully clothed, jeans and a T-shirt pulled tight across her boobs. Her oval face flushed and dark hair windswept. "Charlotte, right?" She drawls, like she doesn't know. She wanders slowly around me, not focused on anything.

"Yeah," I say. I might be weak and my ribs could come loose any second, but I focus on her in case she decides to strike.

"That wolf was pretty cool," she says, impressed in her own

faded way.

"Thanks."

"Damien's was cool too, don't you think?" She stops pacing and looks up. "It's weird you both brought wolves, don't you think?"

"I don't know what to tell you." I keep a hold of my aching ribs. It's not like we planned our matching outfits.

"I mean, he *never* used to run with a wolf, like ever, in all the times we went running together. We went out together all the time, just us, and I've maybe seen that thing three times. Want to guess what his absolute favorite is?"

My breathing thins. "Ellie, I don't know what to say."

"You could tell me you're sorry," she suggests, ripping an unsuspecting King's Crown from its stem.

My mouth is dry. Dots swirl in my peripheral. "For?"

She purses her lips, concentrating on the flower's spikey, ruby bulbs. "Doing whatever you did."

"What do you think I did?"

Her eyes flash. They shine in the scarce light. "I don't know, but it was something. Someone like you doesn't just become interesting for someone like him."

"I'm not going to apologize to you," I say, trying to keep my voice from cracking.

Maybe because she's high from the shift or drunk on actual alcohol, she pauses and nods in my direction. "I'm just trying to help you out. You're in over your head, *little one*."

I watch her, tiny cold veins beginning to wrap themselves

around my too-tense chest muscle.

"It's not easy, being friends with him. That kind of family. They're strong people. Leaders. People who matter."

"Don't we all matter?" My voice is soft. It sounds pathetic even before the words get out into the air but I can't stop them.

I can just make out her smile. Or is it a sneer? "Some more than others. They're an old family. This is an old clan, things get done a certain way. Just because you want to be different doesn't mean the way we do things is gonna change for you."

Want to be different?

When I don't respond she just shrugs and disappears into the brush.

I struggle to my feet, taking it slow as the world tilts.

My empty stomach churns and I still feel naked. I haven't let myself get this bad in years. The wolf is traumatized. I've never been torn from a skin like that—we've never become one and she's never taken over. She hums barely enough for me to hear, drained, but I keep her tied to my forearm, hoping to provide some comfort. I still hold some guilt for doing what I did. It wasn't my hand that brought her down. She didn't seek me out like most skins do. I found her, vulnerable, and waited to take her. It's not something Dad would have done. He probably would have stayed with her and made sure she went peacefully. But I couldn't leave her, let her go. I pushed myself toward her, and have been convincing both of us that it was for the best.

Voices of the clan help me resurface when I break the tree line. Our tent is on the far side of the clearing. The smoke of the campfire, roasting meat, and weed entice me forward. They've got several fires going, the one in the middle the largest still. Mom's laugh rises above the others for a brief moment and I try to make her out, but then Freddie's body lounging in a folding chair catches my eye and I stumble towards him. Hopefully he's still in his happy, loving mood. There's a few kids emerging from the woods, faces red and a hungry look in their eyes. Soft crying comes from a nearby tent and the unmistakable soothing of a mother's voice whispers above it.

Dad was always the one to console me, and even that was a rare occasion. I didn't have bad shifts often, but when I did, he held me against his giant chest, let me feel his heartbeat, stroked my hair and didn't say a word. A handful of times I've even held Mom in my arms, absorbed her shaking and inconsistent breath. When we were younger, Freddie sometimes would come running to me after a night out with Ro or Liam when Nicole wasn't around, but not anymore. He'd never let me see him in a bad way now.

My hands tremble more and more the closer I get to Freddie, itching to reach out to him. He's turned away from me, a beer in hand. Ro and Bass crowd the fire with him, a couple of Ellie's friends across from them. All at once I wish Dad was here to cradle me in his Viking arms, protect me from the night. He'd soothe not only me, but the wolf, too.

Homesickness hits me hard, the gaping hole of where he once was widening inside my chest.

Freddie notices me first, and by the time he realizes something is wrong it's too late and everyone has seen me.

"Thought you bolted for the border," Ro coughs, exhaling a cloud of smoke and trying not to sound too bitter.

"Want a s'more?" Bass asks, a bag of marshmallows in his hand.

I drop hard into the canvas folding chair next to Freddie, wishing he was just a little closer. "Yeah."

Bass gets to spearing two marshmallows on a sharpened stick and Ro passes the joint to one of Ellie's friends. They give me quick glances.

"You were so fast," Ro says, leaning a little too close to the fire.

"Like a graceful cheetah." Bass laughs, twisting the stick in the flames to get an even toast.

"I didn't even see her," one of the girls says, inhaling the joint.

"I mean you have the speed of a dead fish, so you probably wouldn't," Bass starts, then swears when one of the marshmallows drops into the fire with a hiss.

"What are you talking about?" Ro jeers. "We left you hanging on the back with Tad Adderson." He snorts, the image of the thirteen-year-old stumbling around as a mangy dog spreading around to all of us.

Freddie's fingers brush against my elbow, right above where the wolf's tied, and they both send a current up my arm. My eyelids flutter and my lips part. I turn to him, about ready to beg him to walk me to the tent, but an approaching body from behind stops me mid-breath.

Damien comes to a halt right between us, and the boys fall

silent. I don't have the strength to look up at him, not that I even have the courage.

"Wear yourself out, little one?" he asks, scooping my hand out of Freddie's. He puts himself between our chairs and gently tugs me to my feet.

I warm to his touch, like he's pouring velvet down my back. I sway and he slides an arm around my waist. The burnt glow of the fire casts shadows over his features and scars, making the frown look even more disconcerting.

The second marshmallow drops into the fire with another hiss, but Bass doesn't swear this time.

"Let's get you to bed, huh?" he says softly.

Freddie stands so abruptly from his chair I jump.

"What's wrong, Freddie? Ro, pass this kid a joint."

"Excuse me?" Freddie says. That tone.

I step away from Damien, even though my body screams not to. "It's alright. I am just really tired." I lean slightly to give Freddie a pleading look. Not tonight.

He just stares back.

I pull myself away from the light and warmth of the fire. Damien follows.

"You're limping," he says quietly, once we're out of earshot.

I'm glad the conversation around the big fire doesn't lull while we sneak past.

"I'm fine," I answer, straightening up. I don't want to talk—I want to crawl up in a corner and dissolve into nothing.

"You were gone for a little while," he presses, an urgency in

125

his tone. "I wasn't chasing you anymore. I was chasing a wolf."

His words sting my raw flesh and I clamp my mouth shut, holding my sides.

When we get to my tent he steers me to the back, out of sight. The small part of me begging for his empathy lets him. The spring air brings a chill when it rustles the trees and bushes behind us.

Damien plants himself not even a foot away. A loose thread hangs from his dark shirt.

"Look at me," he says.

I keep my teeth clenched and blink to clear my eyes before raising them to his.

They pierce through me, straight into my brain, hungry. "She took over, didn't she, Charlotte?"

My lip quivers.

"Don't," he murmurs, and pulls me into him.

I gasp as he crushes me into his chest. His head drops against mine and he holds me tight. He sucks the sobs right out of me.

"You're okay," he whispers fiercely into my ear, swaying us back and forth. "You're right here. Right here."

I grab fistfuls of his shirt, shaking. "I don't know where I went. She tore us apart."

He feels down my arm and loosens the pelt, taking it off. Guilty relief floods like blood in my veins.

"Sometimes they like to steer themselves for a while."

A tear slides down my cheek as his voice rumbles through his chest, vibrating into mine. "I let her."

He strokes my hair. "It happens."

"To you?"

"Twice."

"He never told me," I whisper. Dad never warned me this might happen. Why? How could he let me feel like this?

"He probably never got the chance," Damien says, reading my thoughts.

I pull away but he holds me close.

"I've never heard of it happening to a child, Char." He gently strokes my spine. "We feel more strongly as adults, know how to let skins deep inside us. Especially the ones we hold close. You two must think alike. Connect to each other, deeply."

"It was like I didn't exist anymore." The tears overflow. His embrace is so sure, his voice so even.

He pulls back just enough to search my face, like he's looking for something, listening for something. Then he tilts his head and reaches both hands around my neck. My wolf skin, twisted in his fingers, hums between us.

"Feel that?" he asks, a hint of a smile on his lips.

"The skin?"

"She likes you."

"Does she?"

"Her soul beats for you."

"No. I feel like I took her," I whisper. "In these woods. I found her and took her. She didn't call to me, she didn't want me."

He shakes his head and his fingers tighten their grasp. "You saved her."

127

Eleven

A tugging at my side pulls me awake. Sunlight fuses through the material of the tent with the muffled voices of early risers. I roll over to face Freddie, whose mouth is hanging open with an arm thrown over his face. He's spilling out of his unzipped sleeping bag onto the plastic floor. On the other side of him is Mom.

She stares at the domed fabric above us, a soft glow from one of the open screens lighting up her hair. I watch her while she's lost in a daze of thoughts. She's not in a bad place, but she's not here. Freddie stirs, and she blinks a few times and looks over at me.

She smiles. "'Morning, hun."

I pretended to be asleep when Freddie came in last night. He nudged me and whispered softly in my ear but I kept my eyes shut and breathing even. He didn't buy it, but after several minutes of one-sided conversation he unrolled his sleeping bag noisily and slipped into it next to me. I wasn't pretending when Mom came in; by that time I was knocked out cold, exhausted.

I smile back at her. "Hey."

Her eyes fill with concern at the hoarseness of my voice. "Are you alright?"

I tighten the sleeping bag around my shoulders. The early morning chill touches my skin like an octopus pulling itself across my back. "Yes."

"How was your run?"

I should tell her. I know she won't judge me. If anything, she'll be worried. But the thought of her realizing Dad didn't explain that a soul can take over holds me back. Would that make her sad? Would she feel responsible? Does she even know it can happen? I shiver. "It was a rough one."

"Rough how?"

"I think I just went at it harder than I'm used to." Not a lie.

She cocks an eyebrow. "Why was that?"

"It's just been a while, okay? We haven't got to run like this in forever. I'm just sore."

She squints at me, senses sharpening. "If you say so. I mean, you're not the type to try and impress anyone, after all."

I set my jaw. "You're right, I'm not."

"But then again..." She sighs, sitting up. "You've never wanted to impress anyone before."

I struggle to face her, my entire right side screaming in

protest. I see black spots. "I don't need to impress anyone. I'm impressive all by myself."

"And stubborn all by yourself." She folds the top of her sleeping bag over and stands in the cramped space, careful not to step on Freddie. She slides on her flip flops and manages to smooth down her wild hair. "But you're right. You've always had that something in you—something that strikes people before they can strike you. It's something Sam had. Drove me nuts."

"But everyone liked him." I don't mean it to sound accusatory, and I'm surprised to hear the jealousy in my voice.

Her sad smile crosses her lips. "He liked to impress people. I bet it'd be easy for you, too, if you wanted to."

I let my mouth fall open just a little as she ducks out, leaving the tent open behind her.

"I never saw it like that," Freddie says, making me jump. He's peeking at me from under his arm.

"Saw what like what?"

He's quiet, gray eyes holding me steady. The wheels are turning in his head.

"What are you even doing here?" I quip, getting into a sitting position. The muscles along my ribs try to hold my grinding bones in place. I grit my teeth.

"You said I was staying with you. And you'd never rescind an invitation."

"Seemed like you patched things up with Ro and your parents."

"Oh, I did."

I throw him a look. "So this is about last night."

He bolts upright. "Of course it's fucking about last night. Christ, Charlotte, what the hell was that?"

Why is he so frustrated?

"Would you give me the truth, right now? You and Damien."

I rub my face. "I have been telling you the truth." Most of it. "It's not a thing, yet."

"Yet?"

"It might be," I say. I don't know. Damien was so attentive, cared so much. At least, he acted like he cared, more so than he would've done before he vanished. Blood rushes to my head, like my heart thinks by sending it all there I can sort myself out. Have an epiphany on what to do, how to make sense of what's going on.

"What aren't you telling me?"

"Like I just said to Mom, I went too far."

"Bullshit. He did something." His eyes are cold.

"What I did last night I did to myself. He didn't push me." My voice is solid. I leave no room for him. Squashing his doubts, setting the story. I did this to myself. Whatever I did, if I was trying to show off, it led the wolf to separate herself from me. Damien being there was just coincidence.

He knows he's lost. "Fine. But if you're covering for him—"

"You'll what?" I cut him off, finding a smirk. "Roofie him?"

"Maybe," he confirms. "Roofie you too, if you don't know what's good for you."

"Can't wait."

I shove Freddie out of the tent to change, and he doesn't ask me about my side when he notices me grimace. He knows what it feels like. Oddly bent bones, sore tissues, creaks while everything eventually fits back into place. He's gotten used to the pain. He likes it—reminds him of who he is. After we're both dressed we wander through camp and pick up food. Ralph's cooking sausages and a big pot of chili. No crazy rumors reach us about Damien walking me to my tent last night. At least not yet.

I avoid Ellie's gaze when we pass her cluster of girls. Their voices drop and Freddie makes it a point to keep talking so I can't hear what they're saying. Damien is nowhere to be seen, and neither is Ro or Bass, so we assume they've all gone on a run. My weekend is ruined—only someone wishing for a slow and painful death would shift after a night like that. I turn down Freddie's offer of pills, so he suggests we smoke instead. The food helps, but a good high will numb me for as long as I need.

We venture into the woods. Distant roars and howls reach us from far-off groups doing their own thing. Freddie brought his bowl (Ro packed it for him): a bulbous piece of glass with blue clouds frozen in its stem. We pass it back and forth and soon the pangs in my side to become little itches.

"See, it's really not so bad out here," I say. We straddle a fallen tree. The dead bark prickles my legs but the creeping moss provides a nice cushion.

Freddie lies on his back, head towards me, holding his bowl to his chest. His eyes are glazed over. "We're not meant to live outside."

My laughter spills out uncontrollably.

"We've evolved past that," he whispers.

I comb my fingers through his light hair. "We can't do what we do without the wild."

He squints at me. "What do you think clans in the cities do? They find a way without living like savages."

"What cities?"

"San Francisco. Vegas. New York."

"You're so full of shit," I laugh, pulling his hair.

He grabs onto my wrists. "You came from Virginia. Hadn't you ever heard anything from D.C.?"

"You're the first skinwalkers I've ever met, remember? You might know a lot of things, Frederick, but you can only guess what's out there, like the rest of us." Except Damien. I nudge him with my knee, and he rolls off the uprooted tree, landing on his face.

He grunts into the ground. "I've heard things, from some of the older guys. The ones who remember what it was like before Ray." He lifts his head. "Sanders has been to D.C. Said there's hundreds of us, Char."

"Well Sanders came back, didn't he? So I'm sure D.C. couldn't match the magnificence of Ruhn Roads." I start laughing before I can finish the sentence, but an uneasiness creeps into my stomach. If the world wasn't tilting I'd be more concerned, think harder about what Freddie's saying about cities, clans elsewhere.

He stands with a grunt and snatches his bowl out of the dirt. He huffs, throwing me a sideways sneer, then sits against the tree.

His shoulder is bruising but the wound is now a good kind of red. A dead leaf has buried itself in his hair.

I smile at his turned head. "I think you just need to get out here more. We were doing really good this winter, no matter what you say about being drugged up."

He pretends not to hear me.

The world spins and I lie flat, watching the clouds. They're a second grader's clouds—flat on the bottom and puffy on top. A warmness spreads up my body and into my limbs. Blood slows and settles in my veins. Freddie leans his head back against my leg and I feel his blood pump, too. The sky lightens and the treetops sway like beckoning hands.

"Why don't we take the fox?" Dad suggested, pointing to the auburn fur I tried to hide in the wood box. He stood in the dead center of my room and surveyed me while I packed my bag, eyeing everything I shoved into it.

I shrugged without turning. "I'm already taking the owl and the wolverine."

"Well I'm talking about the fox."

"I don't want to take the fox."

"Why not? You need to get used to each other and you've only run with her a couple times."

I scooped the box up from the floor and snapped it closed. "I just don't want to." We'd barely moved to Ruhn Roads, and not even ten days in Dad had made me go out and hunt down the fox. Only a few weeks later and we were going on our first camping trip with the clan.

"Char," Dad said, taking it out of my grasp. He pushed me by the shoulders and I fell backwards on my bed. "Why not?"

I zipped the duffel bag closed, jaw tight.

Dad squatted in front of me and waited, gaze trained on my movements.

"She doesn't like me," I whispered.

"That's stupid," he said, standing. He filled up almost all the space in my room.

Anger flashed through me and I stuck out my chin at him. "She hates me. She's so loud when she's in my head, like she doesn't want to be there."

He raised an eyebrow and sat on the crumpled comforter. "She doesn't hate you. You're just strangers."

"No, it's more than that."

He leaned against me, and I tried to handle the weight. "Not all animals are as complacent as an owl or wolverine. Some don't like to go quietly."

"They put up a fight, too. She's different."

He watched me pick at the loose fabric of the bag for a few moments. "Animals are a lot like people," he said quietly. "Especially when we let them into our heads. We feel the same, to different degrees."

I didn't respond, still ticked about the *stupid* comment.

"How would you feel if someone took you? If they tried taking your skin?"

I bit my lip. "I wouldn't like it."

"You'd put up a fight. I'd put up a fight, and so would your mother. But not everyone is like us, right? Some people aren't as strong as we are, and might go easily."

I shrugged.

"You just have to create that bond with her. Be patient and be gentle. In the end, you're stronger than she is."

I turned to him. "What if I'm not?"

He put a giant hand on my shoulder and his pulse spread across my back. "You are. You always will be, Charlotte. You can't think any differently."

Bass passes the joint to me from my right, but I hand it to Freddie. Our fire's low but not too smoky, and the four of us sit around it. Bass is trying to roast a hotdog. I balance a styrofoam bowl of chili on my knees and tear pieces of bread to throw at Ro across the fire. He has to catch them in his mouth. If he misses, he needs to take a gulp of beer.

There was a moment, coming out of the woods with Freddie, that everything was alright; late afternoon and the sun was still high. Ralph's barbecue calling to us. Laughter and rustling of trees. Ellie nowhere in sight.

I'm taking it as a sign.

"I think he's doing it on purpose," Bass accuses as Ro finishes his fourth bottle.

"It's not like he really needs an excuse to drink." Freddie sighs, balancing the joint between his lips.

Ro leaps to catch a chunk and tumbles out of his chair. "Keep 'em coming!" he roars from the ground, eyes on fire.

Bass points. "You spilled your beer. Game over."

"And you're eating all my bread," I add, popping a chunk of sourdough into my mouth.

Ro struggles to his feet. Apparently, they went out early this morning and he's been drinking since they got back. His giant bulk can take a lot of alcohol, but everyone has their limits.

"If you get alcohol poisoning, I'm not driving you to the ER," Freddie says.

"Good thing, too, since your license is suspended," he slurs, dropping heavily into his seat. The cheap metal folds creak under his weight.

Bass snorts and Freddie throws his blunt into the fire.

We all look up when a crashing sound comes from behind us.

Damien, face flushed and shirtless, stumbles from the brush, and my heart leaps. Ray follows directly behind him, hands on his shoulders and sharing his smile. There's a few other guys, then Ellie.

My stomach contracts around the chili and it turns cold as her smile flashes across the clearing. The spoon, halfway to my mouth, lowers on its own back into the bowl and I spin around to face the fire. The sauce sticks in my throat, salty and vivid.

"That didn't take long," Ro says too loud.

Bass stiffens, and I catch the flash in his eyes.

Jealousy. I think it's jealousy. I sit up a little straighter when their steps become louder, willing my face not to turn red or my ears to prick at Damien's voice. The tension slowly creeps back up my spine, mixed with this new emotion.

My hand tightens around the spoon, and I take a bite, almost forcefully. It's not like I could have gone for a run with him if I wanted to, not with my side sore and bruised, but it doesn't dull the stinging. You're being stupid, Char. He doesn't owe you anything...

Even if he said he did. Even if I want him to.

"Char," Freddie says.

I barely glance at him. "What?"

"He's coming over."

I bite the inside of my cheek and the chili almost spills out of my mouth. Bass shoves his nearly-cooked hotdog into the fire. It sparks with the new fuel and splutters for a second.

Damien's pulse is irregular. There's a buzzing around him that rises goosebumps on my arms. He comes to a stop between Bass and me, barefoot, with his jeans hanging low. I let my eyes wander up only far enough to make out the slight nicks on his ribs before he slides on a dark shirt. Should I pretend last night didn't happen? We seem to be creating all sorts of secrets, tightening unseen tethers that we might not be able to hold on to.

Out of breath, he leans against my chair. It sinks a little into the grass. "Anyone got a blunt?"

"Freddie threw it into the fire," Bass says, not too bitter.

Damien's fingers drum against the top of my chair, brushing against my back. "Freddie, light one for us?"

Freddie doesn't look like he's going to agree, but after a hard stare into the fire he reaches into his pocket.

My blood bubbles. I lean forward, away from Damien's hand. "I'll do it," I say, reaching for the pipe.

Freddie lets me take it from him and I stand. I round the fire to where Ro sits, his head lolling back and forth. When he doesn't make a move to give me the weed I reach into his hoodie pocket. Their eyes are on me while I pack the bowl tightly with the green plant. Bass holds out his lighter before I ask for it, a smirk in the corner of his mouth. I inhale the hot smoke, and dare myself to match Damien's eyes.

His head's cocked to the side, lips parted just a little.

It gives me courage. I hold the bowl for him, over the fire, not breaking his gaze.

He takes it slowly, fingers brushing against mine.

"Want to go for a walk?" I ask before I have time to stop myself.

His black eyes flicker under his hair as he lights the pipe. "Read my mind."

Bass shakes head, the most amused look on his face. I give Freddie a poke in the shoulder when I slide past him, but he doesn't flinch. Ro lets out a snore before Damien and I even reach the tree line. I keep my pace even.

It gets quieter as we walk, and my fingertips tingle. Most of the wildlife has fled from the clearing, but the deeper we venture into the thick the more signs of life we pick up. It's cooler out here, like the clan has turned into a big ball of energy that creates heat and then uses that heat to generate more heat, sucking up the oxygen and building an ozone around itself.

"Doing alright, little one?" he asks, shortening his wide strides for me.

I nod, unsure how to start. It's here—the right time. I've been playing this moment out in my head for years, with a whole range of outcomes—some unthinkable, some devastating, some obvious. Whatever the truth is, I don't think it can shock me. But knowing, for sure, is putting an end to it.

"How's the wolf?"

"We're fine." I take a deep breath.

I can't just attack him with "Hey, how did my dad die?" He'd shut me down like an atom bomb. But how do you lead up to something like that? I've convinced myself that there's more to the story. Years of polluting my own head with ideas that just rip me apart further. Was he attacked by another animal? *Why* couldn't they help him? Or was he utterly alone, separated from Damien and Ray? Maybe they didn't even see anything, maybe they found him hours and hours after the damage had been done. Was there no one around to hear his last words?

The silence grows around us, every second of neither of us speaking lets the doubt in my head grow. I'm chickening out. I can feel the cowardice roll up my throat. I don't want to make

Damien mad. I like what we've got going. Like the attention. Like having him near me.

"Why are you like that to Freddie?" I blurt.

"Like what?"

"You talk to him like he bothers you."

He's leading us now, through the shade. "He's just a kid." He glances back. "A spoiled one."

"Spoiled?" I laugh, picturing everyone clamoring over themselves to accommodate Freddie.

"You've been here long enough to know how things are done. You treat him like—"

"He's equal?"

He stops and I almost run into him. "It's not about him being equal. He's one of the family, of course he's equal."

The sky's gone warm, bathing us in orange.

He turns when I don't respond and slides a hand through his hair. "He's weaker, Char. *You* spoil him."

I open my mouth but he puts a finger against my lips.

"No matter how hard he tries, or how hard you force him, he can only get so far. It just comes down to him not developing enough as a kid, because he couldn't."

I stand still, and he drops his hand.

"You're the reason he pushes so hard. And he'll keep pushing because you tell him he can get better."

"He can," I say. "If he wants to. It's his mind that's stopping him, not his body." Even though forming his own bruises doesn't help, I'm not going to admit my concerns to Damien. He doesn't know Freddie like I do. Doesn't see how far he'll go if he needs to.

He shrugs. "If you're sure."

"I am. And Sam would think so, too."

He falters for a breath, and his eyes go cold. But then he sets his mouth, and they soften. Does he know what's coming?

"Damien," I say. I can't look at him directly. "I've been wondering, for a long time..."

He waits, forcing me to finish.

"Can you tell me what happened?"

He takes a step away from me. "Charlotte—"

"Please," I say, a little too sharp. "It's just, I deserve to know, I need to know."

Now he can't look at me. "It was so long ago. I can't believe you're still holding onto it."

"You were there. I just want to know what you know."

"Why does it matter?" His features tense before he turns. His heart picks up.

"Please. Tell me now and I'll never bring it up again." The tears threaten, but I shove them down my throat.

"I'm not the one you should talk to. You should go to Ray." But he doesn't want me to. His father's name catches in his mouth.

"You're not Ray," I object, voice cracking. "I trust you." The words tumble out, their meaning getting lost in the air. There's something about Damien, something I see in him that I've never seen in anyone. He's got a rawness in him that fuels a fire, a fire that burns and a fire I want to feel the warmth of. "Even if you get back together with Ellie, even if you spy on me again, even if you hate Freddie, or leave, or don't ever want to talk to me after this, I'll still trust you."

"Why?" he demands, rounding on me. His face is hard but his eyes are wet. "How could you trust me? After what I did to everyone?"

I take a step back, not prepared for the severity in his tone. But then I come forward again. "Because you're a leader. You want what's best. That bond goes deeper than anything else. That's why everyone's forgiven you, why Ellie's clinging to you even after you ripped out her heart, why even though Freddie wants nothing more than to claw your eyes out, he does what you say." The next sentence gets stuck between my teeth, but I pull it out anyway. "Why I want to be around you."

He drops to his knees in front of me and I fight not to flinch again. He locks his hands behind his neck and stares at my feet for a very long time. "I watched him go off the cliff face."

My knees shake but I keep my muscles locked.

His voice is low. "One second, his wolf was in front of me, then next he just disappeared. I almost went off the edge, too, if I hadn't slowed to look for him. Ray was miles behind us. I found where he went over, but it was so steep I had to go around a different way." His breath wavers. "By the time I got to him, he had almost shifted back into himself. He didn't have it in him to turn all the way."

My legs give, and I land in front of Damien.

He doesn't look up, but reaches out to me and finds my hands. He holds them tight, so I don't float away. Or run away. "I held onto him, I didn't know what else to do. I was sixteen. I didn't even want to be there, I was scared."

My throat burns. I stare at Damien.

He raises his eyes to meet mine. They're dilated and red. His jaw is tight. "He kept saying your name and Jule's, over and over. And all I could do was hold onto him, feel his life leave. Watch him bleed. There was so much blood, Charlotte, and it just kept coming out." His voice breaks. "And he kept saying your name, like it was you next to him instead of me. Right before it was over, he saw me." He squeezes my hands. Tears spill over his cheeks. He's back with Dad, kneeling in front of a dying man, listening to his last breaths. "He told me not to let you fall."

I lose it. The little monster that gnaws on my heart at night claws its way out and I cry. Then Damien's arms are around me, blocking out the world. He pulls me onto his lap and squeezes me, letting me sob into his neck. His own trembling rumbles beneath me but he holds on, letting our heartbeats merge.

When I pull back he uses his thumbs to wipe away my tears. "I am so, so sorry, Charlotte. I wanted to tell you, and I wanted to do more for him—but I couldn't, there just wasn't any time—"

Before he can finish his sentence my mouth collides with his. He tenses under me as I press myself against him, my lips hot against his.

But then his fingers curl in my hair and he breathes me in. His mouth moves hard against mine and he pulls me closer.

Twelve

My face is warm despite the chilly air.

Camp is quiet and all the lights are out. Stubborn embers from a fire glow from across the field, and the moon overhead gives me guidance as I take the path down to the cars. I focus on praying that no one boxed in my truck so I won't turn back. The memory of Damien's lips makes me shiver and I dismiss him from my mind before he can change it. My ribs ache.

Mom will forgive me for taking off. I've woken up countless mornings with both her and Dad gone without word. Sometimes they left a note, sometimes not. Usually they'd just go on a run, or errands into town. I don't trust myself to not break down again, and if I had to face Mom I know everything would spill out.

Dad's death haunts her, every day. She's loved him longer than I've been alive, and he was all she had, apart from me. She doesn't talk to me about it, so I can't know if the truth nags at her like it does me. Would it even be worth it to tell her? Would she find comfort or would it rip open that scar?

Because the universe decides to give me a break, my Ford has a clear route out of the clearing. It rumbles to life, forgiving me for the abuse and glad to have something to do. We speed along side roads, and the further out of the woods I get the more I start to shake. It's a good thing the truck can't go much faster than the highway speed limit or else I'd probably get pulled over. I crank up the volume on the busted radio, undoubtedly damaging the speakers beyond repair.

Instead of the relief I expected, wished for, a tension grows in my muscles. My fingers are stiff from my grip on the steering wheel. The *Welcome to Ruhn Roads!* sign is a blur when I pass.

I take Main Street, which is just coming to life. Past the ancient waffle house I can just make out the squat roof of the bar, but I keep going. The sun hasn't sprung yet, and the town is coated in a sickly blue. I continue past the high school, and past my old middle school, taking the few turns that I've avoided for so long.

Right when I think they might have moved it on me, I nearly drive past the decrepit old sign. I slam on the brakes and make the sharp turn into the darkly paved lot. It was gravel the last time I was here. My skin is on fire when I throw myself from the truck and slam the door. Blood is pouring between my ears when I step onto the wide dirt path of the cemetery, and colors swarm as I stomp the hollow ground.

It takes me longer than necessary to find where he is. I tread through the graves and the scraggly crows. The sun's morning glare spews across graveyard, getting stuck in thick branches of too-large trees. Dew clutches to every surface, new and corroded, and the divots and bumps in the land capture mist in puddles. I scour the bundles of cut flowers and faded flags.

Dad's grave hosts a small bouquet of yellow snapdragons. His washed-out headstone shrieks above the rest, waiting for me.

My fingers curl. Mom comes to see him, I know, after late shifts at the bar and on holidays. When she can get away with a free hour or when she needs someone to talk to that isn't me. When I can't be there for her like Sam can.

There are no other skinwalkers in the graveyard. Or probably any other. We don't bury our dead. We burn them and spread their ashes in the wild somewhere, and keep the last bit of dust for ourselves. Mom decided not to.

If she'd gone the traditional route, I wouldn't be slamming my fist against his slab of marble. I hit it as hard as I can, over and over. On its curved top, it's face, against the SAMUEL LEE REED carved out in thin block letters. Eyes stinging from being overused, more tears spill and my sobs echo through the empty cemetery. My knuckles start to bleed so I stomp on Mom's flowers.

"You left me. You left me, left me here."

I fought through my anger a long time ago. I stopped cursing and blaming him once Mom stopped crying in front of me. But learning the truth brings it all back. His stupidity.

"You brought us here," I scream. "And now we're stuck, stuck without you." This is all his fault—he did this to us, to himself. The loss, the truth, plants itself in the gaping hole he left behind, right where it belongs.

I gasp, out of breath, wheezing and stinging all over. Blood drips in the grass above him, stains his flowers, smears over the headstone. I grip it and try to pull it from the earth, my rage not spent. "Why?" I cry over him. "You did it for nothing. You're dead. What did you do this for?"

The chunk of marble won't budge, its veins stained with my blood. I fall against it, burying my face in my sticky hands and trying to breathe. The sharp sting of the scratches takes away from my side but my head throbs. "Did you really tell him not to let me fall? Did you really think he would?"

Dad doesn't answer. I wipe my face and try to clean his headstone with my shirt.

"I'm sorry I never came to see you," I whisper. After I get most of the blood I sit up against him again, looking out through the still cemetery. "And I'm sorry for beating you up." I pat the earth beside me, let my fingers pinch the destroyed yellow petals. "I just don't know what I'm supposed to do. What you want from me. For us. You did this because you thought it was the right, but you were wrong."

Now I'm expecting an argument, but it doesn't come. He's quiet. Or maybe he's turning over in his grave, calling me an idiot because he knows something I don't. Or maybe he's gone.

My eyes burn with the brightening day and I lean my head back, watching the bunches of flowers sway on the graves around me.

In the beginning, right after he died, I'd wake up in the mornings and have that blissful moment that made me believe nothing had changed; it took a few months for my brain to store the knowledge that Dad was dead.

But that morning, I was so aware of reality that it woke me, threw a black sack over my head and dragged me to the guillotines. It was the day we had to say goodbye. Mom didn't have to pull me out of bed. I didn't complain about how hungry I was. She wasn't rushing for work. I wasn't rushing for school. We were quiet. She brushed my hair. I got our shoes ready by the door.

The clan had never been to a proper funeral, and never would again, so almost everyone showed up in black and played their part. Even though most were disapproving of Mom choosing to bury Dad, it didn't change their feelings for him, so they saved their gossip for the wake. It wasn't a very nice day; the sky was dark and the clouds were moving fast, but the rain held off.

I stood by Mom at the front, to the left of the pastor. We weren't religious, and didn't care who sent him off, but Ray insisted that if Dad were going to be buried, it should be done right. The pastor they found was a kind-looking guy. His face was soft and he had light eyes. When he looked at us, he wasn't wary. He didn't squint or avoid us. Mom and me got there early, and as we waited for the rest of the clan, the pastor actually took my hand and squeezed it. He felt my pain.

They put a few chairs out, but nearly everyone ended up standing around his dark, plain coffin. Freddie, ignoring Nicole's hissy voice, elbowed his way to the front to stand by me. Ray and Mona and Damien sat in chairs across from us. Damien looked ill. He'd been held up at his house ever since they returned from the camping trip, and even Ray's eyes were red. My hatred for them was still fresh, and their faces made me sick, so I kept my eyes on Dad. His casket was closed the entire time, and I fought the urge to look into it to make sure he was even there. I just kept thinking that if this was all some sick joke, the funeral would be the punchline. If it wasn't real, Dad wouldn't be in the coffin.

The soft-hearted pastor was not a lingering man. Maybe because he felt the uneasiness creep in on him from all sides of the clan, or because he sensed my own discomfort, his good-bye to Dad was brief. "The righteous perish," he began, chin high and voice low, "and no one takes it to heart; the devout are taken away, and no one understands that the righteous are taken away to be spared from evil. Those who walk uprightly enter into peace; they find rest as they lie in death."

Thirteen

After being mistaken for a homeless person by a groundskeeper I numbly make my way home. The ride seems too short. Years of consciously avoiding it almost wiped it from my memory, like a black hole in Ruhn Roads.

I pull into our driveway behind Mom's car and sit. From the outside, our little hovel looks like it could be sitting in a time when Dad was alive. My stomach gurgles even though I have no desire to ever eat again. I slide from the truck while it ticks angrily and thank it for making the trip. My heavy feet carry me up the porch and into the house. The air is stale from lack of circulation, but I ignore it, climbing the stairs onto the narrow landing.

I'm already sliding off my clothes, piece by piece, the smell of campfire radiating off me. I plug my dead phone into its charger and slither into a too-hot shower. The water loosens me up, the tense muscles in my stomach soften. My hands sting from their new wounds and the bags under my eyes make it uncomfortable to look down.

My lips tingle.

Oh, God.

I kissed Damien. Or we kissed each other. He didn't shove me away, didn't sit unmoving. He held me. I can still feel his arms keeping me upright, his hands on the back of my neck, his fingers weaving into my hair. My first kiss. What possessed me to do it? What told my body that it was okay? Because it wasn't my brain. My brain was exploding, firing all the wires, absorbing Damien's story. And my heart was breaking. Something pulled me towards him, made me believe his lips where what I needed, right then.

The water runs cold.

When I get out of the shower I slowly unpack my things and wait for Mom to get home. There aren't any messages on my phone, but we've never gotten good reception at the campsite, so I can't worry that she or Freddie are mad at me for leaving. Yet.

I straighten out my closet, do the laundry, pull out the vacuum cleaner. Manage to find a fluffy duster and run it over every flat surface. Wipe the thin coating of dust off the mirror standing in the corner of my room (avoiding my reflection) and the one in the bathroom. Even after I take my cleaning frenzy into the hall and down the stairs, through the living room and into the kitchen, there's still nothing to do but wait. I start *The Scarlet Letter* for

English (leaving *Frankenstein* undone) and hope it won't be as depressing as it seems.

Jessica's car rumbles up our driveway around two. I hover by the stairs, wiping any remnants of last night from my face, and open the front door for Mom.

One look. "What happened?"

I take the bag with our tent from her, but she just dumps her duffel and purse on the floor.

Her hair is windblown and her hoodie hangs off one shoulder.

"I felt sick. It got worse after that shift." Not a lie.

She latches on and hugs me around the neck. "At least you made it home safe. Nobody could get ahold of you, and we were trying."

"We?"

She releases me and hoists her bag off the hardwood. "Me, Freddie, Damien."

"Damien?"

"You left without telling anyone, what did expect? I trust you, but men are irrational." She shakes her head and pushes past me, up the stairs.

I follow involuntarily.

"I mean, I was just surprised you didn't stay the whole weekend. It seemed like you were getting along with everyone. You used to live for these trips."

"I was having fun," I assure her, pausing in the doorway to her bedroom. "I'm sorry."

"I'm not the one you need to apologize to." She empties her

153

bag onto the bed and picks at a shirt.

"Then who is?"

She sighs. "Who do you think? I know you're playing hard to get, Char, and that's every parent's dream, but now you're bringing me into it and it's really not my battle—"

I throw my hands up. "What? What are you talking about?"

"Damien, hun, cornered me this morning. He had a freak-out when he realized you'd left."

"He did?" I didn't realize Damien might worry. I was too embarrassed to think much further than my kiss-attack.

"Oh, yeah." She gauges my reaction. "He was talking about going after you, like maybe you'd…"

I finger the fabric of my shirt. "I'd what?"

She can't bring herself to say it, but we both know.

"I would never leave like that," I whisper.

She huffs, disguising a sigh of relief for one of annoyance. "*I* know. But like I'm saying, men are irrational." She plucks up an eyebrow. "I lied to him, told him you left me a note saying you were heading home. After that, he asked me."

I step into the room a little more. She's going from her bag to the closet and back again, tactically avoiding my gaze. "Asked you…?"

"Permission."

She laughs when I cringe. "Permission to do what?"

"To date you, hopefully."

Oh, no. I throw myself on her bed to die. There's no way. Freddie's face flashes through my mind. He's going to eat me alive. "What did you tell him?"

She pats my foot. "That it's not my permission he needs." The bed moves slightly when she sits next to me, but I bury my face deeper into her comforter. "Did something happen last night, Charlotte?"

She has a mocking tone, getting way too much of a kick out of this. She likes it, probably glad I have a shot at a real boyfriend. A reason to stay here with the clan. With her.

Two thoughts pull my brain to opposite corners of my head— to tell her about Dad, or let her have this moment of peace at my expense?

"I kissed him," I say quietly.

She punches my leg. "I knew it! He was acting weird, jumpy, couldn't look me in the eye."

I almost can't look her in the eye.

"And that's why I asked him to come over for dinner."

Mom insists we cook, even though we both suck, and sends me off to the grocery store to get a ham. A fucking ham.

I try calling Freddie, scanning the frozen food for pizza (just in case), but he doesn't pick up. He's probably mad that I left him to fend for himself in the wild. He'll cool off in a day or two. Or three. Or maybe never, if he knows Damien wants to date me. I pick up a bag of lollipops. Maybe I'll mail them to him one by one until he forgives me.

When I get home, Mom's passed out on the couch, mouth open and snoring. I put the groceries away noisily, hoping to get a stir from her, but she's out cold. Uneasy, I search her cookbooks for how to cook a ham. Then I go to the internet. Apparently these things take hours. By five I'm panicking, and Mom's still sleeping, so I preheat the oven for the pizza.

When she finally opens her eyes and smells the melting cheese, she gives me a thumbs up and goes upstairs to shower. I make a salad, not sure of what else to do, and countdown until Damien gets here. My stomach is in knots by the time Mom comes back down.

"What time did you tell him?" I ask, hacking up a cucumber.

"Six."

The clock on top of the stove reads 5:53.

Mom hums as she grabs plates and bowls and I do my best not to throw up.

"Just breathe." She bumps her hip into mine and winks, reaching past me for the napkins on the counter.

My stomach settles a little. The pizza, cooling on top of the stove, almost smells good.

"I didn't have the guts to ask to meet Sam's parents." She laughs.

"Why?" I don't think about my grandparents, because I've never had any. No pictures, no funny stories, no cute names for them like Papa or Meemaw. When I was little I'd try to imagine couples that looked like older versions of my parents because I was convinced that grandparents worked like clones.

Mom shrugs, laying out three plates on our little table. I can't see her face. "Things were just different for us. And Damien already knows me." She looks over to smile. "This'll be nice, so relax."

The doorbell chimes, and the front door bangs against our bench-stopper.

"Evening, ladies!"

Mom and I both freeze at Ray's voice ringing through the house, and only Mom starts moving when Mona and Damien's murmurs reach us.

"In the kitchen," Mom calls out. She doesn't hesitate.

I drop the knife into the sink. "Did you know they were all coming?"

Her lips go tight. There's a light behind her eyes. "I had no idea."

Ray appears first, hands on his hips and a smile plastered on his aged face. He looks around sentimentally. "Hello, Jule. Hope you don't mind us dropping in."

"Of course not." Mom matches his molded smile.

"When Damien said he was coming for dinner we thought it'd be the perfect opportunity to check in on the old house." His eyes glaze over me. "How's the new dishwasher?"

Ray replaced our broken one last year, after Mom mentioned it to Mona in passing. We haven't used the thing once.

"It works great," she says.

Mona appears behind him. Her eyes are so bright, so different

157

from her son and husband's. She moves deliberately, and she and Mom share a look.

Damien takes up the rest of the space. His dark hoodie doesn't have any holes, and his hair is damp. His eyes are hard as he follows his Dad's gaze to us, but when he gets to me they soften and he grins.

A smile. A smile is good. I try to do the same.

"You painted the kitchen," Ray says.

"Just a lighter blue." Mom grabs my salad and plunks it on the table. "Really brightens it up in the mornings."

Ray opens his mouth but Mona cuts him off. "I love it. It looks more and more like a home every time I see it."

"Yeah, since we never intended to live here forever." Damien winks at me.

Ray sends him a warning glare, which he doesn't see.

"Do you need help with anything?" Mona asks, ignoring them both.

"If I had known everyone would be over I would've done a little more than pizza," Mom apologizes, cutting through the Digorno with our well-worn pizza slicer.

Yeah, like figured out how to cook a damn ham.

"Oh, no, that's our fault." Mona sets two more plates, brushing Mom away when she tries to help. They're both preparing for something, something I can't grasp. Something only Moms can sense.

Mom keeps her smile light, gesturing for everyone to sit down. Mona gives Damien her eyes, but he takes the chair next to me at the table. Mom passes the salad, which I take with shaky hands. Mona keeps babbling, and Ray continues looking around the room and back to us, getting caught in his own memories.

I fumble scooping some leaves out and finally give up after a cherry tomato bounces onto the floor. I pass the large bowl to Damien and make the mistake of looking at him.

He's watching me with his head bent and a smile on his lips. As he takes the ceramic bowl his fingers brush against my hand and he notices my scratched knuckles. The smile disappears and he takes my wrist under the table.

I try to pull away, but he holds onto it tight, passing the bowl to his mother. His touch is like fire as he holds my hand in his lap, running his thumb over the raw skin. The feeling of his jeans on my wrist burns into my brain.

"How's school, Charlotte?" Ray asks, interrupting Mona mid-sentence, apparently done taking a mental tour of our kitchen.

I ball my free hand in my lap and Damien squeezes my other. "Good, on track to graduating."

"Char works really hard. What are you now, top ten in your class?" Mom says, lifting a slice of pizza onto her plate.

Before I can answer Ray speaks again. "And college? Going to State?"

"Maybe." My eye twitches. Why can't I capture the light tone Mom's got?

Damien shifts in his seat next to me. "You're going to college."

I glance at him and hold back my smile. Ray stiffens.

"And what will you do then, Jule, left all by yourself?" Mona

159

questions, grinning.

"Haven't given it much thought. Probably take up knitting or join Nicole's book club," she replies, biting her cheek.

The two laugh at the thought of Freddie's mom letting mine in her book club, and Damien winks again. He knows it, too, what's coming. I'm the only one who's going to be blind-sided.

It only takes Ray a few moments to recover. "Well, I'm glad you're feeling better, then."

"Huh?" The word cracks in my throat.

"You left camp early. Thought you weren't feeling well?"

My bloody knuckles are warm. "Yeah, I'm feeling better."

He nods. "Good. Things aren't as fun when a Reed isn't around."

My insides bubble. Ray's never treated me with hostility. From our first meeting he's been nice, welcoming. I've seen his wrath, but never been on the receiving end. Is this what's coming? Any second is he going to leap from the chair and go for my throat?

Before the silence becomes too much Mom says, "What about you, Damien? Going to try school out?"

Mona laughs for them both and Damien goes on like Ray isn't even here. "No, not me. I'm lucky I graduated."

"Only because you're lazy," Mona says. "I told you that then and I'm telling you now."

"You should know better than to think I'd listen to you then."

She rolls her eyes. "Or listen to me now."

Ray puts his palms on the table. "Enough."

My heart picks up. The air's heavy.

Ray sighs, leaning back in his chair. "What is this, Damien?"

I try to take my hand back from Damien, and this time he lets me.

He sizes up his father. "I think you've already got this figured out."

Mona makes a move but Ray holds up a hand at her. "No, I don't. Tell me."

Damien's gaze is even and his heartbeat is steady. A smile creeps onto his lips and he looks at me. "Do you know what this is?"

Ray's voice raises only the slightest bit. "I'm asking *you*. What are you doing?"

"I like her," Damien answers, not taking his eyes away from mine.

"You *like* her?"

Well, I've lived a good life. At least I've had my first kiss before meeting my gruesome end.

"Yeah. What's so dangerous about that, Ray? What about that is so threatening that you had to bust up the pizza party?"

"Sorry, son, it's just that the last time we spoke about your liking a girl, it was right before you left."

"That was six months ago."

"Six months ago you were talking about marrying Ellie. Now all of a sudden you're not and you've got a new crush."

Marriage. I glance at Mom, and she just looks at me steadily. I stand.

"Ray!" Mona exclaims, reaching for him.

"No." He brushes her off. "Charlotte, sit down."

Damien jumps to his feet, nearly knocking his chair backwards. "Don't tell her to sit down. I was gone for half a year. Did I take Ellie with me? Tell her where I was going?"

Ray stands too, struggling to keep his voice down. "You didn't tell anyone where you were going."

They're both radiating, and I'm torn between sitting down and running away. Mom's mouth is a thin line, eyes blazing, and Mona looks like she's ready to knock Ray to the ground.

"That doesn't matter now, does it? What I said before doesn't matter. The things I did don't matter."

"So what you put us through means nothing to you?"

This is the first I'm hearing of anyone being resentful for Damien's disappearance. Ray's voice drips with hurt, betrayal. Maybe he isn't so quick to forgive Damien. Maybe big bad Damien *can* do some wrong.

"I'm saying it's over," Damien says, lowering his voice. This feels like a conversation they've had before, but I was probably not involved in the previous. "The only thing that matters is what I want now. I'm not fighting you on this. I want your support."

Ray smolders. "We had a plan before you decided to run away and put a hold to everything."

"I'm not running away now, am I? I want the clan. I want to do all the things we laid out. It's just now I want one more thing."

They turn to me.

"What do you want, Charlotte?" Mona asks.

It takes a moment for her words to register, and another moment for me to realize they're waiting for a response.

I look at Damien, and his eyes are fire. They look just like they did the night he got home, in the woods. Something happened to him out there, all by himself. Something none of us can understand. Something that made him rethink who he was, made him open to the possibility of being with someone like me. It made him tell me the truth about Dad. Made him ask permission from Mom to date me. I was so sure, terrified, that he'd never look at me like this again after I learned the truth. But here he is, in my kitchen, trapped between his father and me.

If he's sure enough to argue with Ray, turn his back on Ellie, let me kiss him, accept whatever torture Freddie could have in store, then I should be sure enough to admit that I like him, too.

Even though I can't hear past the blood in my ears and Ray's eyes are trying to pry into my skull, I nod. "I want him."

Fourteen

Ray and Mona leave, but Damien stays. As soon as the door shuts behind them, and I don't have to breathe the same air as Ray, his words hit me like a meteor that was circling and circling, waiting to bust through the atmosphere.

Marriage. Damien was talking marriage with Ellie. What a strong concept for a pair of twenty-one year olds. He almost went all the way with her, built a family with her. Now he's going through the motions of—what, likeness? Love?—for the second time, with me. Are we going to be that intense? Is that even possible? It's like I'm watching a horror movie with someone who's already seen it. He knows what's going to happen, but the jump scares are new to me and I'll have to cling to him to get through it.

"I'm sorry, Jule," Damien says, picking up the plates from the table. The pizza's a quarter gone and almost everyone's food is untouched. Except for Mom's.

"It's alright, hun. Ray just doesn't like surprises." She turns so only I can see her face. "You alright?"

Damien's eyes are on me. "I am." My fingertips are cold and my head buzzes.

She squeezes me and kisses me on the cheek. "Good, you two got this?"

"What?" I block her exit. She can't leave me alone with him.

"Promised Ralph I'd close the bar tonight." She winks.

And spill all the gory details to Jessica.

"No worries, Jule, we'll clean up." Damien takes a slice of pizza from the table and leans against a chair.

She slips past me when I get distracted by Damien's chewing mouth.

His gaze is steady. "Did you mean what you said?"

I want you. "I think so." My mouth is dry. "Did you mean what *you* said?"

"What part?"

"About Ellie."

He drops his crust on the table and closes the space between us. "I didn't bring her up, remember. Ray did."

"But marrying her was the plan?"

His hooks a finger around the strap of my dress and gives me a tug closer. "It was."

Don't get distracted. "What happened?"

"Other things became more important. And when I was out there, alone, a lot of things became apparent."

"Like what?"

"Like there's more to life than what she was offering. Us together was a sickness. We were just poisoning each other. I couldn't do that to her, to myself." He pauses, like he doesn't know if he should continue. "And running into you the night I got back, I saw something I didn't want to poison."

Blood pools in my feet.

He points to my hands. "But I don't want you trying to poison yourself, either."

I put on my I-don't-know-what-you're-talking-about face.

"You can't disappear like that, Charlotte." His eyes are hard. "Especially after what we talked about. You can't scare me like that. Where did you go?"

"You were scared?" My lips quiver and I try to keep the smile under control, despite my heart quickening. I scared him. "That must've sucked, having someone run away and not know where they are."

"It did suck." His face is stony. "I told you something I've never told anyone. Ray doesn't even know what happened." He stares at my balled-up fists.

I stand my ground and push Dad's face from my mind, even if his frozen eyes are staring at me from the hallway. "I came home."

"Rough up some people on the way?"

"Only a few."

166

He runs his fingers over my raw knuckles and nods. "What about the rest of you?"

I shake my head. "Looks worse than it is."

His hands move down to the hem of my dress and start to lift it.

I instinctively shove him. He moves maybe an inch. "What the hell are you doing?"

Ignoring me, he raises the light fabric above my hips. "I'm just checking, sorry if I don't trust you. And how many times have I seen you naked, now?"

I cover my face as he exposes the ugly bruise. And underwear. Pretty underwear, thank God.

His eyes probe my skin, fingertips brushing my ribs. I'm too mortified to flinch. "You've got to take it easy, little one. Only seen these bruises on little kids."

I hit him. "Shut up."

He catches my forearm, letting the dress fall, and pulls me into him. His arms wrap around me like barriers, and even though he showered I can still smell the campfire. Like last night, he strokes my hair, letting his fingers tangle in the locks.

I want to kiss him again. But stealing two might be pressing my luck. So I let myself consume him; his breath, the softness of his hoodie, his body pressed against mine. I can't remember the last time someone burned a hole into me.

We break apart when Mom comes bounding down the stairs.

"Can I trust you two to finish the leftovers?" she says, adjusting her white T-shirt.

"You can trust me to eat anything," Damien answers, taking his last bite of pizza from the table.

She hugs me again. "You're sure you're alright?"

I want to ask her how she knew. How she stayed so composed. Why it felt like she'd been through it before. But I can't. Not in front of Damien. And I don't want her to have to lie to me, so I pluck up a smile. "Yeah."

Her full eyes hover over my face before she gives me another peck. "Goodnight, Char." And to add to the horror, she pecks Damien's cheek. "Goodnight, Damien."

I watch her leave. The house goes silent.

Damien breaks through the quiet. "Show me your room?"

"What?"

He takes off.

I stumble and try to grab the back of his hoodie. "No, not okay."

He takes the stairs two at a time. "Why not? Used to be my old room."

"Well it's not anymore." I chase him through the narrow hallway and cringe when he flicks on the light. Clothes everywhere. Messy sheets. Bras hanging and books toppled over the hardwood. The air is stuffy and there's a half-eaten bag of chips on my desk next to a paused Netflix movie. As he stands in the middle of the room and surveys the den, I noiselessly dart behind him, scooping up clothes and throwing them into my closet. I straighten out my comforter and slam my laptop closed. I'm heaving the window open when he turns toward me, a book in hand.

"I remember this one," he says, flashing my copy of *To Kill a Mockingbird*.

He seems completely undisturbed by the rancid state of my room, so I lean against the windowsill as casually as I can. "You read it?"

He grunts, flipping through the yellowed pages. "'Course not, but we talked about it in class."

"It's one of my favorites."

"It wasn't very fair."

"Fair?" I can't help but laugh. "You believe in a fair world?"

His gaze locks with mine and he closes the book. "Life isn't fair, but this is a book." He steps toward me. "Stories should have happy endings. Everyone should get what they want."

"Happy endings aren't as common as people like to think."

He cocks his head to the side and tosses the book on the bed next to us. "Maybe in real life."

"Well you don't read, so you shouldn't care, right?"

He shakes his head, surveying my room. "You do."

"I think if someone's meant to have a happy ending, they will. Doesn't matter if it's in a book or not."

The corner of his mouth lifts.

"I mean, if everyone gets a happy ending then what's the point?" I don't like the way he's looking at me, but I can't shut up with him so close. "Fighting to get what you want makes the victory that much sweeter."

"Can't argue with you there." He brushes the hair from my

169

face, letting his fingers rest on my collarbone.

The breath leaves me, and I step closer to him, tilting my head up. This time it's up to him to kiss me, since I can't reach.

His smile breaks and he leans down into me, pressing his lips against mine. His hand cups my neck and the other holds my hip.

I take his hoodie into my hands and pull him closer so his whole body is up against me. He breathes into me, parting my lips with his tongue. All I taste is pizza and sweetness, and I dare myself to reach his tongue with mine. His heart jumps, and he lets out a small moan.

I gasp, I can't help it.

He pulls me into a bear hug and spins us around. "Happy, now?" He laughs. It rumbles through his chest. "See what you're doing to me?"

"I'm sorry!" I plead.

He drops us on the bed and stretches out on the small mattress. I grip my side for a moment, the collage of bruises stretching. He watches me. My knee is pressed against his thigh and the scent of boy is foreign on my sheets. I want to taste him again.

He props himself up. "Take it easy the next few days?"

I share his smile. "I will."

"I know it's hard for you."

"What is?"

"Not shifting. Freddie makes you out to be an addict."

There's so many things wrong with that sentence. "You've talked to him?"

"He came after me when he realized you left camp. It was impressive. I think you might be right about him."

Of course I am. "He's my best friend, since day one."

He nods, slow, like we're sharing the memory of meeting on my porch. I'm not going to let him down again. I'll do whatever it takes to make him believe I'm a cool kid. "I know. You two used to smoke in my front yard at meetings."

My jaw goes slack. "What?"

He licks his bottom lip. "In the bushes, out front. You remember, when Sam used to make you come. You two hated being dragged over."

Oh, I remember. Back then, meetings could go on all night. After a certain point, once dinner was over and Mona could chill, and Ray said anything he needed to say, everyone would drink and drink and drink until there was no alcohol left. Then they'd get some older guy, usually Tanner if he hadn't relapsed by then, to go get more. Music got louder, voices got sloppier. Damien and his circle would disappear in the trees beyond the backyard and once the coast was clear Freddie and me would break into Ro's truck and steal the weed he kept under the driver's seat.

"How do you know that?"

"Saw you a couple times." His eyes glint. "And you should thank me for not ratting you out to Ro."

"So even then you were a nasty little pervert spying on children?"

He shrugs. "Only one child."

"That's disgusting." Even though my cheeks go red.

"Speaking of—got any weed now?"

We smoke. He plays the skinwalker band; The Becoming of Lions, they're called. I try to explain *To Kill a Mockingbird*. He peels off his hoodie and I use it as a pillow. I finally give him my number. He talks about the concerts he saw while he was gone, my first glimpse into where he went, but I get a little too high to remember the venues.

I forget I have school in the morning. I forget Mom and Dad and Ray and Freddie and Ellie. For tonight, it's just Damien and me. And pizza.

Fifteen

The sun is bright today. I pull Damien's hoodie sleeves over my red knuckles, turning the steering wheel. The fabric's soft on my skin, threaded with all the places he's been. His clean scent fills the truck, fills my head. I make a quick detour down Second Street for gas, and pick up a couple cereal bars inside the 7-Eleven. I light a joint in the school parking lot and wait for Freddie.

The lot fills up quickly, and the buses come and go. He totaled his sixteenth birthday present (suspending his license in the process), and Liam refused to buy him another car until he finished his Junior year, so he's had to get dropped off or take the bus. Sometimes I give him rides, but volunteering to be the one to get him out of bed in the first place means leaving my house an hour and a half early. An hour and a half.

At quarter to eight I finish the joint and head for the front doors. Freddie's still not replying to my messages. I rip open a cereal bar with my teeth and I trek through the horde of high-schoolers into the courtyard. Cinnamon sugar coats my tongue.

I take up my usual spot on the concrete bench and keep an eye on the doors for him, expecting his thin frame to stumble into the sunlit square with his stupid grin. Or glare of pure hatred for abandoning him—it could go either way.

Maybe that's why I don't immediately recognize the high-pitched squeals coming from behind me. I turn a little too slowly to see a crowd gathering near the gym's exterior wall. A group of sophomores are gaggled together, hollering at something I can't see. Could be a fight or some dare. I start to turn back around, but then I hear Joey's laugh.

And a little heartbeat.

Before I tell my feet to move I stand from my perch and cross the cement to the huddle. Even though most of the boys are taller than me and the girls are hysterical, it just takes a nudge for them to give me room. They separate out of my way to reveal Joey. His black eye is in its worst stage, muddy and puffed. My side and knuckles will be long healed before the traces of his confrontation with my best friend are gone. I'd never admit it to Freddie, but a wonderfully sick satisfaction fires through my brain with the knowledge.

I might let it consume me now, if blood wasn't dripping steadily into the green grass at his feet. If he wasn't waving a frantic raven by its talons. Up above there's a smear of red on one of the many squat windows that line the brick building.

Joey's boys are behind him, minus the one Freddie called gay, and he shoves the squawking animal into the faces of a couple of freshman girls. The black bird's mangled screams get drowned out by the crowd. It flaps and flaps its broken wings, desperate to get away from Joey's sausage fingers gripping its legs. He lets it swing, using its frantic panicking to stir up the adolescent children around him.

My blood curdles.

"Put it down." I step into the circle. My buzz simmers and dies when the junior turns his attention to me.

A hint of alarm crosses Joey's features and he scans the crowd behind me. His pudgy face twists into a sneer when he doesn't see Freddie. "Make me, bitch."

There's a low *oooh* from the lower classmen and I take another step towards him.

He jeers at his boys and propels the raven towards me. It lets out a startled squawk, its tiny heart racing and racing, over-pumping what little blood it has left.

I reach out to take it from him, but Joey jerks it back and drops it onto the grass. Howls of laughter.

He shrugs, drawing courage from the crowd. "My bad."

The bird writhes on the ground.

"Just leave it be," I whisper. Last chance. I'm being kind. Give him a way out, make it seem like I'm asking, like he could save himself all on his own, before I make it too late.

"Leave what be?" He points to the bird with a fat finger. "This?"

He raises a foot—to kick the bird or stomp it in—and I come forward. Before he can knock me away I shove him by his face, his bruised eye warm on my hand.

He falls backwards, into the dirt with a force more than gravity bringing down a heavy load. The boys behind him leap back.

The shouting, the voices, cut off like I've closed every one of their stupid fucking windpipes.

"What…" is all he can manage, the breath knocked out of him. He blinks into the universe, his brain trying to catch up. His arms splay about him, grasping for something that isn't there.

I stand over the raven and look down at the boy. Then up at his friends, daring them to come forward. Blood rushes through my veins and my hand burns where our skin met. I'm grasping, too, but for a totally different reason. The raven's soul reaches out to me, and every muscle pulls toward it. Joey's hate and fear and determination all emanate out at once, overpowering the crowd's adrenaline.

After a few labored breaths he scrambles to his feet without the help of his friends. Joey looks me right in the eyes, his momentum all thrown. He doesn't believe I knocked him over with one hand. Doesn't believe the sensation of my palm on his face, the ferocity of my skin touching his. He wants to hit me.

And a part of me welcomes it. I'm stronger than he is. Stronger in all the ways that count. My brain is sparking so bad I'm surprised I'm not shooting fire out of my fucking eyes.

I've never gotten into a proper fight. Ever. Tumbled a few

times with Dad and Freddie and once even Ro, but damage has never been an intention. I've never wanted to hurt anyone. Never wanted to taste another person's blood.

"You done?" I question.

He glances around the circle, seething.

The mob is lost. Without their voices filling the air, the raven's labored breaths pierce their ears and bring them back to their humanity. I feel every heartbeat. Every nervous shudder. Every shift in every eye and every step of every kid already turning away, ready to act like they weren't here at all.

"Done for today." He spits on the ground in front of me and points at my face. "But we're not done."

He means it as a threat, but we both know he's just saying it to save the little dignity he had to begin with. He and his boys take off, careful to walk slow. The rest disperse quickly, thankful for the cue. The bell rings from very far away.

The small raven lies between my feet, and as the courtyard clears I squat down on the grass. Blood oozes from his beak where he broke it on the window, and a wing is caught at an odd angle. He keeps trying to tuck the other one into his body. His little heartbeat is fleeting and he doesn't even struggle when I take him into my lap. I carefully bring in his good wing and hold him still in my hands.

"Go on," I whisper into him. I'm buzzing, the hairs on my body reach out to the wind, all my cells want to flow into this little bird.

His soul flutters in my grasp, begging to be released. I can't take him. Like most of us, I only connect with animals of my gender. And his body is too mangled. It would only hurt both of us if I tried.

In his last few breaths, he gives into his fate, as all of us do.

I only cry once I get into the truck with the raven, which I wrapped up in Damien's hoodie.

Did Dad meet his end like this? Did he face his fate in his last breaths, when Damien made his promise? Most animals sense their time is up when they feel me coming. Even though I resemble them, they know better. Some try to run; need the threat of my teeth in their flesh, my desperation. Others cling to life until I'm right inside their chests, tugging at their heartstrings. But in the end they all give in, one way or another. They know that there's more after death. Know that it won't extinguish their souls.

People, Dad told me, are no different. When we come near the end, right before we face death, we all welcome it. How did he know? The thought of people dying used to petrify me so I never asked. But after his last camping trip I thought about it a lot. Parts of me obsessed over it; the same parts that obsessed with knowing what happened to him.

I know better than to shift in my condition. The only times Dad ever got really mad were when I shifted while I wasn't at my best. He would lock me in my room and threaten me from the other side of the door, painting horrible pictures of skinwalkers who got stuck between skins. Spouted blood from gaping holes from missing limbs. Deformed bones. Misshapen organs. Pockets of skin gone forever. I heard it all, and even though Mom lectured me, too, she never told him to back off.

The message sunk in, it really did. And I can't help but hear his stern voice as I carry the raven to the creek. I break off the path before I reach the water, and start crying again when I kneel in a mass of gnarly roots to dig a hole with my hands.

The dirt is dark and wet, and it feels good to get it stuck under my fingernails. The bird sits quiet beside me, the sunlight above reflecting in his empty, unblinking eyes. When the grave is deep enough I slide him in and watch a few stray tears drop onto his ruffled body.

"You're not alone," I whisper, layering some earth over him. We go through life alone. Every being there ever was. No matter how many friends we have or how close we hold our families; in the end, same as the beginning, we're alone. But when it's over, after death, our souls move on to something else. Somewhere else, where maybe we're not alone anymore. Maybe we become a part of something bigger.

I cover him with a layer of rocks, and another layer of dirt, and strip my clothes. My muscles are stiff, my side still the color of some nightmarish galaxy, but while I bend into the owl I try to imagine the pain the raven felt. The pain Dad felt. I think of how beaten and battered they were in their last moments, and hope when my time comes, there'll be someone there to hold me, too.

The pressure brings me to my knees, but even when the human skin transforms, the sweet release doesn't come. I rise, body shaking and wings beating against the air. She purrs in my ear. The owl's always embraced my fear. She loves it, feeds on it. She tasted it when I took in her soul, drank it up before I plunged off the branch of that tree, and after Dad died, soaked the insecurity in like a sponge, cleansed my body of it.

The more I spread out, the lighter I feel. High above the trees, with the sky going on forever in all directions, I let us breathe. Tall mountains beckon in the horizon. I let us coast on the wind. Everything is loud and quiet at the same time. Where on land there's always the constant noise of people and animals just *living*, up here there is nothing. Nothing but the wind, letting me fight my way through it.

And all at once, it's too hard to breathe, and the owl is silent. The earth is eager to claim me.

I become heavier than air. We descend, and my vision blurs. I hope I'm close enough to the spot by the path. She guides us the last few feet to break the tree line, but it's not enough to get us to the ground.

My skin turns to fire and I stop flying and start falling. I come crashing through the branches and brush, landing hard on some rocks. The owl releases me but my form doesn't break through her skin.

Not good.

Blood boils into my mouth and I choke, unable to breathe.

Flesh strips from underneath, bones try to bend into the right places. My lungs won't inflate and I wheeze, struggling to inhale. Really not good.

Hot blood spills from every pore, drowning me. I writhe in the dirt and like the raven trying to tuck in its broken wings, every push gets me a little closer to becoming whole. When my body stops strangling itself and I get a good breath, I roll over and listen for the stream.

It's a little ways off. I grit my teeth and through the tears crawl to it. My whole body feels like dead weight, ready to leave a piece behind with one sharp tug.

Just focus on the stream, the water. The water. The water. The water.

I climb over prickly bushes and decaying branches, everything sticking to me. There's a loud sound coming from my mouth that I don't recognize. I shove over some roots and get caught in the shallow part of the stream.

The chilled water flows over me, blanketing every crevice and cooling the raw skin. My fingertips burn. Rocks dig into my tender back as I lie flat, but it's enough to finish the change. Water floods my mouth, but I still taste blood.

I look down. My skin is red and angry, but I count four limbs and no gaping wounds. All my toes and no feathers.

When my body cooperates, I pull myself out of the stream and struggle to my feet. I manage Damien's hoodie over the seared skin before I throw up onto a patch of Old Man's Whiskers. I abandon the rest of my clothes, fighting gravity the entire way to home.

Fumbling through the sliding back door, I call out for Mom. My bare feet hit the cool tiles in the kitchen.

No answer. Was she already gone when I came home? I can't remember if I saw her car in the driveway. She definitely would've stopped me when she heard me come in, saw me carrying a dead bird with tears on my face. I try calling out to her again, but my stomach contracts and I heave a thick red liquid onto the floor. Every step brings needles on the balls of my feet.

I get more and more exhausted with every step and I have to choose between water or my bed when I get to the top of the stairs.

My body shuts down. I grasp the door, the desk, bed frame, and finally collapse onto my mattress. I have to keep my mouth open just to breathe.

Mom's name escapes my bleeding mouth one more time before blackness overtakes me.

Sixteen

A dull thumping brings me back up. Knocking? It comes from my body, deep in my chest.

Just ignore it.

You need sleep.

"Char? Where are you?" Mom's voice penetrates the fog. Her clunky shoes on the stairs. "Char? School called me. Who the hell do you think you are picking fights with a Mahone?" She laughs. "But thanks for getting me out of doing inventory. Ralph was just about to have us—" Her amused tone stops short, right when it gets loudest. There's a choking sound, and I'm not sure who it's coming from.

I try to open my eyes, but my lashes are stuck together. I

struggle to get one apart and tilt my head up.

"No, stay down." She's right beside me, holding me in place. But she sounds so far away.

My skin burns at her touch, and there's a creeping sensation spreading up my back. "Mom?" No sound comes out.

"Don't talk, stay down," she says, more forcefully.

I can just make out her small mouth pressed tight.

"Mom?" The tingling sensation is on my arms and legs, like they're asleep, and I move to shake this uncomfortable feeling, but my body is wet and heavy.

"I'm starting you a bath," she says evenly. "Stay down. Don't move."

She jumps up from next to me and disappears. I reach out for her. The sound of water splashing into the tub rushes my ears, and she's talking again, but too low for me to hear. Her tone rises. She's on the phone. Who is she calling?

I try to shift positions again, but I'm so sticky. It's like a sopping blanket's been thrown over me. I can just barely bring a hand up to my face to wipe my eyes and get them open.

When I do, all I see is red.

A terror flares in my chest and I force my head up. There's a crimson coating over everything. My limbs are tangled in my once-white comforter, and pools of red creep into every surface. Joey. The raven. My owl.

Where's my skin? Did it fall off? Searing pain shoots through me and a scream I've never heard comes hurtling out of my mouth. And then Mom's back in the room, cupping my face in

184

her hands.

"You're alright," she says, over and over, wiping the blood from my face.

But I keep screaming. I start to choke.

She says something else, but I don't understand. She pulls me from the bed. My sheets stick to me. They're dripping in it. There's so much. Her voice is a constant stream in my ear, but her words don't make sense. Arms sure around me, she takes us out of my room, through the hallway, and into the dark bathroom. She doesn't turn on the light. The tub is half full.

I don't want to get in. I can't let her go. She holds me by my waist and slowly lowers me into the tub. The water isn't hot or cold. I can't even feel it.

"Just lay back," she says, holding my side and stroking my face. I reach for her but she gently pushes my arms in the water. "Close your eyes, Charlotte." She cracks on my name.

An older, croaky voice brings me out of the deep blackness. It hums through the dim and I open my eyes. The bathroom lights are off, but candles burn on the edge of the tub. Dusky light pours from the little square window above the shower. The water isn't red, like it should be; it's a deep purple. Clumps of leaves and herbs and weird knotted things float in it with me. My skin doesn't sting.

"She's coming around, Jule," a woman says, ending her hum. It's familiar, but only vaguely.

I blink at the little old woman crouched over the sink crushing up something in a marble bowl. Candles sitting on the back of the toilet illuminate her weathered features. Her long, black hair falls around her in a curtain. Gnarled fingers deftly perform their tasks.

Erin. The Clan Healer. She dips a cloth into the sink and rings it out, and moves towards me to drape it over my bare chest. A cool sensation spreads over me. Erin is the oldest in the clan, and her family has been taking care of it since the beginning. Her daughter Sofia will be the next Healer when Erin's gone, and she's usually the one to make house calls. It takes a lot for Erin to abandon their cabin.

Mom appears in the open doorway. The light from the hall at her back makes it hard to see her face. "Are you okay?" Her voice is shaky.

"Mom," I rasp, sitting up.

"Stay down," Erin commands, pointing at me with a crooked finger.

I slide back into the swamp water.

Mom drops onto the edge of the tub to hug me. "You scared me to death."

"I'm sorry," I whisper. My throat and mouth are clear of blood. Smooth and new.

"What happened? The school called and said there was a fight with Joseph Mahone? You took off?" Her voice is getting more

186

and more stern. The kind of stern that takes over when the threat is out of the way, when she knows I'm going to be alright. She holds me at arms' length.

"There wasn't a fight." You can't call what happened a fight. It was a confrontation. Though it could have been a blood bath if I had lost control. "Joey was flinging a raven around by its foot, torturing it. It was dying, and I had to make him stop. I had to do something, Mom. Someone had to do something."

Erin pauses in her crunching. Mom's mouth is thin. She looks at me a long time. "That doesn't explain this."

My lips part but no words come out.

"Your ribs were nowhere near healed enough to shift," Erin butts in, resuming the grinding in her witch's bowl.

"Your bad shift from camp?" Mom's eyes narrow. "You made it seem like it was nothing."

I just barely hold back my glare at Erin. "It didn't feel that bad," I lie. "I thought I'd be okay if I shifted, and... I had to. It was all too much, Mom." Where is that cracking in my voice coming from? This is bigger than a bird. I know I wouldn't have gotten so riled if this weekend didn't happen. If I didn't learn the truth about Dad. If the thought of him dying in the woods alone didn't hurt as much as it does.

Mom searches my face, and hers becomes softer. She pulls me close, stroking my damp hair. Her clothes have my dried blood on them. "You're always so careful. You should have called me. If the school hadn't, I wouldn't have been home for hours..."

"Looks worse than it was," Erin says. "If she'd completely

burst out of her skin then we would have had a real problem." She lights her concoction on fire. Smoke rises in little wisps and she sets it on the toilet seat.

"It looked like a lot of blood," Mom says softly, still holding me.

Her tight embrace stops me from making up more excuses.

"She's got two big tears." Erin's face is clouded by the thick smoke rising and taking up the room. "One on her shoulder and the other on her back."

I shudder, making the water ripple. "What's the smoke for?"

She waves it around so she can see my face. "Clearing the air."

I'm about to ask what she's clearing the air of, but she picks up again.

"Just mind the tears. I'll have Sofia check in on you tomorrow." She fills a small drawstring bag with crushed somethings. "Bathe in half of this tomorrow, and the rest the next day. Stay in the water for at least a half hour."

I nod quickly.

Erin passes the velvet bag to Mom. "Stay in bed, and don't stretch out my stitches because I'm not coming back."

A soft panic sweeps through me, but Mom breaks from our embrace as Erin starts gathering her herbs and roots. "She will."

From downstairs, the unmistakable bang of the front door hitting our doorstopper rattles up the frame of the house.

"Charlotte?"

Damien. My stomach lurches into my chest and nearly busts my stitches.

"Up here," Erin answers, only a little annoyed.

Mom stands, and I grab onto her wrist. "Don't let him see me," I hiss. I sink lower in the water.

Several pairs of footsteps bound up the stairs, and I get a quick glimpse at Damien before Mom blocks the doorway, closing the door partly behind her.

"What happened?" His voice is rough. Too hard. "Ray said you called for Erin."

"She'll be fine," Mom says, putting on her Mom Tone. She can't fool me, though, I felt her heartbeat, weak and shallow. "It was a bad shift. She wasn't ready after camp."

"Camp?" Freddie.

I sit up straighter. A sharp tug comes from my back, like someone pinching my skin. I wince an inhale, waiting for it to subside.

"Lay back," Erin says, shoving the bathroom door closed completely. Their voices muffle when Mom herds the boys downstairs. Is that Ro's rumble?

"You called Ray?" I ask.

Erin flicks on the bathroom light and blows out her candles. I get a good view of her folded skin, stretched and bent more times than I can count. I've heard Ray refer to her as *little one* more than a couple times, but I've only seen her in the flesh twice. At Dad's funeral, and Damien's twenty-first birthday party. I managed to catch her even gaze a few times at both, but we never spoke.

She doesn't respond.

"You're a miracle worker," I push on.

189

Her old eyes are a little cloudy when they move over my face. "We'll see."

I watch her put her things carefully away in a big threaded bag. "Thank you."

She pauses, then slips a small jar from the sack. She sits on the edge of the tub with a sigh, taking Mom's place. "Let's see those hands."

I let out a sigh of my own before raising them out of the water for her to inspect.

She scoops some white goo out of the jar and smears it across my knuckles. "It's a good thing your bones are strong. Punching blocks of marble isn't generally a good idea."

I blink. "You know?"

She nods, rubbing the lotion in. Her fingers are sure and strong as they knead my hands. "I saw."

"At the cemetery? What were *you* doing there?"

She gives me a concentrated frown, but speaks anyway. "I know someone."

"Like a dead person? Who?"

"You're awfully curious for someone who nearly died."

I flinch. She kneads and kneads before letting my hands plop back in the water.

"I toned it down for Jule's sake, Charlotte." Her voice is thick, like she's never tried to spare anyone's feelings before.

"Why'd you do that?"

"Because she's right."

I squirm a little. "You won't tell her about the cemetery?"

"No." She rubs the excess goo into her hands. "You're a lot like Sam."

His name sounds weird coming out of an old lady's mouth. Especially when I'm not expecting it. "You knew my dad?"

"Of course, child. Everyone knew him."

"I mean, you knew him well?"

"He came to me first, when he found us."

I push myself up, careful not to do it too fast. "You met him before Ray did?"

"He made sure of it." She gives me a sideways glance. "He was feeling us out. Knew the best way to do that was through me."

"Why?"

She stands with a grunt and feels over to the sink. "Do you ever wonder why you are so much more advanced than the others?"

She wants a specific answer. "He taught me everything, I guess because I started off young?"

She goes back to her bag, and I know I've failed the test. "You're a lot like him," she repeats. "When you fall, you fall hard."

I won't let you fall.

She levels with me and she heaves her bag over her shoulder. "So you've got to be careful, Charlotte. Don't be so stupid."

I know how to be careful. And I'm hardly ever stupid. Why is it now, when I feel like I'm finally getting a grip onto something, finally figuring out who I'm meant to be, or who I *want* to be, there's someone at every turn trying to shove me backwards?

The door opens just a fraction and Mom pokes her head in.

"The boys are going crazy," she says. Bumping noises come from behind her and Freddie's unmistakable swearing echoes down the hallway. "I have them getting the mattress out of here. There's no saving it. How much longer do you want her to soak for, Erin?"

"She can get out for today, but I want her lying down. Lots of sleep."

"I'm setting up the couch. We'll be able to get you a new mattress tomorrow, hun." She's pasty and her smile doesn't sit right.

"If your wounds start to irritate you, put some of this on them," Erin says, setting the jar of goo on the back of the toilet. She hobbles past Mom into the hallway, where Ro's back is shoving my mattress down the stairs.

Mom clicks the door shut behind her and comes to help me out of the tub.

"I really am sorry," I whisper. Erin's words confirm that this was the worst decision of my life.

Her bottom lip trembles. "I just... I can't see you like that, Char. You're my baby, and I can't see you like that."

We slide on one of Dad's old shirts over my head. As I dry off my skin starts to prickle. The room tilts and I sit on the closed toilet lid.

"I set up the couch for me, so you can have my bed," She pulls the stopper out of the tub.

"No, it's fine, I'll take the couch." I pinch the soft fabric between my fingers. "You know what it does to your back."

"My back is the least of my problems tonight."

"I know, but I'll be fine. Your room gets too hot anyway."

She clenches her jaw, sizing up the argument. But we're both exhausted. She sighs. "If you say so."

I grasp the counter and hoist myself up, the steam and smoke from Erin's herbs making my head fuzzy. For the first time since I got ready for school this morning I see my face, but I can't remember what I looked like before because today was supposed to be an ordinary day. I was supposed to fantasize about Damien kissing me to get me through Greer's class. I was supposed to force Freddie to forget camp. I was supposed to ignore Joey like always. I was supposed to look the same as I did this morning, so why would I have memorized myself earlier?

I'm pale. My eyes are dull and my lips are drained of color. My hair hangs stringy around my face and my skin is blotchy. But no blood.

Mom puts a hand gently on the small of my back and pries my grip from the counter with the other. "I'll help you downstairs."

I lean into her familiar body, and when she opens the door Damien's standing on the other side.

He fills the doorway, like a statue. His face is stony and he glares at me, coal eyes on fire. A black beanie covers his head and his plain white shirt is stained with blood. My blood.

He steps forward, scooping me up into his arms. "I got her, Jule."

I wrap my hands around his neck as he maneuvers the narrow

hallway toward the stairs, just in case he decides to drop me. His body is tense and his jaw is tight. It hurts to lean against him. He's burning up.

"What did you do?" He doesn't look at me.

He's mad, like I planned to bust out of my skin and scare my mother to death. "I made a mistake."

"You told me you'd take it easy." His tone is only slightly softer.

"I know." It all seems so dumb now. Joey. The raven. But I couldn't let it go. More than once, when I first started going to school, I'd come home crying because of kids teasing me. They'd play a game pretending they couldn't hear or see me, and it made me believe I didn't exist. Mom would be there to calm me down, and Dad to give me a pep talk. He was the first one to teach me to rise above, let things go. After a while, taunting didn't bother me. I coped well with people acting like I was some outsider, and once I really understood why, I took it with ease. But something I couldn't learn to handle was when other people, those who couldn't cope, got singled out. Especially animals. Beings who couldn't fight back or wouldn't. That was something Dad didn't have to teach me.

There's one light on in the living room and all the windows are open. It's a welcome relief when Damien lowers me onto the couch. Mom already tucked a spare sheet over the old cushions and brought down a few pillows. I try to get in a comfortable position. She passes behind us.

"I'm making soup," she says. Her voice is shaky. Her

adrenaline is draining. Soon she might not be able to act stern or angry. A warm scent drafts through the room.

Damien stands in front of me, and I can't stop staring at my blood on his shirt. He crosses his arms. A gesture he's never used towards me.

The front door opens. Freddie comes first, his blond hair tangled. There's blood on his hands and on the knees of his jeans. He's got blue bags under his eyes and they avoid me. Ro's bulk comes up behind him, shirtless. Any excuse.

"Freddie," I say, getting to my feet. Damien takes a move toward me, arms unfolding in case I collapse, but I hold my hand up at him.

"Jesus, sit down," Freddie snaps. He barely crosses the threshold.

Ro pushes past him to leer into the kitchen. He gives me a glance. "Glad you're not dead, Char."

"Thanks," I answer, watching Freddie and standing tall.

"Sit down," Freddie repeats, eyes wandering down my raw legs.

"I'm fine," The living room spins. My hands are shaking. Freddie's face makes my sore eyes hurt even more.

"Please sit down," Damien pleads in a low voice. The look of fury is gone from his features.

I lower myself back onto the couch.

Mom appears, wringing a dish towel. "Not too long, boys. Char needs sleep." She eyes each of them, especially Ro, who's inching toward the kitchen.

Guess no one's staying for dinner.

"You're taking the mattress?" Mom asks Ro, grabbing his attention.

He looks down at the woman half his size. "It's in the truck, Jule."

"Thanks," she says flatly, trying to wipe the memory from her mind. After a second she adds, "And you can have some soup to go."

He doesn't miss a beat and hops from view. She follows him to make sure he doesn't take off with the fridge.

Freddie turns towards the hallway.

"Where are you going?" I ask.

He pauses, and my chest tightens.

"Let him go," Damien says. "They'll be back tomorrow." Like he can see the future, or make it.

"No." My voice drops out. "Freddie, come here."

He turns, and when his eyes find mine, they're steel. "You're a fucking idiot."

Damien makes a move, but I reach out and grab his arm. He freezes under my grip.

"Why were you trying to kill yourself?" Freddie's revving up, ignoring the one person on this planet he should be afraid of.

"Why are you all assuming I have a death wish?"

"Oh, I don't know…" Freddie gives Damien a pointed look, like he's genuinely confused.

Ro skips back into the room, causing the lamp in the corner to shake, with a Tupperware bowl in his hands. "Ready to—?" He cuts himself off and his eyes dart around the room.

I keep a hold of Damien, and Freddie's fingers curl.

Ro creeps behind his brother. "I'll just wait outside." He squints at me right before he disappears. "Again, Charlotte, glad you're not dead."

The front door slams behind him.

"What's this about dying?" I say, on my way to being as angry as they are. "I'll be fine."

"Well you almost weren't, were you?" Freddie holds his bloody hands out for me.

Damien pulls out of my grasp and plants himself up against Freddie. "You need to calm down, kid."

Oh, no.

Freddie looks Damien up and down. "Calm down? This is all your fucking fault. Putting ideas into her head, making her do stupid shit."

"Damien," I say, willing him not to throw my best friend out the window. "Can you give us a second, please?"

He doesn't move. He just glares at Freddie, and for a second I think he might actually hit him. Freddie's been fighting since he could talk, but I've never seen Damien lose anything.

"Please," I repeat. "Everyone is just really pissed off right now and I'm the one you're mad at, not each other."

Damien looks like a volcano due to erupt. In a swift movement, he pulls the beanie off his head and slips past Freddie without a backward glance.

Now Freddie shifts his glare to me. "A bird. You did this for a goddamn bird."

"Look, I'm sorry, okay? You think I wanted this? And I only put myself in that situation because you weren't around to help me."

"Don't you dare try to blame this on me. You went too far, disappeared in the middle of the fucking night from camp, and took on Joey alone. Learning a few tips from your boyfriend, aren't you?"

"This isn't about Damien," I say, bottom lip trembling. I can't handle him tonight. Not after today.

He stops short, taking me in. "No. This isn't about him." He crosses the room, rubbing his hands on his shirt, and sits close to me on the couch. He breathes easier when there's only two to take up air. "You really fucking hurt yourself, scared us to death."

He's paler than usual, and his eyes focus on me completely. "Are you sober?"

"Of course not," he lies, looking away. He takes my hand and runs his fingers over my knuckles. "This isn't you. You're the responsible one."

"I made a mistake. I'm allowed to make mistakes."

"But you don't. I just—I didn't think you could. You're indestructible." His voice breaks.

I squeeze his hand. "I would never leave you alone to deal with these people."

He rubs his face to hide his smile. "Everyone was talking about you today. I rolled into school a couple hours late but as soon as I heard what you did to Joey I left and came straight here. Met my

198

brother and Big Bad in the driveway." He looks at me. "I wish I was there. Finish that fucker off."

"Instead of making me do your dirty work."

He laughs, but it's harsh, like he's not joking about going after Joey again. I ignore the pinching in my back and hug him. His body is always a shade cooler than anyone else's, no matter how worked up he gets.

"It's over, me and Joey," I assure him. "He's not just scared of you anymore—he's scared of me."

This time Freddie's laugh is real, musical. "No shit. But he'll be back. You think his family will let him live down getting his ass kicked by a girl?"

I shrug, hoping my pulse doesn't deviate. "Next time I won't be alone, though, will I?"

He runs a finger across the bandage holding me together, no doubt jealous. "No, Char. Never again, babe."

I give him a smug smile.

"You should lay down. Ro wants to burn your mattress tonight at Bass's house."

"Yeah, you better not miss that."

"I'll come back tomorrow, promise." He grins, standing from the couch, and yells a goodnight to Mom.

After he slips out, Damien comes into the living room with my soup.

"And you're not done with me yet, are you?" I sigh and lean back into the pillows.

Damien gives me a twisted smile and sits on the edge of the

couch. He's going to play nice. "Sounds like you got it all from Freddie."

"You know how he is. You don't need to let him get to you when he starts talking shit."

He stirs the soup. "He shouldn't talk to you like that."

"Compared to how he talks to everyone else? I thought I got off easy."

The spoon drops into the bowl with a loud *clink*. "We could have lost you today, and no one would have even known if you bled out in your bed."

I sit up, my stomach twisting. "Don't think like that. Even Erin said it's not a big deal."

"I don't care what Erin says—you didn't see Jule's face when we took down your mattress."

I put my arm through his and scoot closer to feel his warmth. He smells like sweat and blood, but his sweet, woodsy scent lingers around him. "I'm sorry."

He watches my lips as I speak, eyes full, and runs a hand through his tangled hair. "No one's ever scared me like you have."

I lean my head against his shoulder and pull him closer. "I won't make a habit out of it."

"Why do I feel like that's going to be a hard promise for you to keep?"

I nudge him with my elbow and he picks up the spoon, but instead of a mouthful of tomato soup he brings his lips down onto mine instead.

Seventeen

After Damien, Ro, and Bass haul up my brand-new mattress I don't leave it for nearly a week, which is fine since that's how long I'm suspended for. I'm just lucky they're letting me graduate. Apparently, a few kids stepped forward when the principal questioned the witnesses about the blood in the grass. Sophomores with consciences.

I sleep through most of the first forty-eight hours, only breaching the surface to guzzle water. Food makes my teeth tremble and I'm constantly itchy. My skin pulls tight and my bones ache, but Sofia's regular visits settle me. She's just as capable as Erin, and better at dealing with people.

"What if we cook the ham?" I say on day six. I left the house

201

briefly last night to go on a short drive with Damien. He, Freddie, Ro, Bass, Ralph, and Jessica have been on rotation, checking in on me when Mom can't. The attention feels a little undeserved, overwhelming, but it's the only stimulation I'm allowed. My skins call out to me every night when I try to sleep, begging like dogs on short leashes, but Mom's already threatened to take them from me twice, so I don't give in to temptation.

"We don't know how to cook ham," Mom replies, flicking through the channels.

I sprawl out on the Lazy Boy across from the TV. "Ralph does."

"He has a bar to run."

"He spent two hours with me the other day making me sharpen his knives. I'm sure he can spare a couple more teaching us to become housewives."

"I was a housewife, thanks."

"Apparently not a good one."

She groans and picks up her phone, evidently sick of my constant company.

Ralph's over in less than twenty minutes.

"Where are your spices?" He opens all the cupboards, letting pots spill onto the floor. He coughs on the dust collected in our blender.

I'm working on clearing the table of mail and take-out containers. My arms and legs are weak, and my side pulls, but it feels good to be on my feet. "There's salt and pepper by the stove."

He turns on me. "Oh, child, you poor, starved thing."

Ralph rings Jessica and rambles off a list of things she needs to pick up on the way over. "... and don't forget the liquor store."

Freddie calls me in the middle of searching for the biggest covered pot we have. "Yes, Freddie?"

"What are you doing?"

"Cooking a ham."

"I'm coming over. Is Damien there?"

"No." But if this turns into a party, he should be. A thrill starts in my stomach and works its way up my chest.

"Liam's letting me have the car to pick up Ro from work since his cock machine is in the garage."

"So you're bringing Ro?"

"I was just going to leave him at the site, make him run back."

"Bring him, and Bass, too."

"Why?"

"It'll put more people between you and Damien."

He hangs up.

I text Damien. *I'm cooking a ham just for you.*

It doesn't take long to get a response: *Are you literally cooking, or are you just trying to flirt?*

Ralph's at the helm, I'm just supervising.

See you soon.

Mom turns on some music. Halfway through her tango with Ralph, Jessica barges through the front door, laden with plastic bags. I help her unload the sacred spices, booze, pasta salads and chips. Heat rises in the kitchen from the stove above the adults' loud voices. Before too long I have to sit down. The air is heavy.

Ro and Bass make a loud entry, immediately going for the food. They're dirty and bring the smell of freshly chopped wood with them. Bass is in a good mood; he must've not of thought of Ellie in a while. Or maybe it's because Damien's spending his time with me and not her. Freddie drops into the chair next to me, pretending to be annoyed.

"Get out of the way, boy." Ralph shoves Ro away from the stove. He's got a pot of mashed potatoes going on top.

"So what's the occasion?" Bass says, hunting for beer in the fridge.

"Back to School Party!" Jessica raises her glass of boxed wine.

Mom winks at me. My incarceration is over.

"You're coming back?" Freddie says, leaning on the table.

"Looks like it." I grin at him.

"Thank God. School's been so boring without you to nag me."

Before long, Damien appears in his perfectly messy way. When he enters the kitchen he leans down to press his lips against mine.

I love his taste. Subtly sweet, like honey, with just a hint of smoke today. I blush when he pulls away, heart racing in front of everyone.

"Finally joining the real world?" he asks, flashing his chipped tooth.

"Yep, we're celebrating. See, I'm cooking and everything." I point at Ralph.

Ralph waves a spoon.

"What a lovely meal you're making," Damien compliments.

Ro gets him a beer and Jessica twirls around the kitchen, pulling Bass along with her. Mom turns up the music. All my favorite people, together. Happy.

If it could stay like this.

I get up early for school, gathering the homework I bribed Freddie to get for me. *The Scarlet Letter* was just as depressing as I hoped it wouldn't be. I take a long shower to rid myself of recovery once and for all, and dab on some makeup. I keep my hair down and slide on a bralette for good measure.

The sun peeks cheerily at me on the drive over, and I almost fall over dead when I see Freddie waiting for me by the front doors.

"Are you feeling okay?" I ask, coming up to him and pressing my palm against his forehead.

He brushes me off, sending the faint tang of weed floating in my direction, and gives me a cheesy smile. "I'm doing just fine, babe."

"Then why are you so happy?"

"Told the office you might need a wheelchair. Mono is no joke."

"Mono?"

He shrugs. "It was either mono or pneumonia, and getting mono from me is way more believable than pneumonia in April."

The six people who contracted it from him (this year alone) would agree. I'm proud to say that I don't have it, even prouder to say that I've never hooked up with Freddie, despite rumors. "But why do I need it? I got suspended."

"Joey forced me to it. He's been talking shit, won't shut the fuck up about how he got rid of you."

"But *mono?*" Mono is his excuse for everything and probably the only reason they push him forward with all his absences, even though it doesn't affect him nearly as severely as normal people.

"Because that's bullshit. Are you listening? You can't let a guy like him take responsibility for you being out of school."

I squint. "But he *is* the reason—"

He catches me around the neck with his arm and kicks the front doors open, dragging me through.

Before I can open my mouth again I feel the buzz. More looks than usual in my direction. Lower voices. Even teachers look away. A small path opens before us and Freddie leads us onward, through the halls. The hairs on the back of my neck stand on end.

"See?" he says, low. "It's been your actions against his words all week and people are already starting to forget how you stood up to an asshole to save a small, defenseless animal. You're turning right back into that freaky girl who's not nearly attractive enough to be seen with me—"

"No more freaky than usual," I snap. But the scar on my shoulder throbs.

He cracks his neck. "I just haven't been able to get him alone."

"Freddie—"

"What?"

"You can leave it. This won't be for much longer."
Graduation.

"That bitch rattles you, and it's not fair that you don't care when he does. When I do. I'm just looking out for your health."

I don't believe he's actually worried about my well-being, and am about to tell him so, but a familiar scent reaches my nostrils after we turn down the hallway to my locker. It stings just a little. The fumes of fresh paint swirl around us and I don't let myself process it until the black mark comes into view. The crude portrait of a raven with blood dripping from its body glares at us from my locker door. The paint is still wet and the bird's crazy-looking beak wants to peck my eyes out.

Freddie and I stop in front of it and stare. Everyone around us gives a wide berth, like I'm going to attack.

"Just leave it alone," I repeat, but the words hold no meaning.

Freddie steps forward and smears his hands through the black and red paint. He wipes them on his white shirt and raggedy jeans and starts spinning my lock. "As long as you don't care."

Despite my best efforts to avoid it, I manage to get some paint on my fingers. After school I go right to the kitchen sink and start scrubbing, but it won't come off. When I graduate, it'll end. I'll be gone and Joey will be stuck here. I won't have to see his ugly, pudgy face ever again. Why does he waste his time? He must like Freddie's attention; who doesn't? Or maybe he likes my attention—that would be a first.

I'm going at my nails with the scrubby side of the sponge when the front door opens.

"Where's the invalid?" Damien sings through the house.

The knot uncurls in my belly and I answer him. "The kitchen."

"How was your first day of freedom?" The air in the room changes when he enters.

I twist the sink off and turn around to face him. His smile is warm and his eyes are hazy. "Tiring."

He comes right up into me and pushes me gently against the sink with his hips. His hands trace up my sides. "Anything exciting happen?"

"Nope," I whisper.

"How are you feeling?" His face is getting closer and closer.

"Better by the second."

His face breaks into a smile and our lips meet. I pull him by his shirt. He breathes me in deeply, cupping my face in his hands. "I want to take you out," he mumbles into my mouth.

I pull away. "Out?"

"Like a date." He pecks me again on the mouth. "Even though we're way past that by now. I've seen you naked, nursed you from the brink of death, and you've been threatened to be murdered by my father—"

"He actually wants me dead?"

"No. But if he does I'll be the first to know."

"You can't joke like that. I have this recurring nightmare—"

"Did you hear me, Char? I'm asking you out on a date."

The knot tightens up like a noose. "When?"

His smile freezes. "Do you not want to?"

"No! I do." I nod with resolution, the confused look on his face sending a jolt through my heart. "I've just never been on a date before."

He bites his smile, recovering. "No kidding?"

"I know it might be hard to believe, considering my never-ending charm."

He weaves his fingers through mine and pulls me with him. "Then let's do it, right now."

"Now?" I try to keep the panic from my voice. "Shouldn't I, you know, shower or something?" Shave my legs? Rehearse some flirty dialogue?

He runs his free hand through his knotted hair and flings open the front door. "You're right. Go clean up."

"Really?"

"Fuck, no. I like the way you smell." He grins. "Go grab a skin, though. Something on four legs and fast."

I wait to make sure he's serious before turning and running up the stairs. I'm going on a date. My fingers can't grasp anything as I search through my skins, gathering courage. The fox. She whispers seductively at me and I feel past the wolf fur for her.

When I come back downstairs Damien's waiting for me on the front lawn. He's staring at the house.

"Wait," he snaps when I shut the door behind me.

"What?"

"Go back inside and close the door."

"Huh?"

He hops up the creaky steps and ushers me inside, slamming the door between us once I'm over the threshold.

The moments tick by and my heart stammers. Maybe he's running away.

The doorbell chimes and I jump. I pull the door open and Damien's standing there, hands behind his back.

"H-hey," he stutters, tilting his head.

I glance around, looking for something that's changed. "Hey?"

"Sorry I'm a little early." He rolls his eyes sheepishly. "I just thought I should meet your Mom."

"My Mom?"

A smile plucks at the corner of his mouth. "I want to make sure she knows I won't keep you out too late. Curfew's ten, right?"

I bite my lip, mouth pulling. "I mean, it's a school night."

"No, it's not," he whispers. "First dates are always on a Friday."

I nod quickly. "Right, yeah, ten it is. But she's at work right now..."

His eyes widen and they do a quick roam over my body. "Really? Home alone?"

I choke a laugh. "Yeah."

"Well," he shrugs, and thrusts out a handful of weeds at me. Stems picked from our front lawn. "These are for you."

I take them. "Thanks."

He's openly laughing now. "Maybe we should wait until she gets home. So I can make sure she knows my intentions are pure."

I push out onto the porch, right up against him. "Thank you," I say softly.

He winks. "Anytime you need a first date, just ask."

"One is probably going to be enough." We drop down the front steps and I toss the weeds into the deranged garden.

"What's your favorite flower?" he asks. "So I don't make a fool out of myself next time."

I shrug. "I don't have a favorite."

"You have every name of plant and tree in this state memorized and you don't have a favorite?"

"I've never thought about it. They're all pretty great in their own way." I point at him. "And besides, all the really pretty ones die too fast."

"Flowers are a symbol of love, Char. They're not meant to last forever."

It takes half the time to get to his secret mansion in the middle of the forest, and when I question Damien about it he shrugs. "Missed my exit last time."

"I find that hard to believe."

"You were distracting me."

I keep the smile to myself. The fresh air and loud music clears my head of school and the clan. I breathe a little easier with Damien around. I've never had someone be mine before, not like him. Other than Freddie, no one's ever made a point to hang out with me. Really wanted to.

We park just outside the gates, like last time. The ground is damp from the rain last night and the trees converse loud as ever in the wind. I slip through the wrought iron fence first, and Damien weaves his fingers into mine as we walk. The forgotten home welcomes us back, wood and stone orange from the sun's glow.

Damien tugs me forward, through the bushes that border the garden. "You were so nervous the first time I brought you here."

"I was not," I lie.

"You're nervous now, little one." We snake through the uneven paths and ivy. Bees bumble from perfect little flower to flower, fountains overflowing with rainwater shimmer while birds bathe themselves, and statues peek at us from underneath moss. The garden spans out before us like a confused maze, and when we reach its center Damien spins me around into him.

The fox hums in my pocket.

He smiles down at me, wide and open, that raw look in his eyes. His irregular heartbeat reaches out to mine and he holds onto me like he won't ever let go. "Do you miss it?"

I miss a lot of things. "Miss what?"

Without blinking he says, "Sam. Before the clan, before us. Do you still miss it?"

He doesn't skip a beat when saying Dad's name and it takes me by surprise. It almost hurts.

There's no way to avoid the truth with his gaze burning into me. Even if I wanted to lie, I couldn't. Not with the statues spying and cherry trees listening. "I do, every day."

He watches me, face unreadable.

"I'm always going to miss him." My voice is quiet. "I'll miss him for as long as I remember him. Then after that."

He stops spinning us, a mangled expression of pity and sadness on his features, like he was expecting a different answer.

"You gave me closure," I add. Why is he looking at me like that? "But that doesn't change anything. He's still gone. Now I just know how he left."

He shakes his head, pulling me into him. "I don't want you to forget."

We stand together for a while, listening to each other's heartbeats, falling into a rhythm.

"This is an odd first date," I mumble.

He laughs, but he's not amused. It's the laugh of an evil mastermind with something disastrous up his sleeve.

When Damien said fast, I didn't realize he meant *cougar* fast. He transforms into a monstrous cougar with thick shoulders and tan fur, dark markings around his black eyes. He's the perfect stalker, silently gliding though the underbrush on strong, sure legs. Even if I wasn't rusty, I probably wouldn't be able to keep up. I'm clumsy and out of step as I dart after him through the trees.

But the strain is satisfying, and I stay on his heels. I'm actually grabbing for air by the time we come to the large puddle of water, trying to fill the fox's little lungs.

Damien gives a pause at the water's edge, and glances back at me. I stop where I am, still in the tree line. He wants me to watch him change. After all the times he's seen me vulnerable, I guess it's only fair.

But it still stops my heart.

His body trembles and his breath becomes ragged. A tearing sound comes from within him, the sound of muscles shredding and bones rattling. The fur sheds, peeling away to reveal the skin that threatens to pull him in all directions. Veins rove under a protective layer. It's hard to keep my eyes on him; the cougar wants to tear him apart. He lets out satisfied groans and digs into the mud. I don't dare move as his final form takes shape.

He knows exactly where I am, knows that I haven't moved an inch, and turns his head to give me a sly smile before he wades into the water.

The sun has dipped, cooling everything around us. Heavy branches reach toward the water and the waterfall merrily gurgles onto an otherwise still surface. I stand on the smooth stone with the perfect crack.

"I won't look," he calls, waist-deep with his back turned. "Even though I've seen all of you before."

I snap my jaws to warn him, but he only laughs, swimming in deeper.

I do need a break. A week was all it took for my body to slide backwards, too comfortable. Some of the clan go long stretches without shifting; it has to be scheduled, like when you have to make time for sex after you get married. They have to work it into their routine, or it's forgotten. If I don't shift, I burst. It's a horrible feeling, being out of shape.

I ease into my real form, not nearly as dramatic as Damien's transformation. The burn doesn't linger. When I'm left hovering over the damp earth I wriggle my fingers and toes, just to make sure they work. My new scars are still only scars.

I'm comfortable in my body, and even though for every birthday I wish my boobs would grow, I've never criticized myself too harshly. But it's one thing to be comfortable with myself, and a whole other issue to be comfortable around someone else.

Especially someone like Damien.

I watch his broad back from my vantage point, tracing his dripping hair and straight spine. His hands reach out to snatch drops of the waterfall and suddenly he looks at me. "You coming in, or am I going to have to come get you?"

I leave the piece of fox on the perfect stone, wait for him to put his eyes elsewhere, and dart out to the water's edge, barely hesitating before wading in. The water sends a chill up my back but my warm skin welcomes it. Once I'm out far enough I leap off the ledge, diving under the water. Its blackness consumes me and I glide through the dark.

When I break the surface my boy is gone. "Damien?"

Something brushes against my legs and I flinch, kicking out.

Damien bobs up a foot away, his grin wide.

"Asshole!" I splash him.

He laughs and spits water at me. "So jumpy."

"Sorry I wasn't prepared for a shark attack."

He swims toward me, getting too close. "Tell me something."

He's very inquisitive today. "What do you want to know?"

He keeps his eyes level with mine. "Who'd you run around with, little one?"

Too inquisitive. "What do you mean?"

"While I was gone, or before I left." The side of his mouth lifts. "Who got you hot and bothered?"

"I told you I've never been on a date." Where is the bottom of the pond? My limbs are going to fail me at any moment and I need something solid under my feet or I'll drown.

"I heard you. Messing around doesn't mean dating." He's looking at me too hard.

"There's no one."

"Oh, come on." He sighs like he can't believe what he's about to say. "Freddie?"

My jaw locks. "No. Never."

He blinks. "Ro? Bass?"

"Do I seem like the type to give a blowjob in a mulcher?" I don't realize the words until they're out, but Damien doesn't notice.

"Some boy from your school, then?" His tone's taken an edge,

216

like he hates the idea of me being interested in a regular person.

"No." His eyes are too dark; I can't read them.

"You're telling me no guy ever has tried to get with you." He's agitated, like I'm lying.

"You're the first, Damien." Now I'm getting defensive.

"First what?" he presses, reaching out to touch my face.

I pull away. "First guy. Kiss. This. I've never done it before, any of it."

He grabs me before I can dodge him. "Look at me."

It takes a horrible effort, but I manage it. His grasp is cool against my arm. He's going to start laughing in my face, I know it. What eighteen-year-old has never been kissed? Never been interested in anyone, never had a crush? Never felt the way she does now, with a dangerous naked boy in a pond?

"Why?" is all he says.

"Why, what?" Can I just please drown already?

"Why am I the first?"

He's got to be joking. "It's not exactly like I've ever belonged. Look at me."

His eyes falter and his fingernails dig into my skin. "I see you. You're beautiful, Charlotte."

Blood rushes to my ears. "Everyone knows I'm different, Damien, I mean *everyone*. It's hard for me to relate to other people and for them to relate to me because most of them just don't get it."

He waits for more.

"I'm not from here. I don't have that pack mentality that you

217

all do. I learned differently. I just can't get to your level and you can't get to mine. We're in different lanes going down the same highway."

He pulls me against him so tightly not a drop of water survives between us. "We're all going down the same highway, Charlotte," he agrees. "But the lanes don't matter. We're bonded by what we are, not who we are. That bond is thick as blood."

We're very naked, that's for sure. I'm frozen against him. Every goosebump on my body pushes against his flesh. His muscles shift under me. My boobs squish into his chest and the hair on his stomach trails right down into—oh, God.

"You can't think that you're more different than the rest of us, like you're your own breed." Every breath vibrates through me, smothering his words. Concentrate, he's talking to you. "Do you think a normal person could do what we do? Think they could handle it?"

I can't answer. My brain's stopped working. Another organ is taking over.

He pulls back, holding me at arms' length, and I can only stare at him helplessly. "They'd go insane. The shifting, the soul capturing, the weight of running around with another being inside of them would be too much to handle. Too much for any normal person to handle."

I can breathe. His words start to make sense.

"I learned a lot about myself when I was alone. I learned a lot about us."

"Was it good for you? Leaving?" I blink up at him, ignoring the numbness in my toes and fingers.

He watches me, eyes filling with a sadness I can feel. "I didn't think I could actually do it. But once I did, it became that much harder to come back."

"I'm glad you did."

His mouth lifts and his eyes wander down my neck. "Come on, you're freezing. And the date's not over."

He doesn't bring up The Hug, but I can't keep it from my mind. I've never been so close to a naked person, let alone crushed up against one. Every one of my cells was fighting to get to his, like without clothes Damien became one big magnet that I could wholly stick to. Is the pull that strong with everyone? Or was something else taking over?

It's well past dark when we pull up to the bar. "Wow, pulling out all the stops?" I say, determined to make this first date as awkward as humanly possible.

"Hey," he says, giving me a look. "Remember, first dates are supposed to be horrible. And this one is going a little too well for my liking, so we gotta bring you back down to reality."

Just a little too well? "I'll keep that in mind. We going to split the check, then?"

"I could make you pay for the whole thing if it'll get it through your head."

It's a typical Wednesday night (but a pretty sad one for a First-Date-Friday) at Ralph's place and I fight the urge not to turn and run when we spot several of the clan. I scan the meager crowd for Mom but see Jessica instead. Damien nudges me forward when I hesitate and I lead the way to an open booth against the wall. I can just make out a sad tune from one of the jukeboxes.

Ignoring the stares, Damien plucks a laminated sheet from the metal ketchup and mustard stand on the end of the table. "Ralph added fried pickles to the menu? He hasn't changed this thing since I was born."

"Jessica convinced him to pickle his own cucumbers, and now he puts them in everything. They're not inedible."

Jessica springs up on cue, right by my elbow. "Hey, there's my lovebirds."

"Hear that, Char? Lovebirds." Damien winks.

"Oh, I heard her." And so did everyone else in the bar.

"What'll it be?" Jessica says, flipping her now-darker red hair behind a shoulder and throwing Damien a smirk she thinks I don't see.

"Cheeseburger tray," I say before Damien can speak. "With a coke, and some mozzarella sticks. Please." I give Damien a big smile.

"Thought I heard something about fried pickles. Some of those, too?" Her pen starts scribbling before either one of us can answer.

"Yes," I say. "Damien's paying, so why not?"

He raises an eyebrow. "Make that two orders of fried pickles.

I'll get a triple burger tray and a Sam Adams."

"You got it," she says, containing her laughter. "Be back in a sec, lovers."

Damien bites his bottom lip. "I like the sound of that."

"She's the worst out of all of them. You can't encourage her."

He grabs my hand over the table and pulls it toward him. His touch sends pins and needles up my arm. "Don't fight the connection, Char, we're in too deep for that."

I wheeze. "I'm not."

"You can't go back on a first date."

He won't let my fingers go. "If you're trying to be cute, it's not working, Portman."

His grin splits wide. "Say my name again."

I reach to slap him, but familiar voices stop me short.

"It's the walking dead," Ro calls from across the bar. He's crossing the threshold with Bass behind him, and Ellie at the rear. The ex-daughter-in-law.

Damien's hand engulfs mine, refusing to let go.

I've been hoping I could avoid Ellie for the rest of my life, or at least never come face-to-face with her with Damien around, because the three of us in the same room is just too uncomfortable to handle. It's like I can't help but zone in on every little movement either of them make, every small gesture and every facial expression. It would be different if Damien acted like he doesn't completely loathe her, because then at least one of them would behave like a real human being.

"Freddie told me about the locker thing," Ro says, bringing

their party to a stop at our table and patting my head. The aroma of sweat, tobacco, and lumber follows him like a perfume. The stink of a real man. "Someone better reign a leash on that junior."

"Locker thing?" Damien repeats.

"It's nothing," I say quickly. "Just this kid bothering Freddie." Damien has enough to deal with lately, and I know I can handle Joey.

Ro wants to give me a confused look, but Bass steps in. "Sucks you couldn't be there for the Mattress Burning. Went right up in flames. Your blood's flammable as hell."

"Freddie recorded the whole thing for me." I'm thankful for the distraction, but not too thankful. The idea of my blood evaporating into the atmosphere makes my stomach twist.

"Why'd they burn your mattress?" Ellie asks. Even with Ro's big mouth, he's managed not to broadcast my demise to the whole town. She pushes right up against Damien's side, looking worse than ever. Her normally wavy hair is limp; eyes are clouded and red. Her fingers shake. But she keeps her voice steady.

Damien shifts away from her and leans against the table. "Everything good for tomorrow, Ro?"

"Yeah, Bass's place will have to do."

"What's tomorrow?" Ellie looks pointedly at Bass, but he doesn't return her eyes.

"Boys' night," Ro answers when Damien doesn't say anything, either.

"What, ordering a bunch of hookers?"

"Why? You free?"

"Maybe." She turns to Damien and sets her shoulders, letting her voice rise to a playful tune. "If I'm invited."

Compassion bubbles into my stomach, and rises into my chest. I feel sorry for her. She's high off her ass, in love with Damien and not sure why he's sitting here with me. I should be upset by how close she's standing to him, how she's acting like they're just in a bad fight and he's not literally dating someone else, but watching her dilated eyes dart around his face sets something different loose in my chest. Another emotion I'm not used to. Pity.

"You're not," Damien says.

She breaks, her voice falls flat. "I need to talk to you."

"We've talked." She might as well be trying to converse with a pickled cucumber. Damien's a wall she's not getting through, a wall I know he hardly puts up for anyone.

I try to pull away from him, but he holds tight. Bass is watching Ellie's shaking hands.

"Well I'm not done." Her jaw clenches. She's holding back tears.

"Don't start, El. Stop before you do something else you'll regret tomorrow."

Ellie jumps, like she's been shocked.

Jessica bursts between Ro and Bass with two glasses in her hands. "Here's your drinks, kids." She sets them on the table, trying to get a whiff of what's going on. "Food should be out shortly," she adds, glancing around at all of us. "You all staying? Should I move you to a bigger table?"

223

"No, Jess, thanks," Damien says.

Ellie disappears, tears brimming her eyes.

Bass follows her, head bowed. Ro puffs out his chest. "Alrighty, well, see you tomorrow," he says to Damien. He flicks my nose. "See you, Char."

I get my hand from Damien and busy myself with my straw. His beat is steady, but my heart thunders.

"She's fucked out of her mind. She won't even remember this tomorrow," he says.

"It's—I'd be upset, too." I can't manage anything else. He made her crazy. Could he ever drive me to that point of devotion, too?

"She's not upset, she's angry." He reclaims my hands. "Her mind doesn't work like most people's. When she gets locked on, it takes the jaws of life to pry her free."

My thumbs stroke his wrists.

He sighs. "I ended things, before I left. I know it was a soft breakup. I gave her the whole 'I need to find myself' thing, but it was true. I guess I was hoping that when I got home Bass would've already scooped her up, she would've moved on."

"Bass?"

His eyes narrow. "You see it, too. Don't pretend you don't."

I shrug. "He was close."

"If the kid wasn't so afraid to show some feelings before consulting Ro they'd probably be married by now."

I laugh, I can't help it. "One time, when I was over Freddie's, I was on my way to the bathroom and I heard Ro video-chatting with Bass in his room—they were helping each other pick out what to wear for some logging seminar thing down in Chandlerville."

It's good to see his smile. "It was really bad when we were kids. They convinced everyone in the fourth grade that they were twins. Switched shoes on the bus, made sure they always had the same haircut. I'm pretty sure they sat in for each other's yearbook photos one year."

"They're soulmates."

He nods, eyes wandering my face. "They are."

Eighteen

"He can't come," Freddie reminds me.

I put the phone on speaker and drop it in my lap as I turn out of my driveway. My sunglasses slide down my nose. "I know."

"I just don't want him thinking he can show up at my party."

"It's hardly a party, Freddie."

"It's always a party with you around, babe."

"He's not coming, I told you. He has something to do with Ray today, anyway." My stomach knots at the idea of Damien going on a run with his father. Ray's tolerated me these past couple weeks—you know, letting me into their house and stuff—but is still chipping away at Damien. Going on overnights with his boys, making him speak at meetings and having Leanna work him in the logging company. Ray's trying to occupy all of Damien's time, make him feel like he won't have time for me. It's not particularly working, but the old man is persistent.

"Well, *I* told you he can't come, and *you* told him he can't come, but that won't stop him from coming."

"He has better things to do than hang out with you." That, and I just didn't mention the party to him.

"Like you have better things to do than celebrate my birthday?"

"Of course not, you're top priority." Which is why I'm picking up his presents on my way to his house.

"Good. See you in a couple hours."

He hangs up and I bump my way along into town. Freddie *is* top priority. Today. Things have shifted, almost overnight. Before Damien, Freddie was the only one who ever wanted to hang out with me, and beyond that, skinwalking was always enough of a time-killer. There were days when I did nothing but read and eat. Where I didn't have to get dressed or shave my legs or face the outside world at all. But with Damien, there's always something to do—listen to Ray's monologues, help Mona around the house for meetings, sneak away for a run or fly or hang out at the bar. And even when we're left alone exhausted at four in the morning, we'll talk and talk and talk. He's taken precedent over all the little things in my life, filled up the empty space. And when days like today come and he's stolen from me by Ray, I have to go back to having free time.

Tourist season hasn't hit quite yet because school is still in, but the days are getting steadily warmer. It's easy to find a spot on

Main, and they haven't started charging for the meters so I don't have to dig around for change. The maple trees lining the street are blooming late, but the birds are nesting just fine. First thing I do is grab an iced coffee from Rosie's Cafe, then make my way down the sidewalk to Main Sweets.

Freddie likes his retro candy. Salt water taffy is his favorite, even though that's what old people would taste like if you tried to eat them. The glass jars lining the walls paired with the black and white checkered tiles put me on sensory overload while I fill a couple paper bags with candy. There's a new kid working the counter and making the fudge for the day. He gives me an awkward look when I come up to pay for my four bags, like he knows who I am and who I associate with, but in the end he just smiles, his heart skipping a little when I hand him my money and our fingers touch.

I throw the treats into my truck and cross the street, dodging a few cars, and walk along the other side of the road. There's hardly anyone out besides a few people with their dogs and grandmas going to their morning brunch. Brook's Books is a block and a half down, sandwiched between an art gallery and a furniture store. On the second Saturday of every month, for fifteen bucks, you can fill up a burlap sack with as many books as you can fit.

The bell above the door jingles when I walk in, and Memphis comes waddling towards me. She meows, greeting me like an old friend, and rubs her gray body against my ankles.

"Welcome in," Brook says from behind the counter. She

started the bookstore with her husband in the 80s and kept it going, even after the divorce. And the fire. And the flood.

Memphis follows me through the cramped bookstore, rubbing against my legs and meowing loudly when I stop. Animals are tricky. Most of the time they steer clear, especially if there's a lot of us. But sometimes, mostly with cats, they're too curious for their own good. They can smell the wild inside. I love the hum domesticated little bodies give off.

It's easy to fill up a sack for Freddie—he devours serial killer biographies and anything occult. I have a wider range for the type of books I like, so it takes me a little longer to fill up mine. I rub Memphis's tummy before heading out the door, then make my way towards CVS.

One of the many things about Freddie I'll never fully understand is his obsession with letters. He loves cards, anything handwritten with cheesy expressions of emotion. Sentimental would be the last thing I'd call him, but something about letters touches a place in him he'd never let anyone see.

So on every occasion I get him a Hallmark card and write whatever I can think of inside, and watch with secret pleasure while he reads it and stores it in a box under his bed, right beside his old-school porn.

The automatic doors to the pharmacy open before I can step up to the censor and I nearly drop the bags of books.

Mona's walking out towards me.

"Hey, Charlotte." She smiles wide. Damien has her smile. Ray's dark eyes, but her mouth.

"Hi, Mona," I say. We don't talk one-on-one all that much, but she's been nice to me, especially after Pizza Night.

"Doing some errands?" she asks, nodding towards my bags.

"Yeah. It's Freddie's birthday so I'm picking him up some stuff."

"Oh, I didn't know that." She lifts her plastic bags from the drugstore. "Boys are keeping themselves busy so I finally have some time to dye my hair. What do you think?" She takes out two boxes of dye and holds them up for me. One is a dark auburn and the other is a bluish black.

"The lighter one," I say. "Summer's coming."

She looks back and forth between the boxes. "Yeah," she agrees, eyes meeting mine again. "I'm hopeless."

Hopeless isn't a word I'd ever associate with Mona. She's married to Ray, basically making her co-leader of the clan. She keeps everyone in check, completely willing to give orders and orchestrate dinners and parties. I've never given much thought about her social life, not before she became my boyfriend's mother. When I see her, she's at home, doing work around the house, spending time with Ray, or planning something. I've never seen any women hanging around *just because*, or have heard her talk to anyone without a purpose. Maybe she doesn't have a girlfriend to ask an opinion on her hair dye. Having friends you choose and people you have to be around just because of who you're married to are two totally different things. She's intimidating and strong to me, someone's shoes I'd never be able to fill.

"I'm glad I ran into you, Charlotte. I wanted to talk to you about something."

The Talk. "Yeah?"

"I know Ray seems like a tyrant," she says, shifting her bags between hands. "It's just hard for him to see the big picture sometimes. He gets fixated on the little things. It's not you."

"That's good to hear." I cough out a laugh.

"And for what it's worth, I'd take you over Ellie any day."

That's really good to hear.

"The people just don't know how to handle change. Damien's life has been planned since he was born. He was burdened with even more pressure when he didn't get any siblings."

No one's ever talked about Damien being an only child, and I never thought to ask. Another piece to the Mona puzzle.

"And it really isn't you, Charlotte, even if it might seem like it."

Mom's been telling me the same thing for years, but to get confirmation from someone who doesn't have to say it means a lot.

"Shock is good for them," she goes on, smiling. "They've been complacent for way too long, in my opinion. Your dad started to teach them spontaneity, and I feel like you're carrying that on. He came to me so many times with his crazy camping plans. Always last minute, but it kept everyone on their toes. I don't think anyone loved getting out there more than he did."

My eyes go hot. Tears come out of nowhere, and I barely keep them at bay. Since camp, there's been no hesitation when including me to go for runs. Ro and Bass ask freely, which I don't mind, and Damien doesn't make a big deal when he gathers a few of their friends after clan meetings. I'm still not totally comfortable with the larger groups, but I've noticed people follow me sometimes, watch me stretch out my legs or try to fly higher and higher with me into the air.

I don't know what I could do, to live up to Dad. It's not like I'm a teacher or expert, but I do try to help. It's what drew me to Freddie, makes me want to help Damien however I can. I nod. "Thank you, really."

She pulls me into a firm hug. She's bonier than she looks. "Keep it up, Charlotte. And stop knocking on the door when you come over. Just come right on in, okay?"

I laugh. She smells like rosemary. "Okay."

The Randalls live in one of the new developments built a few years ago; the houses have similar floorplans and their exterior colors are mapped out according to the lot. They have little front yards and the backyards are sandwiched right up against each other. Nicole nearly slit some people's throats for a corner lot and I admire her for that. All the streets in the labyrinth of the neighborhood are named after birds. I pull down Robin Lane and park on the curb. The Ford sticks out like a sore thumb amidst the BMWs and Acuras.

Both Nicole and Liam's cars are gone, but Ro has his GMC backed up against the garage. I fish out the cowboy birthday card I got Freddie and scribble a long passage about how much he means to me, then, juggling all the bags, I ramble up the walkway. As I struggle up the porch, the front door swings open. Nicole shelled out a couple more grand to have her own door installed in an effort to show all the other moms who's boss.

Ro catches a rogue book trying to escape. "Hey," he says, letting me slide past him. He's shirtless, with his logging hat twisted on backwards.

"Hey, yourself."

He shuts the heavy Cherrywood behind me, sealing off the outside world. I inhale the artificial air and drop the bags on the glass coffee table. "Who did the balloons?" Black balloons fill up the ceiling overhead, too high up for anyone to reach.

"Who do you think?" He goes for a bag of candy. The flat screen mounted over the fireplace has on a paused video game.

Footsteps bound down the stairs and a moment later Freddie appears with a joint between his fingers and a crooked birthday hat on his head.

"There's the birthday boy!" I pinch his cheek and give him a squeeze.

"Yeah, yeah, what'd you get me?" He doesn't push me away.

I thrust his sack of books at him, and Ro resumes his shooter game.

Once Freddie's satisfied that all the books were written by discredited PhD holders, he moves on to the candy. "Where's the licorice?"

"In this one," I say, holding out my bag.

The joint bobs between his lips. After he finds the red, twisted vine, he looks up at me. "Thanks, babe."

I smile. My little man, all grown up.

"Oh, and this, too," I hold out the blue envelope.

His eyes immediately light up when he tears through the thin paper and opens the card. His eyes scan it greedily, then go through again more slowly, a soft smile spread on his pale lips.

A ton of flirting and ego-boosting later, I convince Freddie to go on a run with me. Ro invites himself, and offers to drive. Freddie doesn't argue, which is a really good sign.

Ro plays his rap loud and rolls all the windows down. He takes us to one of his spots, an old service road near an old logging site. We come to a pull-off and disembark the tall SUV. Freddie and I follow Ro down a short, beaten path. I've never been to the hideout (Freddie always seems to forget where it is or succeeds in distracting me when I mention it), but its parties are legendary.

The path ends, spitting us out at the base of a large ponderosa pine tree. It's not obvious at first, but then the treehouse hits me all at once. Crude, random-looking wooden platforms and beams jut into and out of the tree, propped up on branches and forks, molded to fit. Rope ladders hang freely and tarps drape over branches to serve for roofs. The platforms go up three stories off the ground and there are no railings to be seen. It's like the tree decided to grow itself out to become a house. Sofas and chairs litter the ground at the base and there's coolers everywhere. We squint up at the wooden fortress.

"Did you add another platform?" Freddie asks disdainfully.

Ro grabs one of the ropes and hoists himself up. "Yeah, it's a great jump-off for birds. Plenty of time to catch the wind."

My heart flutters at the thought of plunging off the top story. "Did you build this?"

"Some of it," he says, disappearing behind the trunk. "The original bones were built by some of the older guys way back when. When they got too old to care they told Damien about it and me and the guys helped build it up."

The old guys tell Damien a lot.

The planks creak under Ro's weight. I catch glimpses of him through the branches as he flips furniture and trash.

"What's he looking for?" I ask Freddie, who's going through some leaky styrofoam boxes.

"Probably his buck." He finds a half full bottle and inspects the label.

Ro tosses a chair and it shatters a few feet from me. An image of my oak box at home, all skins tucked safely inside, fills me with pride. "Come on," I say to Freddie, hauling him to his feet. "He'll catch up."

We pick our way through the trees, empty bottles and used condoms becoming few and far between the further we go. The sun hasn't quite reached past the branches and the earth is damp under us. He follows me a few paces behind, heart quick and shallow.

"How long's it been?" I ask, forcing myself not to turn around.

He doesn't answer right away. "Awhile."

"What's awhile?"

He hesitates again. "Camp."

"Why?" I keep the accusation from my tone, but he senses it anyway.

"Dunno, Char. Maybe because the girl who bullies me into shifting suddenly got too busy."

I stop in my tracks and he runs into me. My eyes come level with his nose and he stares at me, waiting. "I'm not going to argue with you on your birthday. Take off your clothes."

He obeys instantly, uncurling the fox fur before slipping off his torn jeans. I step away to give him room and settle myself a few feet away, digging into the ground beneath me to feel for his pulse.

"Your breathing," I say.

"Yes, mother." His tone is soft.

I close my eyes, feeling his gaze on me. "Deeper."

He breathes and breathes and breathes, his shaky heartbeat becoming stronger and longer.

"Feel him. Feel him on your arm, creeping up into your chest. Down your back, in your belly. Crawling through your skin. Listen to him."

His breath picks up.

"Steady. Don't get ahead of yourself. Let him decide when he's ready."

He likes to jump the gun. Take the first wisps of the soul and push it through him, forcing the change. It's why he gets bruises, why it wears him out, why it makes him a cranky, angst-filled boy.

I open my eyes to find him on the ground, head bent. His flesh grows a deeper red, blood pumps to the surface. "Feel him? What's he saying, Freddie? Listen to what he wants."

Freddie grunts, and his back bubbles. The tension in his body causes a few bones to snap. He shakes, but doesn't cry out.

"Take your time. There's no rush." I find myself rocking to his heartbeat. My own skin tightens, ready, but I subdue the pronghorn for Freddie.

The sound of his back snapping sends a *crack* through the woods.

"Feel that pain. Make it into pressure. Let it build."

Fear is Freddie's problem. It's not his body that prevents his growth—it's his mind. He's scared of pain. More specifically, self-inflicted pain. He loves punishment when it comes from others, from outside forces. Doesn't mind drugs, coming down from the highs, fighting with guys who could give Ro a run for his money. No, he craves blood loss, bruises, strained muscles and broken bones.

But the pain that comes with letting a soul take over his body, to allow himself to be overrun by something within his control, terrifies him.

He's worked up the courage, too far gone to go back. I watch the fox break the surface. He twists into the ground, gasping for air and release. But the hard part is over, he let the animal in, and that's the most difficult thing you can do.

Before he finishes I slip my dress over my head and step out of my underwear. The pronghorn whispers softly to me as I tie her around my forearm, and I let her be the only sound in my head. Her soul melts with mine and soon I'm on all fours, walking over fallen branches and leaves, Freddie following noisily behind me.

Nineteen

School is almost over. I can feel it—the end of things. Just two short weeks and I'm free.

I hit *print* on my final English assignment ("The Great Gatsby: Too Bad You Never Learned How to Swim"), and flip through my acceptance booklet to State for the billionth time. The grinning faces of model-college students leer up at me, daring me to infiltrate their school.

Mom knocks softly on my door and pokes her head in. "Got a minute?"

"Sure, what's up?"

She sits on the corner of my desk, hands suspiciously behind her back. "Going to Damien's tonight?"

"About to leave now." I glance at my phone. It's almost ten

and I told him I'd come over so we could go for a fly.

She nods, taking a look around. She's holding her breath. "So, things are getting serious between you two?"

I watch her out of the corner of my eye. "I mean, we're definitely a thing now. Pizza Night made that pretty clear."

"Oh, I know."

I close my laptop to give her full attention even though I'm probably going to regret it. "So?"

She sighs, as if she can't avoid it any longer, and without another word puts a box of condoms on the closed laptop lid.

"Jesus, Mom!"

"I just want you safe."

"We're not—"

"Not yet," she cuts in, flicking the box. "I was eighteen once. Everyone was. I know how things can get. Sometimes the urge just jumps up on you—"

"*Alrighty.*" I knock the condoms into one of the drawers of the desk. My face burns. "I think I have pretty good control over my urges, Mom."

"I know. I trust you. But men, no matter the type, are animals when it comes down to it."

It. I stare blankly at her for a few moments before the will to move returns. "I should get going."

"It's just that things can turn quickly and, if it's anything like my first time, you might not be prepared for it."

I hold back a gag and I search my room for my flip flops. I wanted to change out of this loose T-shirt dress and maybe throw on a bra, but Mom's not leaving me that luxury. "I'm a careful person." Since recent events, I've had to constantly remind her of this. Constantly remind everyone.

"When you're in love you forget how to be careful."

"I'm not in love," I say, trying not to snap. I know she's looking out for me, from someone who's been there, but the image of her and Dad jumping each other's bones because of their *urges* is too much.

"Maybe not yet," she says. "But like sex, that feeling can just creep up on you sometimes. I didn't even realize it happened with Sam until it was too late."

The sex or falling in love? I face her and try to keep eye contact. "I hear you."

Her face brightens. "Of course, most of the time, the sex comes first. Lust and love can be hard to distinguish when you're young and full of—"

"Got it." I throw my hands up. "Please, just stop talking."

"I trust you, Char," she repeats, standing up to give me a hug. "I just want you to be prepared. When you're ready, for sex or love."

I pull up behind Damien's Jeep, and for the fourth time ever, enter their home without knocking. It still unsettles me just the littlest bit when the house is mostly dark. Every memory of it has been bright and loud and full, and when I come over and find only a couple people inside, it feels wrong.

The TV's on in the living room, and I walk in to find Ray and Mona sitting close on the couch, her head on his shoulder.

"Hey," I say, coming to a stop in the doorway.

Mona turns and grins. "Hello, Char."

Ray glances at me before lifting a hand. Progress.

"He's upstairs," Mona says with a wink.

I hop up the sturdy stairs. Not one of them creaks. The hallway is dark and all the doors are closed except for the one at the end. The only room up here I've ever been in. There's a soft glow coming from Damien's room and the low thumping of music. I stop outside the slightly ajar door, letting the familiar scent of weed and the old wood of the house seep into me.

The door swings open and he pulls me inside, crushing me against his naked chest. "What took so long?" he growls, slamming the door behind us. He hugs me close to him, spinning me to the rhythm of the grungy alternative pooling out of his stacked speakers. His window is propped halfway open to let some moonshine in, and the only other light comes from a few candles spread around the room.

"I had to finish my paper," I mumble into his body, enjoying his warmth. He hasn't showered today.

"You already passed your class. You don't need to try so hard anymore." His fingers curl in my hair.

"It's the last thing I'll ever have to do for a high school English class."

He releases me and I go stumbling onto the bed, tripping over a pile of CD cases. My dress comes up just high enough on my thighs for him to give me a wandering look.

Damien climbs on top of me. "I missed you," he mumbles into my neck.

I laugh, but it catches in my throat. The box of condoms haunts me. I half expect to find them floating above his shoulder, destined to follow me around forever. "It's only been two days, and you're very high." Maybe I'm high.

"Ray's on a rampage." He reaches past me for the ashtray on his windowsill. "They're trying to initiate me into the cult." He leans back on his knees, a leg on either side of me, and lights a joint. The orange spark brightens his face and threatens to lick his hair.

"You're already in the cult."

"We're in the cult."

I roll my eyes before I can stop myself and start to sit up.

Blunt between his lips, he leans down into me, pinning my arms to my sides. "What? Still in denial?"

"It's not that."

His body is heavy on mine, the smoke from his mouth falling onto my tongue. "We've talked about this."

"Yeah." Does making plans without discussing other options count as talking? It's almost a requirement after you graduate Ruhn Roads High to apply to State, and unless you're a complete dunce with no ambition, you're in, no problem. So it's not a matter of getting in, it's a matter of throwing it into the mix of other colleges, or (for most townies) using it as a solid backup. But for me, that acceptance letter was my judge, jury, and executioner. My only way out. No other thought was given to any other school, not that I could bring it up without getting a "You're a Careful Person" speech.

"You're going to State," Damien says solidly. "We're together, you've got college, nobody but Ray's been whispering about chopping off your head. Happily ever after. What's there to be restless about?"

I wriggle out of his grasp. "You know what this feeling's like."

"That's not fair."

"We're not that different."

His eyes flash. He retreats off the bed. "I didn't have you when I left."

"You had Ellie."

"I wouldn't have gone if I had you," he snaps.

"It's not like I want to get away from you. I just don't know if I want to stay here." I'm talking too fast. I scramble off the bed.

He puts the joint out on his arm and bends over his desk. "I spent my whole life in this town. How was I supposed to take a clan, lead these people, if this is all I've ever seen?"

"How am I supposed to stand next to you if I don't even know where I come from?" My voice cracks.

He turns on me. "Why do you need to know everything?"

For just a breath Damien looks like someone else. Like he wants to pounce on me, shed his skin to the animal underneath and eat me whole. I flinch and nearly fall back onto the bed.

His eyes soften. He crosses the room and takes my face in his hands before I can back away. "You're here, little one. You've found your way here, to us."

Is that fear in his voice?

He rubs his thumb over my bottom lip. "I just want you to be happy. Happy with me. And when you think about your life before us, you're not. You obsess over it."

Obsess.

He pulls me against him. "Maybe *obsess* is too strong. How about passionate? I like your passion, it makes you strong. But it also hurts you."

"No, obsess seems right." Slowly, I link my hands around him. He might be right. Both he and Freddie could be right.

"I just meant... When you talk about leaving, about not knowing what you want or where you want it, it makes me nervous."

"Then you know how we felt."

His pulse skips. "We?"

"Well not me specifically, but the clan."

"Oh, okay."

I laugh, and soon he's laughing, too.

He releases me and holds me at arms' length, beaming. "I've got a surprise for you."

"It's not some kinky sex thing, is it?" Only half joking.

"Not intentionally." He stumbles over to his dresser and rifles through some papers on top.

I lean against his stereo and flick through CDs, mildly looking for a The Becoming of Lions album. When I move a stack of discs, an envelope tumbles to the floor. I stoop to catch it. In the dim light I can just make out Damien's name scratched on the outside.

"What's this?"

He's next to me in a second, looking over my shoulder. "Oh, remember those guys I told you I met?" He plucks the envelope from my fingers and tosses it aside. "The ones who gave me this scar? They're just keeping in touch. Checking up on me."

My eyes trace the thin line on his chin. "You told them where you live?"

He nods. "Gave them my number, too, but I think they're scared of the grid or something."

"I think they rubbed off on you," I say, remembering his coming-home letter.

He shrugs and pulls me away from the stereo, spinning me again. He presses a thin piece of paper in my hand. "Congratulations on graduating."

It takes a second to register what I'm looking at. His heartbeat picks up. "A plane ticket?"

He grins. "To North Dakota."

"What's in North Dakota?"

He presses his lips to my forehead, fingers circling around my neck. I let him lead me to the bed, let him press his body into mine as we fall back, let his hands feel their way up my stomach. The blood rushes to my face, while his rushes somewhere else.

"Cougars."

Twenty

The first time I saw Freddie was right after we moved here. It was my first day of seventh grade. Lunchtime, and I was too anxious to eat. I'd never had odd looks from other kids, teachers giving me sideways glances, or had a sit-down with the principal as soon as I stepped on school grounds. Dad had warned me the people would be different. They treated our kind warily without realizing it and I would have to get used to it. We were with other skinwalkers now, we would stick to ourselves and to our clan.

I was at the outside lunch area sitting against a wall. It wasn't like my old school's with its tiny trees and mostly concrete walkways, but it was outdoors and I could see the sun. The day was hot and quite a few kids, mostly older ones, were clustered around tables and lying out on the grass. I watched them, playing with the zipper on my backpack and trying to unknot my stomach. Mom packed me lunch—leftover pizza, but I couldn't bring myself to pull it out.

I felt Freddie before I saw him, probably the only time I caught him before he could sneak up on me.

His heartbeat was quicker, lighter, than anyone else's, like it was trying to pop out of his chest. There was an irregular jingle to it, but not in a bad way. I scanned the kids, trying to pick him out (not even knowing who I was looking for), but when I saw the bright blond hair I knew.

He was short and thin, standing on wobbly knees and tugging at the sleeve of his button-up, hanging behind a gang of boys. His small, waxy face was set with determination and his backpack bounced on his back as he walked. He was talking to the boys, who had to be in the eighth grade. They were clattering loudly, pretending not to notice him, turning direction whenever he would get in front.

Finally, he reached down and grabbed one by the ankle, and the lanky kid fell face first onto the concrete.

"Give it back!" Freddie shrieked, standing over him.

"What, you little albino freak?" The boy scrambled to his feet. His round face was red. He pulled a blue bottle out of his pocket and shook it in Freddie's face. "This? Are these what you want?"

One of the other boys took the bottle from his friend and popped the lid. "Maybe he needs these so he won't burn in the sun."

"That's vampires, dipshit," the first boy said.

"Whatever. You want these, Freddie?"

Freddie seethed. He stood rigid, little fists balled. I felt scared for him, standing tall in front of a group of boys who could flatten him with a foot. "I need them."

The boy shrugged, laughing with his friends. "Guess that's too bad, then." He threw the bottle into the air, in my general direction, and the little white pills went flying.

A couple girls squealed and a bunch of other boys hooted. I'm still not sure what compelled me, or what I was planning to do when I got to my feet and made a step towards them.

But then Freddie screamed. High pitched and bloodcurdling, like he was being murdered. He threw himself backwards on the ground and clutched his arm.

A teacher came out and rushed to him. She was heavy-set and older, and jiggled when she dropped to her knees next to him. "What's wrong, dear?"

Freddie hiccupped and wiped away his tears. "Nick h-hit me," he blubbered.

"Nicholas Farthsight," the teacher said, spinning on the bully.

I watched in awe while she scolded the older boy and hauled him away inside, even to the protests of all his friends. The bell rang, and every kid erupted in chatter, gathering up their things. The bottle landed a few feet from me; it was some over-the-counter allergy medicine. I picked it up and walked over to the strange boy, who by then had dried his tears.

He was combing the grass for the pills. "You got that kid in a lot of trouble."

He stopped and looked up at me. His face was blotchy and his eyes were wet, but his features calm. "I did."

I searched his startling blue eyes and held out the bottle. "You could've just said they threw your pills. Why act like he hit you?"

He doesn't make a move. "Not supposed to have them. I would've gotten in trouble, too, if I told Mrs. Jenks that."

I couldn't remember any point in my life where I needed medicine or allergy pills, or why another skinwalker would, either. "You're like me, aren't you?"

He stood, eyes coming level to my nose. "Doubt it."

It's best to tell Freddie about my upcoming adventure in person. I find him in the courtyard before school, propped up on our bench with one of the books I got him for his birthday. He can't have too many left; every time I see him he's devouring a new one. As I get closer he haunches over the paperback and writes something in a margin.

"Hey," I say cheerily, dropping down next to him. It's a foggy morning; the sun can't quite peek out of the mist.

He doesn't respond, and underlines something.

"Just one more week left," I try again.

"Yeah." He leans back on the bench and lets the book close. "Done with this bullshit."

"You still have one more year."

"Senior year's a joke." He winks. "Meeting you out front for graduation, right?"

"Just please don't embarrass me."

"*Can't* promise that. My baby bird's flying the nest." I bite back my smile and lean into him.

"I think Ro wants to go too, since Damien's coming."

My in. "Speaking of Damien."

He shifts and starts digging in his backpack.

"He invited me on a trip, for a graduation present. Just a week of camping, you know?"

The switch flips. It's like his eyes have lasers in them. "Where?"

I straighten up and plaster on a smile. Just stay calm, Char. If you stay calm, so will Freddie. "To North Dakota. For a cougar. You know, if I don't get eaten by a bear first—"

He stands, knocking his backpack on the ground, and wheels on me. "Are you out of your fucking mind?"

"Freddie." His favorite freshman girls go quiet from across the yard. They're not the only ones.

"Fuck you." His voice rises. "You barely survived the last trip to camp, and now you're running off with him?"

Why can't he take shocking news like a normal person in public? Isn't this why people break up in restaurants—so no one makes a scene? "Don't keep putting me through this. That wasn't his fault."

He squints at me, gears turning in his head. "Right."

Now my voice rises. "Blame me all you want, because this is my decision—"

"This isn't like you, Char. You're careful. You don't 'have bad shifts' or pick fights with dumbfucks at school."

"I am careful." Constant reminder.

"Bullshit," he bites. "I get it. You're in love. But it's turning you stupid."

I stand and the world tilts. "I'm not stupid. Just because you can't stand me giving attention to someone other than you doesn't mean you can attack me."

He blinks. The bell rings, loud and shrill through the yard, but neither of us move. There's no movement around us, either.

"This has nothing to do with Damien, it's you and me," I go on. "Sorry I've stopped waiting around for you to find time for me. I can't devote my entire life to you."

"But you can devote it to big bad Damien, right?" His eye is twitching, and I know I've struck the cord.

I reach out to him. "I don't know why you think there's only room for you."

He hits my hand away, my soft tone sparking his fire. "He's going to kill you."

"Stop it, Freddie."

He grabs his bag and shoves past me. "Fine. I'll stop." He takes a couple steps, hesitates, then turns. "But don't worry, I'll act surprised when you come home wrapped in a tarp, too."

I freeze. His words cut through me like a chainsaw, ripping my insides on their way through, leaving me bleeding and raw.

They burn in my brain, in my bones. I've been around to witness the awful things he's said to people over the years, from dead baby jokes to obscenities that kicked off riots, but nothing like bringing Dad into it.

My mouth opens but no words come out, my knees buckle but don't give, my eyes burn while I watch Freddie walk away from me.

Walk away from me.

"Hey," I shout. The wind stops. The four walls hold their breaths. The only thing I hear is my own blood rushing through my organs, and my brain, tick, tick, ticking.

Freddie halts at the sound of my voice, back tense.

My lip trembles. "Apologize."

He whips around, ready. "No. Cunt."

I lunge. I don't feel the ground beneath me as I close the space between us. I aim for his throat and in a second I'm on top of him, hands wrapped around his jugular. Blood is pulsing through me like electricity, deafening me, and his heart thunders out of his chest, into my hands.

Freddie grits his teeth and grabs fistfuls of grass. Push me off, Freddie, I know you can. My fingers encircle his throat and my tears drop onto his face. He watches me through glassy eyes.

I lean down until I'm centimeters from his lips. From all around voices yell and bodies close in, but nothing touches me. Nothing can. "Apologize."

He coughs a little and his eyes flood over with tears.

I shake him. "Apologize."

He goes cold under me. "Don't go."

"Apologize."

I've never seen his face this red. *"Don't. Go."*

I dig my nails into his neck. "I'm not going anywhere."

I'm not going anywhere.

I'm not… going anywhere.

My fingers go slack. Time's up. All these years, the things that I wanted to get away from grew to be the things that tether me here. I got it into my head that Dad's mystery was the only thing keeping me in Ruhn Roads, that once I knew the truth I'd be truly ready to leave. But it wasn't Dad keeping me here—it was Mom. And Freddie. Jessica, Ralph, Ro, and maybe on a good day, Bass. Even now, Damien. If I left, I wouldn't be breaking free, I'd be leaving everything we've built for ourselves. Maybe they've all been right. It's crazy for me to want something I've never known in place of everything that is me.

I release Freddie's neck with a sob and push myself off him. There's a shriek and the world comes into focus. A handful of people spring away from us. My spine ripples and my skin burns.

Freddie coughs, trying to breathe, and a couple girls drop down next to him. He sits up and grabs for me. I keep my hands locked together when he takes hold of me and hauls me to my feet. My skin crawls over my bones and my lungs spasm as I breathe. There's a teacher's voice in the throng and excited hollers.

Freddie pulls me by my waist through the courtyard, into the lobby, and out of the school.

When we get to my truck he lets me slide down onto the asphalt with my back against the rear tire. He crouches in front of me and pries my fingers apart, taking my hands.

"Charlotte." His face is blotchy and his breath is labored.

I sob. "I'm sorry."

He pulls me against him. "You should be. You tried to strangle me."

"You would've let me," I cry, squeezing his shirt.

"I always knew you'd be the one to end it all."

I hold his blotchy face in my hands. "I didn't mean to. I don't know where that came from—I've thought about killing you so many times before but—"

"Glad you acted on it. I really shouldn't have said the thing about the tarp." His metallic eyes wander my face, the hurt in them just a few minutes ago hushed back down to wherever he stores his feelings.

"Freddie."

I can feel his heartbeat in his cheeks. "You're right. I do only think there's enough room for me. I just don't like him, Char."

"You say that like it's news."

He shakes his head. "I don't trust him. I mean, he still hasn't told anyone what happened to Sam. Don't you think that's—"

"He told me." My voice is small, my hands drop.

"What?"

I nod, slow, staring at his grass-stained jeans. "It was at camp. He told me what happened."

He waits.

"I haven't told Mom yet. And I need to, before I can…"

Freddie sighs, leans back against the car parked next to mine. "Before you can tell me."

"You grew up with him," I say. "You got to see all his stages, you were stuck in the middle of them because of Ro. This is the only Damien I get to know, the one he is right now, and it's the one I really like, okay? You don't have to like him, or trust him, but you do need to like *me*, and trust *me*."

"That won't change, babe. What you and me have, that won't change, but Damien's not a creature of habit, like us, like people. He changes, all the time."

"It's for the better, Freddie. Damien's doing all of this to be better. He wants to be dependable, but I don't think he can ever be predictable."

"Is that for the better, though?" He squints at me. "Anyone can see Ray's moves ten steps ahead. Sam may have shaken things but at least we all knew his intentions. With Damien, who knows what he's doing all this shit for? What he'll do to get there? You might be inside his head, because he'll let you, but the rest of them? Clueless. Only they're too stupid to see it."

"But you're not stupid."

"I'm clueless."

I take his hand. "Have I ever let you down before? We've jumped off mountains together. You're my go-to person, and I'm yours. You might not realize this, but you've rubbed off on me through the years. I see more because of you, and I see a lot of Damien. He's not perfect, and there's parts of him I don't get to see, but he's trying. He *wants* to try."

After a long while, Freddie lets out a breath. "As long as he protects you from getting eaten by a bear, we'll be okay. But remember what I'm telling you, Char. He's not a creature of habit."

Twenty-One

"This is horrible," I mutter at my reflection. The white polyester of the graduation gown hangs on my body like a pillowcase. I try adjusting the cap again but my hair won't let it settle completely over my head.

"I can't believe the day's here," Mom whispers from behind me.

I turn to find her with tears in her eyes.

"Now's not the time to blubber, Mother," I say, face going hot. "Can we bobby-pin this thing on?"

She clears her throat and tackles my hair. I babble so she won't have time to think about today. I can't lose her today. She needs to be here, for me, for herself, and for Dad.

This is it. I'm done with high school. Already made it farther than a good portion of most of the people I know. After today, I'll have the summer to prepare Freddie for me going off to the University of Colorado. I'll make Ralph give me a job cleaning dishes and will have learned how to cook and mix a margarita just in time for school. I'll live in the clan's house, crash a Frat party just to rub it in Freddie's face. Come up every other weekend or whatever. Still be a part of things. Maybe I'll even figure out what I want to do with the rest of my life. Mom will breathe easy. Damien will be pacified. Ray won't hate me so much. The clan will be okay.

It's a plan. The most solid one I've ever had. And it feels good.

Mom makes me stop on the stairs to get pictures, and I con her into taking a few of the both of us together. I watch Dad in the family portrait while I slip on my heels, willing him to wink at me.

"He'd be so proud," Mom says, watching me from the hallway.

I laugh, sensing her sadness and letting my own melt away. "I hope so."

Her black lace dress swishes around her thighs as she disappears from the kitchen. "I thought maybe I should wait to give you your graduation present until we got home, but I think we both need this right now."

I stand unsteadily, a few inches higher than normal, and wait for her to reappear with the keys to my brand-new Range Rover.

But she just returns with a dark wooden box not much bigger than a toaster. It's worn and warped around the edges, with etchings and scratches breaking the rough surface. She hands it to me, and I lift the lid.

My chest collapses when the furs start whispering and I drop the top in shock, just barely keeping my hold on the box. "I can't."

She gently pushes it towards me, so the soft wood bumps against my stomach. The skins inside titter, and my heart warms. "For five years I've kept them close to me, turning to them for comfort. Each of these skins has been in him, and he lives through them, Char. He'd want you to have them."

My bottom lip trembles and I pull her into me, the box humming between us. Her familiar arms hold me and her patchouli oil scent fills my head up.

Mom has to fix our makeup before we can leave the house, so I barely manage to find a spot in the back of the school parking lot. I should be in the lobby by now, lining up to walk into the gym for the ceremony. Luckily for me, though, I spot a few white and red gowns gaggling around in the sea of cars.

I keep checking my phone for texts from Damien or Freddie, but nothing. "They know the time?" I ask, almost nervous, as we clip-clop down the tarmac. The sun is high, there's no breeze, and it's weird walking up to the school in heels with my mother.

"They're meeting us out front—look, I see them."

I pause, breath catching in my throat. I spot Damien first,

leaning against the large windows by the front doors. Next to him is Ro and Bass. Freddie's standing on the other side of the entrance with Jessica and Ralph, and all three of them are smoking in front of the THIS IS A SMOKE FREE SCHOOL sign. They look so odd together, like a gang of bouncers waiting for covers, eyeing everyone who skirts past them into the building.

"I didn't know Bass was coming, or Ralph." I had my doubts about Ro, too, but I keep that to myself. "We don't have enough tickets."

"Don't you worry," Mom says. "Ralph has never needed a ticket to get into anywhere and Bass doesn't really count, anyway."

They spot us and break away from the building.

"My groupies," I greet them, smiling wide.

Damien scoops me up into a hug. "You look amazing," he whispers into my neck.

"Congrats!" Jessica squeals, taking me next.

Ralph holds out a yellow rose for me, too dainty in his rugged, tattoo-covered hands. I take it and give him a kiss.

"Damn." Ro's glancing around at a couple of other graduates. "We would've looked good in those gowns," he says to Bass. Even though he did graduate, he was banned from walking because of his Senior prank. Flooding the girls' locker room by clogging the toilets with condoms full of whipped cream turned out to be a more serious offense than predicted.

I laugh, taking in Damien's button-up shirt and Freddie's suspenders. "And you all dressed up."

Jessica gives me a twirl. "It's not everyday we get a graduate. This is special."

"Thanks," I say to them. My eyes want to fill, but Mom would kill me if she had to redo my eyeliner again.

She gives me a bump, taking Ralph's rose. "I see everyone lining up, go on inside." Her voice cracks.

Freddie catches me by the waist as I pass him. "Don't trip."

I make my way inside to find my gap in the long line of graduates. When I near the R's, I spot Greer coming down the hallway. Even though I ignore him not-so conspicuously, he acknowledges me anyway.

"Ms. Reed," he says politely.

I give him a smile.

"Congratulations." He plants himself in front of me.

"Thanks." I resist the urge to look around for hidden cameras.

He puts his hands behind his back. "That spark of yours is going to get you far. Don't ever let anyone knock you around. Whether it be a nasty kid patronizing a bird or a grumpy old math teacher."

I blink and he's gone, walking away without a response. For a second there it sounded like he condoned fighting and the challenging of authority. Maybe he really is a teacher, or rather, an actual human being capable of feeling compassion.

Or maybe I just heard wrong.

Ten minutes later, like we rehearsed, we march on cue to music and take our seats in hard folding chairs in the middle of the gym. The graduating class is a little more than a hundred. The wooden bleachers have all been pulled out from the wall and

262

important people sit in lines behind us. They've set up a metal stage for us to cross to get our diplomas.

We go through a few speeches from the principal, valedictorian, even the mayor. When my row rises, I scan the crowd for my groupies. They're lined up on the far wall, behind the basketball hoop. Mom and Jessica are sobbing, hand in hand. Ro and Bass aren't paying attention, too busy gawking at Ms. Gracey's boobs. Ralph gives me a double thumbs-up. Freddie leans against the white wall, pretending to be bored out of his mind. Damien stands tall, hands in his pockets and eyes on me, only me. The corner of his mouth lifts and he juts out his chin as a sign to keep my head high.

"Charlotte Cameron Reed."

The polite claps get overpowered by hollers and whistles from the back, shocking a few old people from their snooze. I focus on not tripping as the harsh florescent lights beam down on me and the school band plays softly behind the stage, but out of the corner of my eye I catch Ro and Bass jumping like a couple of fleas.

I shake hands with five people who've never given me the time of day, and take the fake leather folder containing the little piece of paper that declares me an adult. Before I hit the other side of the stage, I pause and look at my family, imagining Dad towering between Mom and Damien.

We aren't allowed to throw our caps into the air, but someone liberates several beach balls into the crowd. Once we're all released, chaos erupts. People in my class hug and say goodbye to each other, snapping pictures and savoring their last few moments of mandatory structure before getting hurled out into the real world.

There's only one face I want to see, and as if he knows exactly where I am, Damien appears, sliding between bodies like a snake. A sexy snake. He holds a tiny, potted succulent in front of his face.

"What's this?" I take the fuzzy green and red plant.

"A pretty flower that's hard to kill." He smiles, and lifts me up to spin us.

I laugh, trying not to kick anyone while we turn, and when he sets me down I pull him close and kiss him.

Doesn't get much cheesier than that.

It's no great decision where we go to celebrate. After a few more pictures in front of the school we pile into our cars and trucks and head to the bar. I thought I might be sad, or nostalgic— I mean, my days of free education are over. But as we drive away and I don't have the urge to look back, I realize I've just finished the prologue to a book; a long, complicated novel with a happy ending. (It better have a happy ending.)

There's only a handful of cars in the parking lot, but Ralph insists he sent out a clan-wide invite to my graduation party. I can't tell if he's joking and I don't ask. I let everyone go ahead because the boys are starving and Mom and Jessica need to do something about the mascara running down their cheeks.

The heels gave me blisters. I rummage around the trunk for the first aid kit. After I patch my ankles up I strip off the pillowcase gown to reveal the ivory summer dress I wasted on Damien those months ago.

"Back again, old friend," I mumble to it, adjusting my bra.

A wolf whistle echoes through the parking lot and I turn, already rolling my eyes at Freddie.

But it's not Freddie.

Three figures crunch over the gravel. The one in front stands out above the others.

Joey smirks at me, mouth tight.

I don't recognize the other two, but they're older and larger, easily the size of Ro. They share familiar, beady features. I'm trapped between the side of the bar and Mom's car—the wrong side to make a run for the alley at the back of the lot.

"Looking good, Charlotte," Joey says before I can take a step.

Freddie was right. The Mahones aren't going to let Joey live down what I did to him. I should've let him finish the fucker off. I straighten my back and search over his shoulder for someone—but everyone is gone. "What do you want, Joey?"

"Just a sorry." His brothers, or cousins, or brother-cousins, spread out on either side of him.

"For what?" I take another step, but they've already formed a loose semicircle against Mom's car. My eyes flicker to each of them; dirty, with big arms and wide chests. Close-cropped hair, red faces, and weak chins. They don't seem particularly impressed by me, especially the older one, the only one with any facial hair.

"For being a fucking bitch." They laugh, and I catch a whiff of alcohol. An electricity buzzes between them.

I level my eyes with Joey's, and for the first time he looks me dead on. "I'm sorry," I say in a low voice. I fill it with as much sincerity as I can without showing fear.

A breath.

He shakes his head, grinning wide. "See? How hard was that?" He looks to his boys for confirmation, and they only nod.

The oldest speaks. "But that's not enough."

I'm going to have to run. I'm faster than they are, but if two of them get ahold I might not be able to get free. Not a single person has entered the parking lot, but the longer we stand here and talk the more my chances increase that someone will.

"We've been going back and forth for so long," I say in the same voice. Sound tired and nice, Char. Not afraid. "We've both done bad shit to each other. But it's all over now."

"Is it? I mean, it's not just between you and me." Joey's gaze shifts to the others with him.

"It's your whole damn family. Like a bunch of leeches," the oldest speaks again. Big Mahone—the one leading this witch hunt. I know a man in charge when I see one. And he's already riled. They've decided a long time ago what's going to happen. He prods two fat fingers into my shoulder. "And no one's pushed back."

I don't stumble. His touch sends a blaze through my chest. "I can't answer for them, you know I've only been here six years." I plead with Joey, talking only to him. He's the youngest of us all, the only one who might have some humanity left.

But he shakes his head. "You made me look like a pussy, and

your family made mine look like idiots. Someone has to answer for that."

My breath is too ragged. Panic settles in, nesting in my brain and forcing all my nerves to buzz. All three of them are within an arms' reach of me. "I'm sorry."

Big Mahone goes to grab me, but I lash out with a jab across his face. I duck around him while he staggers, but the third one gets a claw around my arm and shoves me against Mom's car, forcing the air out of my lungs.

Big Mahone coughs, spewing blood as he comes at me. He slaps me. "Bitch. Joey, do it."

My head bounces against the hot metal behind me and both of Joey's guys have me by the arms, pinning me down. The contact sends my senses flying. My vision blurs. I kick out at Joey, but he catches my ankle and holds it.

"Do it!" Big Mahone snaps again. His breath is hot in my ear. Something wet splashes onto me from his mouth—spit or blood?

Joey slaps me. They laugh.

My bully's up against me, holding my chin in his meaty hand. "You gonna apologize for what your family's done to this town?"

My head aches and my cheek stings. A fire spreads through my throbbing lungs and down my arms. I know they can feel the heat because their grip on me shifts like they're getting burned, but Joey hangs on tight, jaw clenched and daring me. Telling the truth—that I'm not really part of the clan, that they don't account for me just as much as I don't account for them—wouldn't do me any good, even if I took the cowardly way out. Generations of

267

submerged hatred are radiating out of Joey, years of being told that everything wrong with his family was caused by us, of irrational fear turned loathing, have become too much for him to handle. And now he has to do something about it. Anything to get rid of the feeling of not understanding. No matter what I say, he's going to get the apology they think he deserves.

"You hit like a bitch," I whisper.

He slaps me again, harder. Sparks dance in my peripheral. "Hold her legs," he barks, and my thighs get pinned by rough hands.

I struggle through the dizziness of getting my head jerked around. I feel fabric, the fabric of my pretty dress running over my thighs, up my hips. I scream, but Big Mahone covers my mouth with a dirty hand. He clamps my lips over my teeth with a force that's going to crack my skull.

"We're going to make you sorry. Make them all sorry." Joey's eyes are filled with a festering, dark monster that's never been let loose before.

His jeans scrape my inner leg, fingers hook around my underwear.

And then he's gone.

Damien throws him on his back and the boys drop me onto the gravel. They spring for Damien, but Ro and Bass grab after them.

Damien's untouchable. He takes Joey's neck with one hand and beats his head with the other, over and over. Blood spews from the boy's mouth.

I'm coughing, trying to catch my breath, a warm and metallic taste in my mouth.

I don't see Freddie until he's right in front of me, hoisting me up. "Are you okay?" he says, yanking my dress down and patting me. "Does it hurt? Char? Are you okay?" He's talking too fast and his hands shake too much.

There's a commotion, and then there's Ralph's voice, and Mom's. Ro and Bass pin the other Mahones on the ground, but Damien is still over Joey. His body is tense and sharp, vibrating. Joey's face is a gooey mess and his blood splatters the ground. He's not moving, and Damien drops onto his knees next to him. His mouth moves fast against Joey's ear.

Ralph has his bat and only glances at Damien before turning his wrath on the boys Joey brought. Mom's running towards me, Jessica on her heels. A couple of the clan follow them, and I do a double-take as the rugged men turn up their sleeves, ready for a fight. A fight for me?

"What happened?" Mom shrieks, running her hands along my face. "What happened, Char?"

I can't speak.

Ro and Bass haul the two boys to their feet in front of Ralph. He's in their faces, screaming something about his bar, his parking lot, his Charlotte.

My eyes find their way to Damien. He rises from beside Joey and steps over him like he's not even there.

"They had her dress up, Jule," Freddie says when I'm silent. He points to Joey, the bloody heap on the ground. His hand trembles. "He was on top of her."

Ralph stops dead, his bat hanging in midair. "What the fuck?"

"Joey's not moving," Big Mahone says.

"He has to go to the hospital," the other one adds. He's crying, and flinches when Bass, only as tall as his shoulders, steps toward him.

"Jonesy," Damien says thickly. He turns to Ray's right-hand man (how long has he been here?) and I can't see his face. "Take this piece of shit to the ER, keep an eye on him. I'll call Ray."

Jonesy and another guy, Pete, help the two Mahones load Joey into one of their pickups. The rear tires kick up gravel and they're gone. After Ralph whispers to her, Jessica ushers everyone else back inside. Only the graduation party remains. Damien won't look at me.

"Do I need to call Erin, Charlotte?" Mom says softly.

"No." My voice doesn't sound like my own.

"What the fuck happened?" Damien's taken off his button-up shirt and is wiping his hands on it.

"It was the hick from school," Freddie says defensively. "The one she got in a fight with."

"A fight?" That makes him look at me.

Ro spits. "He's a Mahone. Those meth heads that went bankrupt."

"What did he want?" Mom says to me.

"What they all want," Ro answers. "To get even. Can't even count the number of times I've gotten in a fight with any one of them."

"But to go after Char—" Ralph protests.

270

"Everyone go inside," Damien's voice is steel. "Give Charlotte a minute."

Freddie and Mom are the only ones who hesitate. "I'm alright." I can't even coax a fake smile. Every muscle is tense; blood roars in my veins. "Can you get some food to go? I just want to go home."

"Sure, hun," Mom nods, kissing my forehead. She knows I'm not hungry. She wants to stay with me, but Damien's tone leaves no room for argument. She pulls Freddie with her. He looks like he might throw up.

Damien's by his Jeep. "Come here."

I don't move. I've never seen a fight like that. Brawls and wrestling, sure, but never anyone beaten the way Damien was going down on Joey. He was trying to pound the life out of him, pulverize him into nothing. Pure anger and raw violence. Tackling and choking Freddie pales in comparison.

He opens his trunk and grabs a bottle of water. "Char, please."

I take a deep breath before hobbling over to him.

He tosses the blood-soaked shirt inside and helps me up into the Jeep before finding a towel and wetting it. He gently cleans off my face. It's cold and feels good against my hot skin. My breath trembles. How can he be so gentle after almost crushing someone to death? He slides the rag down my arms, over the bruises already starting to form, and over my knuckles, red from the one good punch. He moves to my legs, and hesitates. For the first time ever, I see him unsure. I help him, setting his hand on my thigh. He touches the hem of my dress. "Did he?"

"No," I whisper. "He mostly just talked."

His jaw clenches and he holds my hands, completely engulfing them. They're still warm from Joey's blood, badly bruised and cracked. "You've fought him before."

I thread his fingers through mine. "I should've told you, but I thought it was done with. We've had beef the whole year."

"The locker thing? The bird thing?"

I nod.

"I would've listened, if you wanted to talk about it," he whispers. "You should've told me."

"I honestly thought it was over. *This* wasn't Joey. It was his family. If I had known it would come to this…" My voice fails.

He shakes his head, and his grip tightens. "I'm not blaming you—I could never."

I lean into him. "It didn't have to be like this."

He pulls me against him and strokes my hair. "Stop shaking, little one."

"He's just a stupid kid." The tears spill.

He holds me tighter. "It's impossible to know what someone won't do when they absolutely have to—even if they are a kid, even if you know things could've been different. You have to fight back regardless, hear me? When shit like this happens you can't look at him like a kid, someone you can reason with."

I pull away to look up into his face.

"You're a fighter, we all are. It's in our blood. And sometimes you have to let the blood take over. When it's him or you, it has to be you, okay? It has to be you."

Twenty-Two

I've never been on a plane before, and I probably won't ever again. It takes two hours from settling into our tiny seats for us to start wheeling onto the landing strip, and another just to take off. Damien says that it doesn't always take this long, just when something gets backed up, but the grumblings from the other passengers tell me otherwise. It's strange being in the air without the feeling of the wind and chaotic silence. We talk and drink soda and listen to everyone else talk and drink soda. It's just like we're all in a room that's hurtling itself somewhere else, and none of us would know we were in the air without the double-paned windows reminding us we are.

The compact screen on the back of the seat in front of me says we're about another hour away when we hit a little turbulence, which turns out to be the highlight of the ride. I daydream that if the plane goes down, I'll have to shift into my falcon in midair, which would make these endless hours worth it.

When we land, the first thing I sense is the air. We're at a slightly higher elevation than back home, and the air has a different taste to it. Damien leads us through the airport, and I catch glimpses of the new world through the large windows. Each step creates more bubbles of excitement in my gut.

We wait at the baggage claim for another small eternity, and I get a surge of relief when Dad's old camping backpack turns into view. It's green, a little worn around the edges from its years of use. Damien's things aren't far behind, and only on our way to the car rental desk does he mention that sometimes luggage gets lost, too, like we got lucky.

I don't feel so fortunate when we greet another line.

Damien grins at me and I stare at the back of the head of the ninety-year-old man in front of us. "Cool it, little one."

"How far away is the lodge?"

He checks his phone. "About an hour. We'll stop to get groceries before we leave the town, and check in by dinner. I hear they have a really good restaurant."

I sigh, nice and loud.

He throws an arm around me as we move up an inch. "We're not gonna head out until the morning, anyway. Then we have the week. You'll get what you came for."

He can't fool me. I feel his heartbeat. His skin is tingling, too.

He's charging, has been since Ro dropped us off at the airport, like this mountain's been lifted off him once we left the eyes of the clan.

There's a pang of homesickness while we load up the rental car—a little silver Nissan—and navigate out of the airport parking lot. I roll down all four windows and breathe the new air deeply. The unfamiliar trees and flowers wave at us, just confirming we're on a different planet, a one that grew parallel to our own.

"Nervous?" he asks over the wind whipping our hair.

I poke my head out the window to get a blast of oxygen and welcome it into my pores. Though we're still in the heart of civilization, the rolling mountains in the distance beckon. "No."

We pass turnoffs for ziplines and horse riding and camping on the wind up towards the resort. The lodge is all wood and stone, fixed to the edge of a cliff. I don't like that Damien's paying for everything. The plane tickets, the hotel, the food, but every time I bring it up he brushes it off and says something about his savings. I want to bother him about it again when we wind up the stone drive and park outside an ornate glass entryway, cueing a valet to open my door, but he gives me a warning glare.

The lodge is cozy inside, with large brick fireplaces and wooden pillars. Animal heads hang on the walls and woven rugs squish underfoot. Long chandeliers made from antlers dangle from the exposed ceiling and for a second I feel right at home, wandering inside an animal. A boy with a glowing smile takes our bags, and I run my fingers over the polished wood of the front desk while Damien checks us in. On the way to the restaurant we pass a taxidermy cougar. Its soft gray eyes peer at us, and even though it only stands a few feet from the ground, a chill runs down my spine. His torso is long and front paws ginormous, head bent like he knows something we don't.

I can't get Mom out of my head. She'll probably opt to work late tonight so she won't have to come home to an empty house. Ray will be at the bar, and maybe they'll share looks at each other when no one is watching, each wondering if Damien and I are running away. Freddie will be high. He refused to say goodbye, but he'll be at the bar, too, with Ro and Bass and the rest of the clan. They'll be on edge, but hopefully not enough that they'll go for each other's throats.

We eat to the ambiance of over a dozen businessmen getting wasted at the long table across the room. I watch Damien as he laughs and makes a couple shrimp dance, the image of him beating Joey into unconsciousness still burning fresh in my mind. They had to put him in a coma because of the shock. Ray himself went down to the hospital to talk with his grandfather. They agreed to square the fight, since he attacked me and Damien attacked him, both knowing that if they went to the police it wouldn't end well for anyone. Mom wanted to push it, though, wanted Joey to be punished. But I don't know which feeling wins out—the satisfaction of Damien nearly beating my attacker to death to protect me or the fear of seeing my boyfriend lose it and almost kill a boy.

We may be leeches, sinking into any opportunity that comes

our way, but the Mahones are a sickness, rotting everything they touch. Ray's words, not mine.

When I wake up, Damien's already in the shower, the door to the bathroom ajar. We slept in the same bed, even though he got a room with two (just in case I'd think he was trying something), and I made a point to stay far away from his penis.

The morning air is dewy and the sun is just peaking over a far-off mountain. Damien leads us down a walking trail going around the side of the lodge, and we pass a few people with their dogs. He leads us deeper and deeper down the gentle slope, trees and thickets getting more dense, until we leave the path altogether. He huffs every time I stop to inspect some moss or mushrooms.

"How do you know where we're going?" I ask, skipping behind him. The pack is already weighing down on my hips where the straps buckle.

Damien's figure is sure, striding and taking in the air around him. He seems completely at ease wandering around in a foreign forest. "Who's the one who spent six months on his own in the wild?" he shoots back, but there's a smile in his voice.

"I just don't want to get eaten by a bear."

"It's okay to be nervous," he says, catching the stutter in my heartbeat.

I'm not so nervous about him leading us, and I can almost keep

Mom and the clan out of my mind, but I've never skinned an animal with anyone but Dad. He taught me his method, and would sometimes remind me that others did it differently. I didn't know what he meant by that, how it could vary so much that this weird look would overcome him, but now I'm thinking it mattered more than he let on.

"She won't be this close to people," Damien's saying. "They're very secretive creatures. Don't like to be seen."

I watch his back while he babbles on, follow his movements when he stoops to pick up leaves and twirls twigs between his fingers.

"How far out will we have to go?"

"Maybe seven miles. That lodge is on the edge of the national forest. We won't be seeing any more people."

"Great, so if we get crushed by a fallen tree there will be no one to hear us scream."

He stops abruptly and I almost run smack into him.

"What—"

He holds up a hand to shush me and cocks his head. "Hear that?"

My heart stops and I listen hard. The sound of wind and the squawks of birds, the rustle of leaves. "No?"

He turns and flings me under his arm. "Watch out, it's a falling tree."

I try to get out of his chokehold, pulling his hair. "Stop it, goon."

"Don't worry—I'll protect you." He drags me a few paces

before flinging a branch onto the path.

"Almost got me," I mutter into the crook of his arm.

He heaves a sigh of relief. "Jesus, that was a close one."

I wriggle out of his grasp. "You're a regular Natty Bumppo."

We walk most of the day, some spots trickier than others, stopping every once in a while for jerky and water. Finally, as the sun starts its descent back into the earth, we come across a giant rock face. The formation is sand colored and grainy, rough to the touch and unmovable. We call the small clearing at its base Camp, and Damien starts a fire while I figure out the tent. We eat mac n' cheese and settle in on a blanket next to the fire.

"Wouldn't it be great to bring the whole clan out here?" Damien murmurs, staring up at the stars. They cover the sky like a net, and it's so dark out here we can see the milky way.

I'm on the verge of sleep, head in his lap. "Too far from home."

"Too far for Ray, maybe. But us? You, me, Jule. Some of the guys. Freddie, if he behaves."

Freddie shouldn't be away from civilization for any stretches of time. "Don't think they'd survive the flight."

"I'd want to travel again."

My head snaps up, the flames of the dying fire coming into focus. "What do you mean? You said you wanted the clan."

"I do," he says, stroking my hair and gently pushing me back down. "I think we should all experience what I have. It could be fun."

"You've never said anything about this before," I mumble, wide awake. Something in his tone reverberates through me; he's been thinking about this a while.

"I forgot what this was like. The openness."

"The *freedom?*" I guess, rolling my eyes under my lids.

He tugs at a strand of my hair. "Yes, exactly. Out here, we can do what we want for however long we want without worrying about going back home later. Without worrying about people there to judge us when we do."

"I'm the last person to argue with you there."

"It's being alone Ray's afraid of. It's being alone they're all afraid of. You and me, we know what it's like. We feel things they don't."

"Probably because we're freaks, not because the clan might benefit from travelling around like a circus."

"We're all freaks. Some just don't want to admit it."

"So what are you saying?"

An owl hoots softly from a nearby tree.

"Nothing in particular." He taps my cheek. "We should get you tucked in. Big day tomorrow."

I buried my face in Dad's shoulder while the werewolf ripped the girl with the big boobs into pieces.

He nudged me. "Come on, this is the best part, Char."

"I'm not watching that."

"It's educational."

"Sam," Mom shouted from the kitchen. "Stop being an asshole."

Dad shifted his arm so it was around my shoulders. "You know it's fake," he said, turning the channel.

I peeked to make sure the movie was off. "It's only educational if I'm able to shift into a werewolf."

His laugh rumbled. "Who said you can't? Why don't we just go out and find one?"

"Yeah, and a bigfoot. A mermaid."

He poked me and made me giggle. "You used to pretend you were a mermaid all the time. Every time you saw any body of water you were in it, flapping around like you had a tail."

I laughed. "Oh, I got a better one—Santa Claus. Could you imagine me sliding down Freddie's chimney? He'd have a heart attack."

Dad's chuckle got caught in his throat, and he tried to keep his smile from wavering.

I held up my hands, preparing for a sneak attack.

"I don't think that'd be a good idea," he said softly.

I rolled my eyes.

He sat up straight and looked directly at me. "Charlotte," he said in a steady voice. "We don't skin people."

I blinked. "Wasn't planning on it." I grinned, thinking he was messing with me.

He studied my face. "Walking as another person is dangerous."

I waited for the smirk, but it didn't come, so I stopped smiling. "I didn't even know that was a thing." My stomach curdled.

He rubbed my shoulder reassuringly, getting his thoughts together. "I don't mean to scare you, Char, but some of us, in different clans, practice it."

It got hard to breathe. "They *kill* people?" I whispered.

"It's more than that." A sort of glazed look came across his eyes and he looked away. "When you take an animal in, she becomes a part of you. It's the same for a person. But people have a much deeper soul than animals, a much stronger voice."

I clasped my hands together.

"I've seen it drive men crazy. We're only able to carry one human soul in our bodies at a time. Do you understand, Charlotte?"

I nodded. There was a question burning on the tip of my tongue, but I couldn't ask my own father if he'd ever taken a person's life.

He watched me a moment, knowing what I was thinking, but he didn't answer. "It's not a common thing," he said instead. "Not many skinwalkers are even capable of it, doing it right at least, and that means something. It's an old practice, a horrible one."

Mom stood in the doorway. She watched Dad, arms crossed over her chest. She gave me a smile. "Help me with dinner, Char?"

I grimaced. "Do you want to take the chance that I'll burn the house down?"

Dad pulled a grin and poked me. "Go help your mother." His eyes were still dark.

Twenty-Three

We fly most of the day, perching on jutting boulders and skimming the tall, spiky pines. Damien's scouting around for where we might find my cougar, but right now it's all about the ride. We'll find her if she's here, wants to be found.

The sky darkens in the late afternoon; heavy clouds roll in, and we race to camp. We get a grazing of cool rain, our rock protecting us from most of it, and when it passes Damien says it's time.

I lean against our cliff, chin nesting in a crevice, and follow a vein in the rock all the way to the top, out into the sky. My bones settle. This hunt isn't going to be like any other before it. She'll be the fiercest animal I've ever taken down, and the farthest I've gone from home to do it.

Damien muffles the fire and peels off his shirt. His face is grim in the fading light, hair blocks out his eyes. "Are you ready, little one?"

I adjust the thin strap around my torso holding the knife.

He kneels in front of me, head bent, waiting.

I let my feet anchor, feel his confidence wash over me, his trust. No one has ever given themselves to me before, let me lead. Hunting for a skin has never been a pack thing; with Dad it was a partnership. We guided each other.

But this is different. I've got something to prove to Damien. Show him who I am. This is how he was raised, how things will be from now on, and I won't let him down.

I slip the wolf pelt around my arm. She's hungry with anticipation, waiting for her moment to make it up to me, an apology for splitting me open. I take the ground quick, eyes on Damien for as long as I can, but he keeps his head bent. He's vibrating, skin rippling, and only when I take a leap for the trees does he move.

I howl loud enough to let the forest know I'm here.

We travel up, squeezing between rock formations and cliff, Damien leaping and crashing through the underbrush without a care. I take my time, adjust to the terrain, keep my ears open. Eyes alert. I see much clearer through the wolf, every branch defined and root accounted for.

Soon darkness overtakes us and the wood grows quiet. The night dwellers rise from their beds.

I switch between a walk and a run, and lose Damien's heartbeat in the tall, spikey trees. I climb higher and perch myself on a peak, waiting for any signs of movement from below. The wind almost howls up here, treetops sway and dance, and the chitters of night dwellers get lost in the air. The sky is dark, neverending, but the stars give me more light than I need. I let my body rest, let the wolf simmer, let our spines tangle and our lungs fill each other.

Eventually Damien resurfaces, picking his way around the base of my cliff, sticking his nose in bushes and pausing at every little sound. Does he really expect me to find my cougar on the first night? He doesn't know I'm watching from above him, so I take my time. The wolf stirs, hissing in my ear when his back is turned. She wants to pounce, and scaring him seems like a good idea. When I lose sight of him, I rise from my crouched position and hop down a few ledges, gearing up for the chase.

But a flicker of movement catches my attention—

A cougar, emerging from its nest.

I change course, a magnet pulling me. Her heartbeat is slow, steady, and so, so attractive to my ears. She's not full grown, her body hasn't reached its full potential yet. Her color is deep. I watch, bent low, as she stretches her legs and bites at an itch on her behind.

Beautiful.

I close the distance between us softly, padding down the rock face and dodging around anything that can make a sound.

She stops. Listens. Ears prick and she swivels her head,

catching the wind.

She bolts.

I stay with her from above, the wolf gathering courage. She's mine. The cougar doesn't turn, but she feels me. Feels my soul, reaching for hers. When we're only meters apart, I bound down the mountain, almost vertical.

One foot after another, just one after another.

She spins to meet me, ready to fight. Her jaw opens, too late, and I'm on top of her.

The guttural roar fills my ears when our bodies collide. She rolls me, and I come at her, trying to flip her. If she snags me between those teeth, I'm done. I snap at her heels, and she snaps right back, snarling. We circle. She's got a large stomach; her last meal is making her slow. Slow enough.

Just get her on her back. I feign one direction, then spring in another, striking her in the side.

Taking the chance while she's knocked off balance, I pierce her throat. She claws at me, but my bite is just deep enough to fill my mouth with blood. A steady stream darkens her fur but she keeps going. From the ground, she lashes out, snapping my knife strap and grazing my chest. She manages two feet but I throw myself at her, making sure she stays down. It would take more strength than my body weight to keep her grounded, but she's losing blood so fast it only takes a few struggled heaves for her head to bob.

The wolf wants to finish her, but I'm not letting go. Having to take a life is hard enough, and not being able to save the soul makes it murder.

She's fading fast.

I force the shift, giving us space while I push the wolf from me, severing us. I have a much stronger hold on her than the last time we shared a body, and I'm ready for the resistance. Tears stream down my face while I shed the fur, but soon it's just the cougar and me. The ground is wet from the rain, sending a chill through the earth.

The cougar's head is on the ground. She's fighting for her lungs. Her betrayed eyes pierce through the abyss at me. They're so big, like little skies inviting me to fly through them.

I crawl to her, ripping off the wolf pelt and reaching out to stroke her massive neck. She doesn't flinch. Her fur is thick and coarse, my fingers get lost in it. My hand warms with her blood. I feel my way down, listening to her organs grind.

I was wrong. She hasn't just eaten. My insides twist as I stroke a quiet pregnant belly, void of heartbeats. They were gone the moment she rose from her den tonight, the moment her soul reached for me.

"I'm sorry." My voice is the last sound she'll ever hear in this world.

She eyes me steadily. Claws at me when I dig into her chest.

Reaching into a living being isn't like stuffing a turkey or busting open a piñata. It's hard. Skin and muscle and tendons and bones are tough and blood just makes it thick and slippery. Paired with the heat of body temperature and the struggle that comes with organs still trying to function, it's like ripping through a whole universe. One that's established and evolving and successful and endless.

Her heart holds on, but she's lost so much blood. Deeper and deeper I go, into her ribcage in search of her heart. Her breath slows when I grasp the muscle.

"Thank you." I squeeze. "You're not alone with me. I'll never let you go, okay? I'll always be here."

Her heart stops, and she's in me. She didn't fight it, not like I thought she would. She's tired and sad, like she's already known all the heartache and is ready for the relief.

"Here," Damien says from behind.

I hold out my hand, and he presses a cool blade into my fingers. I cut her pelt and take a large sliver of it—the link we're going to share forever.

I hold her piece of soul to my chest.

She latches on at once, grasping at my skin and weaving herself into my soul. Her voice already feels familiar, like she's been inside my head all night. The change is slow as we meet for the first time, and the new shape my bones take pull me unfamiliar directions. Her universe flows into mine through a black hole. Her stars fill my skies and my sun gives her life.

As my body turns to hers, the animal's voice grows stronger, and all the sadness and lethargy disappears. When I stand, her power fills me, overtakes my heart, controls my blood and bones. My body is thick and strong, not wily the wolf. I can see further into the dark, under the thicket and between the trees. I hear Damien blink.

We make eye contact. His tail flicks.

Come on, Damien, let's see how fast you really are.

These woods are different through her eyes. She's used to them, was raised in them. I'm home with her. She guides me, guides Damien. The cougar doesn't shy away from him like the wolf does—she wants him. Craves him. His body moving through the trees, pace in step with mine, his glances to make sure I'm still here, his heart beating with hers. She wants it all.

Dawn is about to break by the time we stumble into camp. Damien shifts by the dead fire, tugs on his shorts, and collapses in the dirt. His chest heaves up and down, whole body flushed and raw.

I will the change, staying by the trees. It's long and slow. Patience is essential the first couple shifts; both our souls need to get used to each other's bodies. When it's over, and I'm left naked in the grass, I stand.

Breathe.

He's pouring a bottle of water onto his face as I approach him, and I stop when I'm at his feet. His skin is red and his hair drips with water onto the blanket. I wait for him to look at me, but he keeps his eyes closed.

"I've never seen anything like that before." His voice wavers.

My toes curl into the grass. "You've skinned a cougar."

He shakes his head. "She was still so alive when you caught her. So full of life."

I drop to my knees in front of him, every instruction from Dad passing through my mind all at once. "Was it wrong? Did I take her too soon?"

289

His eyes fly open and they look right into mine. "No, it was magnificent. No wonder you have such a strong connection with them, you turn their life into yours. You're amazing, Charlotte."

Satisfaction radiates through me. I beam at him.

"She got you," he says, reaching out to trace the thin scratch on my chest. His eyes study the thin red line, then move down the rest of me.

It's time. For a blind leap of faith. For a prayer. For anything that won't let me lose my nerve.

I push his legs apart and crawl between them. "You really think I'm amazing?"

He breathes me in, fingertips brushing goosebumps on my arms. "You are."

I kiss him on the lips. Earth and sweat.

He pulls me on top of him, kissing me deeper. "Charlotte," he whispers against my mouth.

I wrap my legs around him and his grip tightens. "I want to do it, now."

"You're sure?"

"You said I'd get what I came out here for."

"I don't think we should," I say, watching Damien pull on his shorts.

He rubs his head. "We have to sometime."

"I like it out here," I counter, burying myself deeper into the sleeping bag.

He grabs the sleeping bag and pulls it out of the tent with me in it. "Come on," he grunts, landing heavily on top of me. His hand wanders inside, sliding down my body. "Can't do this to them again."

I laugh when he reaches between my legs. "I'd be running away for the first time. They'd cut me some slack."

He shakes his head, fingers finding what they're looking for. "We have to go back."

My smile fades with the sensation spreading through my body. "I know."

It's easy to let the rest of the world slip away when you build a little one of your own. The last three days were filled with laughing, lovemaking, running, eating, stalking, sleeping, stargazing, flame-watching, rain-dancing, more lovemaking, more laughing...

Camp became my home and Damien my family. These woods have become a part of me, Damien a part of me.

The walk back takes half the time, and the lodge is almost unsettling compared to the first time we set foot through its sparkling glass doors; all the wood and stone cut and pasted specifically together with no room to grow now seems like a cage, not a living thing.

I get goosebumps at every person who glances at us, like they know. Know we just spent the week in the woods, know I killed a cougar, know we had sex, know I'm not a virgin. In the elevator on the way up to the room Damien slips his hand into mine. The small gesture shuts up the little voice in the back of my head.

We take a long, hot bubble-filled bath in the jacuzzi tub. Damien picks out rogue leaves and twigs that've buried themselves in my mass of hair. I watch him shave his face. We get room service (the best ice cream I've ever had) and as we sink into the soft sheets, a feeling creeps in.

It could be not enough rest. Or too much oxygen and sun. Not enough food, too much sex (if that's a thing). Maybe it's not enough human interaction and too much Damien. Or a combination of all those things. But it starts. A change—shift into womanhood, maybe. Or the beginning to a new part of my life, the next chapter. This feeling of something new burrows in my pores, swims between my cells, travels through my veins, uses the labyrinth to my heart.

What happens when it gets there?

Twenty-Four

We land well after midnight, confirming my suspicions that planes are a horrible idea because our touchdown was supposed to be eleven. It's raining. Mom's asleep on the couch. Her figure, eyes closed and heartbeat slow, welcome me home. Standing in my dark room, with the rain pitting against my window and bouncing off the roof, I breathe it in. It only takes a couple minutes for my body to get accustomed to the scent of the house before it fades away to the familiar.

I peel off my clothes and crawl into bed, under the covers.

Sleep doesn't take me.

I cup my hands around my boobs, testing their size. We had sex—made love? It was more than two people just getting it on, mechanically fitting together. It meant something. I run my hands down my body, tracing Damien's path, poking and prodding; everything is still the same, except for one part of me. The anatomy is just like it was before, obviously, but there's a sensation that holds a different gravity—like the atmosphere of my body has changed and it orbits a different sun. It went from being just mine to shared with someone else. Someone who knows what the inside of me feels like.

It really is too late to turn back.

Mom wakes me in the morning to make sure I'm alive, and I have to swallow the taste of Damien in my mouth to answer her.

"Feel okay?" she asks, rubbing her back.

I shift my comforter around. It's tied around my legs. "Good, just tired."

She sits on the edge of the bed. Her hair's sticking out to one side. "Make it out okay?"

"Just a few bumps and bruises."

"Find your cougar?"

My heart leaps. I can't contain the grin. "I did. She's on my desk."

Mom wriggles her eyebrows and reaches over to stroke the fur. "Was it scary?"

"Just a little."

She nods, and all of a sudden we're not talking about the

cougar anymore. "But you were safe?"

"Yes."

Those eyes. I must look like a hot mess, but her eyes wander me like I'm some sort of beautiful painting. One that holds all the answers.

"It felt right," I say, taking her hand to distract her from unwrapping my innermost soul. "I'm glad I went out there with him."

She releases the breath she's been holding all week and leans over to kiss my forehead. "Was it fun?"

I groan and take my hand back. "Don't you have work?"

"Yeah, yeah, in a few hours. Jess and me are going for lunch. Want to come?"

"So you can both attack me for details? No, thanks."

Her hug lingers. "I love you, Charlotte." Her words say more than that. She trusts me, happy I'm home, happy I'm living.

"I love you, too, Mom."

Her eyes are watery when she stands and I catch the faintest smile as she leaves.

My phone's been quiet all night. I text Freddie and tell him I'm coming over. He's going to know as soon as he sees me that I'm not a virgin anymore. Even though it's really none of his business, I want to get to him before too much time passes and it becomes a deliberate secret. Plus, I want it out of the way. After our fight he backed off about Damien, but this might open the wound.

The bath washes the last of my trip down the drain. Tired eyes stare at me in the mirror, but I still look like me. Maybe even have a spark?

I park in front of 2189 Robin Lane and tread lightly up the sidewalk. Liam and Ro's cars are gone, but Nicole's is here. I ring the doorbell politely, admiring the freshly swept porch, but no answer. Peering through the frosted glass I ring again, and still nothing. Nicole must not be home. I bang on the door.

After a couple minutes, a form stumbles down the stairs and a shirtless Freddie pulls open the door. "You're back," he says, voice gravelly.

"Good morning, sunshine," I say, and slide past him before he can get a good look at me. He smells like stale alcohol and weed. "Where's everybody?"

"They all start their day at, like, six." He shuts the door and turns back upstairs.

I follow. "How was your week?"

"Boring." His sweats hang dangerously low on his hips and he's got an ugly purple mark on his ribs.

When we get to his room I open the black curtains blocking out the sun. Anita, their housekeeper, comes on Sundays, and Nicole makes sure Freddie's room is the first on her list. His carpeted floor is freshly vacuumed and nearly bare; things are stored and his closet is closed. We're only a day or two into the week, and so far he's only managed to clutter the room with some greasy pizza boxes, clear bottles of vodka, and some clothes thrown just around his laundry basket. He flips open his laptop.

I drop down onto his bed in a pile of black sheets. "I know

you're not one to ever answer me when I call you but I was hoping you'd at least check in on me to make sure I didn't get eaten by a bear."

He turns to scan me through his hair. "Doesn't look like you got eaten by a bear."

I lean on my elbows. "Cougar almost got me."

His gaze lingers on my chest where the thin scratch has healed over, leaving nothing but a pink line that'll soon fade, too. As his eyes focus, they trail down my body and back up again, and land on my face. They flash, a look in them he's never given me before. He watches me like I'm a girl on his bed and he's a boy, almost a man. It's a look he's given to other girls, some guys even, but never to me.

My dress hangs too low and is scrunching up around my thighs, and the moment he turns away to pack his bowl I adjust myself. I ignore his skipping heart, and try to control mine. Oh, Freddie.

"So you got her, then?" he asks on his exhale, sitting at his desk chair like he doesn't trust himself.

I scrutinize his scabbing knuckles to distract me. "She's amazing. We'll go out, and you'll see her."

"Sounds like fun."

We watch each other. He's going to make me say it. "Well? Are you going to ask or not?"

He stands and saunters over, swinging his hips and eyeing me. "You have that glow—"

"Okay, I did it, alright? I had sex with Damien." The words tumble out louder than I intended and I'm almost surprised they

297

come out of my own mouth.

Freddie drops down next to me and pulls me back so we're lying side by side. "Come on," he coos. "Tell baby boy Freddie all about it."

"What?"

I can't ignore the jump in his heartrate. His fingers are cool on my arm. "How was it? How did he make a woman out of you?"

I cringe. "This is why I need girlfriends."

"Was it everything you ever dreamed of?"

"Freddie, stop."

"How big is he? I bet he's thick."

I put my hand over his mouth. "Don't be a dick, please. I have no one else to tell and you're ruining it."

His eyes sparkle and his mouth is spread wide under my palm. "Sensitive."

"Stop smiling."

He lets it fade, eyes not leaving mine. "It's gone."

When I'm sure he won't throw another crack, I pull away.

"But you can tell me everything. I'll let you know if it was good or not."

"I think it was good," I whisper. Just by thinking about Damien I can feel his lips, taste his breath. His body pressing into mine like he needs me, his mouth not being able to move fast enough.

Freddie's voice drops, too. He's watching me; dismembering my expression. "Glad you enjoyed yourself."

What's that in his tone? Bitterness? "It's about time I joined the club, right?"

The bed shifts as he stretches. "At least you made him work for it."

"When did *you* do it for the first time?"

The laugh gets caught in his throat. "You know."

"No, I don't."

"I told you."

"No you didn't."

"Well somebody must've told you."

"Nope."

He looks at me out of the corner of his eyes. "I was fourteen."

He could be nervous if he was anyone else. "I'm sure you were an expert on pleasure, even then."

His head bobbles to the side to look me straight on. "It wasn't all romantic like yours."

Sweaty, with dirt and animal remnants caked in all the wrong places does sound like a plot stolen from a porno. "Who with?" Do I want to know?

"They weren't together for the first time yet. Just talking. He was jumping around with a couple girls. She really liked him, though, you could tell. I wanted some shit she had—can't remember what—and she offered a trade."

My heart chills a little at his detached features. He's seeing something I can't, something I won't ever see.

"It was Ellie. She pretends she doesn't remember, that she was too high, but I know she does."

What? I try to keep my surprise to myself. I can't remember a time when things between them were awkward or oops-I-regret-having-sex-with-you weird. How could I not have seen anything? He was fourteen, so I was fifteen… My Freshman year. We were in different schools. An uneasy feeling turns my stomach. "You never wanted more?"

He laughs. It's harsh and bitter. "No. She's way too fucked up and after she got with Damien and he found out—"

"He knows?"

"Yeah." His tone is flat. "But Ellie's been with everyone and is going to get with everyone eventually. It's not news."

I stare up at his ceiling fan. Freddie's exploits aren't exactly secret within the clan, or the town. He flirts with any girl that's already taken, lures boys from our competitor's swim team under the bleachers and gets caught in compromising positions on every major holiday. He can go on about drugs and fights all day, and considers it a bonus if I'm a witness, but sex has always been off-limits. He wants to keep the most intimate parts of himself away from me, like I'd judge him. It's pulling teeth to get him to shift with me, to let him even see that part of him, but I've done it. I've seen more of him through his soul than he realizes.

I want to tell him that I don't care, that he means more to me than who he's stuck his penis in, but he gives me the don't-go-there look and the words catch in my throat. So I reach out and take his hand.

He squeezes my fingers. "So, I gotta know."

I raise my eyebrows.

"Is he into, like, kinky shit?"

I punch him in the arm and jab his ribs. "You're not funny."

He tries to catch my hands and goes for my armpits. I spasm, laughing too hard, and end up kicking him off the bed.

"What?" he says, breathing heavily. "I just feel like he's really hardcore. Am I wrong?"

"Oh, he's hardcore alright." I laugh. "One time a wasp flew into his face while we were running and he tripped over a tree stump. Ran headfirst into a boulder."

Freddie nods. "Big bad Damien."

"And something even more hardcore"—Damien's face, glowing from the fire in front of the night sky, floats through my mind—"One night he was talking about living out there, just us travelling through the woods."

"Go rogue?"

"Not go rogue," I say. "Just maybe take a long trip."

Going rogue means severing yourself from your clan, cutting them off permanently, stripping any mental ties and loyalty. A year or two ago, a rogue skinwalker stumbled into Ruhn Roads, an older guy. Harmless, travelling in a rusty Volkswagen van. Just showed up one night at the bar, drawn by us, and Ray threw a conniption, made him out to be some deranged lunatic. After putting everyone on edge and making sure we were all unnerved by his alienness, Ray sent him on his way.

Mom was jumpy for weeks afterward. It was weird of her to be scared of anyone, especially someone that had been *us* five years ago. But she denied being shaken, even though I'd catch her looking at our portrait in the hall and phoning Ray, like she was waiting for something.

301

Freddie shakes his head. "Sounds like rogue territory to me."
Better not mention that Ray wouldn't have been invited.

When I tell Freddie what I'm planning to do today, he threatens to tie me to his bed. But he can't stop me. I'm a woman now (dating the next Clan Leader and no longer a virgin and all).

I've been trying to push it from my mind since it happened two weeks ago, but I can't. I asked Damien about it once, and he snapped at me. Don't worry about it, he said. They were taking care of him.

Joey would be fine.

But he's still in the hospital and no one is talking about him.

I have to travel an hour south, to Chandlerville, where they moved him. I've never been to a hospital before, obviously, so it's a new and strange experience. The building is big and there's a dozen entrances, like they expect you to already know where to go. The smell is overwhelming and sterile, like Freddie's house on steroids. There's people everywhere. Nurses and doctors and patients and visitors. Everyone adhering to their schedule or trying to beat it. I find a desk and ask the girl in pink scrubs where I should go to see Joseph Mahone, and she sends me to the ICU, which I learn is short for Intensive Care Unit.

Which doesn't sound very good.

I pass a small gift shop in one of the main hallways and buy a small pot of flowers (giant sunflowers, lime-green poms, bubble-gum pink carnations), since that's what they do on TV. And I need something to do with my hands.

"Hospitals are where people go to die," Dad said to me once, when I was little. Of course he was just trying to keep me from getting too curious about them, since our bodies are different and hospitals could mean exposure, but his voice rings in my head, even now. At any moment someone might pop out of a room and stick me with a needle and then I'll be gone forever.

When I get to the ICU I sign in, too anxious to think of using a fake name once I learn Joey had surgery this morning while I was smoking weed with Freddie. I want to ask what surgery and why and if he'll be okay, but I don't want to make it obvious that I hardly know him. My nerves kick up a notch right before I hit room 4307. What if his parents or brother-cousins are here?

It's empty.

The blinds are half closed and there's a light yellow curtain drawn around his bed. A beeping and puffing noise comes from behind the curtain, and I brace myself as I step inside Joey's bubble.

The whole right side of his face is tightly wrapped. His left side is swollen and only half of his mouth is visible, pink and puffy. He's got thin tubes running in and out of his body and his bedsheets are twisted around him, like he's been wrestling with them.

I squeeze around his bed and set the flowers on his bare bedside table. I pull up a chair and sit beside him.

His eyelid is so droopy I don't realize his eye is open until he says, "You've got to be kidding me."

I jump, I can't help it. The last time I heard his voice it was in my ear, full of hatred. Now he's a real human being, battered and tired and alone. I swallow. "I just—I didn't know what happened to you."

"Here I am." His words slur.

I blink at him. "Are you okay?"

He points to the bad side of his face, or at least I think he does. His hand moves slow and he can't fully extend his fingers and he gives up about halfway. "Last surgery."

Out of how many? "What for?"

He lets out a cough. It could be a choke or a laugh. "More fixing my face."

I sink a little in the chair. "Oh."

"Reset my jaw. Something with my eye. Take some skin from my ass since they couldn't save all of it. Gonna have a fucking beat scar."

My stomach gurgles. Damien did this. With his bare hands. "Are you in pain?"

He presses a blue button on a tiny remote next to him. "Not till I leave."

I want to reach out and touch him, but I don't dare. "It shouldn't have come to this."

He tilts his head. He might be looking at me, it's hard to tell. "What's your name again? I can't... remember."

My bottom lip trembles. "I'm Charlotte."

"Oh." Pause. "What are you doing here?"

What *am* I doing here? "I wanted to make sure you weren't dead."

"The dick who did this…?"

His name gets stuck in my teeth. My hands won't stop shaking. "D-Damien."

He coughs, like he got a mouthful of water down his throat. "He wanted to kill me."

I lean forward. "What did he say to you? He was talking in your ear when you were down on the ground."

Joey's quiet for a second, staring. His breathing labored, lips cracked. Just when I think he might have not heard me, he speaks. He's slow, his words fade in and out. "It was weird. He wanted me to go somewhere with him, together… Or stay with him, but still go… My chest was killing me… He kept saying…"

The beeps on the beeping machine slow. He's asleep.

I don't cry until I'm in my truck, driving home. It doesn't make sense—Joey was drugged up, gurgling words. Talking to me like we didn't hate each other. But his voice was so small. He looked like a child in that bed.

Damien did that. Beat him into nothing. Took his face, a bit of his life he will never get back, gave him a reminder of what he almost did to me—a reminder he'll never forget as long as he can see his reflection.

He changed that boy's life.

And that changed mine.

Twenty-Five

"Come out with us, show off that cougar," Damien says, sliding on his jeans.

I lie sprawled on his bed, naked except for one of the deep blue sheets wrapped around me. Music plays out of his stereo; the singer's cracked voice filled any empty space between Damien and me just minutes before.

"Why don't just the two of us go out?" I suggest, burying myself deeper.

He pulls the sheet off me. "You need to learn."

I get the allure: taking down animals as a pack. But what does it help? To kill an animal for the bonding experience doesn't build skill. Push limits. It's a pissing contest. Hunting was something

Dad never imposed on me, though he enjoyed it. It left me feeling empty, like I'd finished something prematurely. "I already know how to hunt."

"Do you?" He takes my ankle and pulls me to the edge of the bed.

"Of course."

"I've never seen you on a hunting trip, not once."

"Because I don't need to. Or want to."

"We eat what we kill, it's not like we're doing it just for sport."

"I know."

He takes my face between his palms. They're warm, smell like me. "You haven't come out with us. You really should."

"Why?"

He holds back a sigh. "Because I need to do this Ray's way if I'm ever going to get him to give me the clan."

"You'll get it, regardless. He doesn't have a choice."

"Sooner is better than later."

"Will I have that big of an impact?"

"When he and Mona were dating, she never left his side, even though she hated running with Jonesy. He always had to be right behind Ray."

"I'm not your mom."

He laughs, then bites his lip. "And I don't want you to be, but the more you show these guys what you can do, the more they'll trust you. They just don't know you, and I want them to."

I pull my head out of his grasp. "They do know me. They've

had six years to get to know me. They know exactly what I'm like, and I promise you that me coming along on your hunting trip will put them out more than if I stayed behind."

"This isn't about you." His voice is still calm.

"It's about you."

"It's about the clan, and us."

The clan. I almost laugh in his face. They're either the clan or the cult to him; today it's the former and he's going to be the dutiful heir. "Why does it matter? Did they expect anything from your exes?"

"This is different." He turns away from me before I can see his face change.

"It's not."

"You're different."

"When you were marrying Ellie they had no objections to her shooting meth—"

"You're different," he barks, spinning on me. A storm brews on his face, eyes like hurricanes, wild and fast.

My mouth snaps closed. The room gets too big, him too tall. I reach for my clothes.

He stoops and snatches up my dress from the floor. "I'm sorry."

I hold my hand out for the dress.

He opens it up and waits for me to bend forward before sliding it over my head.

I stay quiet. He's trembling.

He squats in front of me and holds me around my knees. "I just care about you." He doesn't look at me. "I was serious about Ellie, but she was born to us. She didn't have anything to prove. And she'd do whatever I asked." His eyes find mine.

I jut my chin out. "I can't change for the clan. I don't like hunting and I don't like shifting with people I don't know would have my back if something went wrong."

"I'd be there."

"If you had to baby me it'd be worse. I can hunt, Damien. The clan knows exactly who I am, and they haven't formed their mob, yet."

He nods, squeezing my thighs. "You're right. I'm just... impatient."

"What happened to 'plenty of time to do everything'?"

He laughs. The tension eases. "That was before I was so close."

I lean down and kiss him, and he kisses me back.

I let him be the whole rest of the day and the night, trying to keep him out of my head so I can think. Everything goes fuzzy when he's near, like he's disrupting my broadcast. He's getting serious about this whole taking-over-the-clan thing. The way he goes back and forth all the time—doesn't want to listen to Ray, but wants to respect his guys. Doesn't care that they don't approve of me, but wants them to accept me. He wants everything, and can't compromise. Where is that going to leave him when he takes over? How will he handle it all?

When I enter Brook's Books, the fat Memphis doesn't come running. There's more people in here than usual for the Second-Saturday Grab Bag Day, but the soft stream of voices and bodies puts me at ease. I stroll between the shelves and stop at tables, and get a few good suggestions from an old lady with a peach sunhat.

As I'm checking out, a familiar figure walks past the window outside. I don't hesitate as I throw my sack of books on the counter and tell Brook I'll be right back.

Tourist season is in full swing, but Ellie's untamed, brunette hair stands out in the crowd. I call her name.

She turns with the couple of girls she's with and her eyes find mine in an instant, like she was waiting for me to flag her. For a second I think she's sober, but as I get closer to her I notice the haze that's taken over her features.

"Charlotte?" she asks, like she doesn't exactly remember who I am, again.

Don't roll your eyes, Charlotte. "Yeah, can I talk to you for a sec?"

She glances at her two girls, and they wait for a signal. One of them, Cassie, is going to be a freshman this fall.

After some intense deliberation she smiles, but it doesn't reach her eyes. "Sure."

The girls take off across the street and Ellie leans against a parked car. She crosses her arms over her perky boobs and tilts her head. "So."

Maybe this isn't such a great idea. She's staring at me, expecting me to dance, so I link my hands and put innocence in my voice. "Remember the camping trip when we talked in the woods?"

She nods once, twice, eyeing me like a bug.

"You said something—that Damien's family has always done things a certain way."

"Our clan's way." Emphasis on *our*.

"What did you mean by that?"

"What do you think?" She pushes herself from the car and gets close enough for me to get a wave of something putridly sweet on her breath. "Clans as old as ours in towns as small as this don't just lay roots and call it a day. It's strict business, carrying on a *legacy*." Her voice draws out the word.

I avoid her gaze even though I want nothing more than to pry her eyes open. "Strict business?"

Her shoulder bumps into mine as she circles, sending a jolt through me. "When they say jump, everyone needs to know how high."

How high.

"And when they take someone into the Portman family, that person needs to jump the highest of all."

I can't imagine Ellie jumping as high as me, or living up to anyone's expectations for that matter.

She catches my stare and cracks a dry-lipped smile. "Not literally, but the willingness to jump is what counts. Has Damien asked you to jump, yet?"

I stare at her.

"When he says jump, it's really hard not to, isn't it?" She looks off at something I can't see. "Really don't want to let him down."

What I want is to tell her that the only jumping I ever do is for myself, but she needs to keep talking. The words spill out of her mouth like a faucet and I'm under it, catching them all in a bucket.

She leans on me, her breath tickling my ear and sending chills down my neck. "After a while he has you jump higher and higher and higher until you don't come back down. He's funny like that, bringing out the most he can out of people, bringing out more than they knew they had."

He's taken too much of Ellie, that's for sure. My mouth is dry and I can't move a bone, my blood almost coming to a standstill in my body.

With a last sigh she steps away from me, into the street. "That's what I meant by expectations."

I watch her swing across the street, not looking for cars. Only when she disappears around a corner, the opposite direction of her friends, does my blood resume pumping.

I abandon my sack of books and head straight to the truck, fumbling with my keys. She's insane, and I'm insane for thinking I could get any sort of answer out of her. I don't even know what I was asking. I know how the clan is, I know their rules and what they think of themselves.

The cemetery parking lot is half full. There's a funeral across the field. If I start yelling, I'll have to do it quietly.

I find Dad's grave with ease, right where I left it, and sink to my knees in front of him. "I don't know what to do," I whisper. "I don't know the kind of person I need to be."

Dad's quiet. There are no flowers today, and all evidence of my blood is gone, washed away into the dirt above him. Did it trickle down through the earth to his casket?

"You knew how to fit in. Everyone loved you. But did you hate it, acting like them?"

I wait, but only the faint voice of the pastor rises up to me.

"Or was there a part of you that wasn't acting? Did you really feel at home here, think we could all fit in? I know that never mattered before, but—"

It never mattered before.

It *never* mattered. I stare at SAMUEL LEE REED.

They don't care about my cooperation, they never did. I mistook their glances, averted eyes and whisperings for disapproval—but that's not what it was. They never made me to go to meetings or hunting trips. Never outright suggested *I* go to State, or particularly cared about any of *my* decisions. They weren't offended by my choices, or the things I did, they were offended by *me*.

I can't believe it's only because of my relationship with Damien. I mean, *he's* the one putting pressure on me. He's the one shoving me into the middle of all of it—pulling and stretching me to conform for a group of people who clearly don't give a damn.

My palms sweat. Stomach hurts.

Dad finally speaks from his grave: *They treat you different because you are different.*

"Am I?" My voice cracks, gets broken by adrenaline. "Am I different? How? Why'd you treat me like I am—and why is Damien? What do you two know that I don't?"

Twenty-Six

I leave early for the clan meeting, partly because I really need to talk to Damien and also because Freddie told me something was going to go down. Big bad Damien has a surprise.

The sun is still a ways off from setting when I pull up to the house. These are the longest days of the year. A few of Ray's guys' cars are already on the lawn. Mom, Ralph, and Jessica are closing the bar tonight, and depending on how the meeting goes they might need to stay open late.

I'm too early to smell the campfire or barbeque. A laugh erupts from inside as I pull the screen door open. There's a few guys in the living room and Mona's voice rises from the kitchen. All the windows are open and summer lets herself in.

Damien and Ray are in the dining room, seated across from

each other with platters of untouched cheese and crackers, casseroles, pies and cookies spread between them. Their table is twice the size of ours. I bet it doesn't even rock.

"It'll be fine, Dad, they'll be fine."

Ray stands. "These kinds of decisions affect us all."

Damien rises, too, glancing at me in the doorway. "No one's going to be affected. We're more level-headed than you give us credit for."

Ray starts in on him, but Damien's quick to walk to me. He squeezes me around the middle and presses his lips to my forehead. "Give us a sec, please?"

I nod, not mistaking the fury in Ray's eyes. He doesn't acknowledge me, though, and I know whatever he's got going on with Damien is for Damien alone. I go back out front, grateful to get away from Ray's murderous heart rate, and prop myself up on the railing. The only sounds that drift through the house are the men's voices rising above the TV and the occasional clink from the kitchen.

Decisions that affect us all. Sounds about right, if he was referring to me. But Ray barely noticed I intruded; the conversation couldn't have been about me, not this time. I grip a chipped pillar, letting the worn wood sink into my palms, and gaze around the yard.

It's not too much longer before cars start rolling in. I'm not the only one anxious about tonight. Everyone's been waiting for something—anything—to happen with Damien, and this might be it.

"Charlotte," Clay Wilnot greets, climbing the steps on ancient legs. He nods at me, and so does his wife, Thora. I've never talked to them before.

A couple more people pass, and someone acknowledges me again. Pete, the one who helped Jonesy take Joey to the hospital. Looks me in the eye and everything. Then there's a group of Ro and Bass's friends, the guys who they throw treehouse parties with. Almost every single one smiles at me, and their gazes don't linger.

I'm about to take a dive for the bushes when Freddie's voice reaches me through the throng. He slams the passenger door of Ro's truck, shouting at him to go suck something that I don't quite catch.

A hand slides into the small of my back.

"Sorry," Damien mumbles into my ear.

I turn and his mouth is on mine. I break free. "What's going on?"

Totally unconcerned, he tugs a lock of my hair that's hanging down by my left boob, fingers brushing where my nipple is under my shirt. "You'll see."

"We need to talk," I say, hoping my urgency breaks through.

He bites his lip and leans into me. "We'll talk, little one."

"I have questions, Damien. I ran into Ellie today."

He pulls away, face dark. There's bags under his eyes and his pupils are dilated. His skin looks thin, like it was difficult to regrow it after a shift. "What did she say to you?"

I stutter. "Nothing, I—"

"I've told her to leave you alone. You shouldn't have to deal with her."

"I was *trying* to talk to her."

Ro's voice picks up from behind me, his boom drowning out Damien's words. "Hey, hey, hey!"

He and Bass and Freddie crowd up the porch. Bass bows. "Your majesty," he says to me.

Ro drops on his knees. "I am your humble servant."

"What have you smoked today?" I snap as Damien steps away. He runs a hand through his hair and cracks his knuckles.

Ro winks. "The King's chosen his Queen. A weekend getaway to the mountains make it official, if you get what I mean." Snorting, they both bow low to the rough wood.

"Alright," Damien says, yanking them both up by their collars. He shoves them towards the door. "Go see if Mona needs help with the steaks." He turns on me. "I'll talk with Ellie, and you and I will talk tonight."

And then he's gone.

Freddie whistles.

"Something's wrong," I say quickly. "Did you see him?"

"He looks like a fucking train wreck," Freddie says, leaning against the railing.

"He was fine yesterday, before they went on their hunting trip."

He raises an eyebrow. "He looked fine last night, too."

"You saw him?"

"When I stopped by the bar he was there, pounding drinks

318

with the guys after they got back."

"Then something must have happened."

"He tell you about the meeting?"

"No."

He lights a cigarette, too slowly. "Really?"

"What did you hear?"

He shrugs. "Big Bad and Ray were arguing last night."

My fingers twitch. "And?"

"Something caught the old man by surprise."

I snatch the cigarette out of his mouth and throw it onto the lawn.

He exhales the last of the smoke with raised eyebrows, then pats my knee like he's cracked my frustration. "I told you not to go see Joey."

I slap his hand away. "What do you know about Joey?"

"More than you do. You can't help him, babe. Can't crack his code, teach him how to breathe. No use in obsessing..." He spits into the bushes.

"This isn't about Joey."

"Then who's it about?"

I want to shake him. "It's about Damien—"

Tha-dump, thump. Thump. Tha-dump, thump. Thump.

The heartbeat penetrates my belly. My head snaps around and I scan the trees. The sun is just dipping over their tops and the pines reach out their spidery shadows towards us. I don't see him, but I feel the blood flooding his veins and his heart skipping beats.

Then there's another heartbeat, and another.

"Char?" Freddie says, uncurling my fingers that are balled up in his shirt.

I still can't see them, but even without their faces I know I've never met them before. Never heard their heartbeat or felt their eyes on me. They're skinwalkers, but they're also something else. My stomach plunges.

Freddie speaks again but I push past him, into the house. Ray's in the living room, holding a beer and talking with a woman. "Ray," I say, louder than I intend. I can't control the pitch of my voice.

He turns, a confused and maybe even angry look on his face.

"There's people outside."

Realization hits him like a brick while everyone else in the room chitters away. He drops his beer onto the coffee table and strides toward me. "Jonesy, Jack, Pete," he commands, gaining everyone's full attention.

Three men jump up and follow him, and the rest of the crowd barely hesitate behind them.

I pause in the foyer, finding it hard to pass through the doorway. Their heartbeats are hard, but something about them feels almost familiar. The way their pulses tear apart like they're struggling between two souls reminds me of something, like a song. A hum, similar to an animal's heart beating fast as it runs from me, only it speaks a language I don't know, can't translate.

Damien comes out of the dining room, Ellie in tow. "Come on, Char, we need to go outside." His voice is hushed and breathless.

I don't move, but he takes my wrist, not breaking his stride.

Ellie's wide eyes lock with mine.

The strangers still haven't emerged. Ray is furthest out in the yard. Damien moves through the bodies, his grip on me iron. I stumble down the porch steps and he releases me, but throws a look behind him telling me not to go anywhere.

Damien stops beside Ray, and everything is still. They stand side by side, shoulders almost touching, staring into the dusky tree line.

The first person steps out—if that's what he is.

The man is tall, gangly and bony with a leather bag slung over his bare chest. Ribs poke out under bluish skin, an ugly white scar running across his belly. A thick black beard hides his jaw and matching, ratty hair is pulled into a bun. His sickly eyes pierce the fading light. They wander over each of us and when they find mine his beard moves slightly. He's smiling.

One by one, others come out of the trees, all in varying stages of his same decomposition. Four men and a woman. Their heartbeats form a grotesque orchestra with each one trying to play too many notes at once. I want to reach out to Damien, to pull him away before the tall one can sink his claws into him.

"Welcome to Ruhn Roads, guys," Damien says, patting Ray on the back.

Twenty-Seven

I told you so, the little voice says. *I knew something was wrong. Who the fuck writes letters?* I take a small step back from Damien. Away from him and Ray and the rogues, toward the clan.

All six pairs of foreign eyes snap to me.

"Find the place alright?" Damien asks the tall one, the leader. There's a ripple of movement from behind me.

"They found my lawn, all right," Ray answers. I can't see his face, but I imagine it resembles the one he made when Damien confessed to liking me.

"Sorry about that, Dad," Damien says. "Told them we'd meet in town."

Dad? That word has never passed Damien's lips.

The tall one gives Damien an easy, apologetic smile, and his eyes shift over to me again. "Didn't mean to intrude," he says. His voice is low and smooth and his southern accent is deep. "But it's a real trek to get up here, made us think like y'all didn't want to be found." Smirks from the rogues. "Carson got so excited when he caught wind of y'all we just couldn't contain ourselves, ain't that right, Carson?"

A bulkier rogue to his right with thick, tan skin and a missing left hand starts to speak, but Ray cuts him off.

"We keep to our own," Ray says, crossing his arms. The tension creeping up my neck eases a little at Ray's voice. Never thought I'd be glad he doesn't take change very well.

Damien gives his shoulder another squeeze and turns back to us, the grin I've seen so many times sprawled across his face. "Sorry for the scare, everyone, I was going to make a whole big thing of it tonight when we got the meeting going, but my friends jumped the gun. This is a little group I met on my travels. They saved my life a couple times—"

"And nearly took a couple more," the tall one cuts in. The other five laugh in a soft, non-threatening way, remembering some joke. An inside joke they share with Damien. My Damien. Our Damien.

A black lump sticks in my throat, its fumes fog my brain. My instinct to run hasn't been this strong since Joey had me cornered. I want to slap the easy smile off Damien's face, tell Ray to go primal on the rogues.

"I wanted to try something a little different. Let everyone

meet some people who know what the outside world is like, give us some experience. I wanted them to meet my clan, my people, my family." Damien's fixed expression, the way he's touching his father, the way the tall rogue peers past them to me like he can't help himself claws a warning right into my pores.

No one moves, and no one speaks. I can't take my eyes off them; the animal in me snarls.

"And we're just passing through, good townspeople, no need to overstay an unexpected welcome." The tall one makes a step forward, but still no one moves an inch. He lays a grin matching Damien's when he scans us again.

"Three days," Ray says, tone cold.

Too long, the little voice seethes.

"Leave the locals alone, this is a permanent residence."

Like we could stop them if they wanted to burn down the town.

"And stay off my lawn."

All our lawns.

He turns to us, folded face set tight. "I don't know about the rest of you, but I'm starving."

And that's it.

Ray passes by me without a glance, and that's when I realize he's already discussed these rules with Damien. He must've told him last night, and the argument carried over to today. Mostly everyone follows him. A small chunk remain outside, people Damien runs with, the usual crowd of Ro, Bass, and Ellie. Freddie's eyes lock with mine from the porch.

"Come on, little one," Damien says, making me jump. He

locks onto my forearm. "There's someone I want you to meet."

I keep my back straight as Damien leads me up to the rogue in charge, skin prickling under his touch. Late twenties and six and a half feet tall, easy. Aside from the massive puncture wound on his stomach, he's got a mesh netting of scars along his whole torso. A thick one disappears into his beard. His eyes have a yellowish tint to them that makes him look ill. They're alert, though, jittery. His veins and muscles pulse.

A body of someone with something to hide.

"Charlotte, this is Lark," Damien says, like he's introducing me to his mailman.

I can't bring my mouth to open, to form words. If I make a sound the little voice might start raving like a lunatic.

Lark watches me. His eyes dart around my face and down my body. "So, you're one of us, then?"

I look to Damien.

"A dirty, no-good wandering rogue," Lark clarifies. He bends down to get in my line of sight.

Damien told him about me?

Lark's beard twitches and he tilts his head. His face is hollow, skin pulled tight over bone.

Damien laughs. "Hardly."

"A well-placed boy like you couldn't know how it feels, not belonging to a clan." He winks at me.

I don't think he's joking, but Damien gives him his genuine smile, the one he shares with me. "Char knows where she belongs."

Do I?

I see the smile through his beard now. "Lucky girl."

The other rogues step forward, more at ease with the smaller crowd. They're all long, unkempt, with scars and tattoos. Like a pack of wild dogs, hunting for a meal.

Damien rings off their names, but I can't take my eyes off Lark. I haven't been so put off by someone in a long time— probably since meeting Damien himself in the woods—and what's frustrating is that I can't read him. His heartbeat, all their heartbeats, mangle together and never change rhythm.

Damien's boys and Ellie's group slither their way over. Ro gives me a small nudge, using his gigantic laugh as a diversion, and my excuse to go pee goes unheard over his massive voice. Despite what Freddie believes, his brother knows more than he lets on. I make a break for my truck.

Freddie tries to intercept me. "Char—"

"Not now," I say, making the mistake of looking over my shoulder after I pull open the door. Ro's distracting Damien well enough, and the girl rogue with impossibly high cheekbones can't keep her gaze off him, but Lark's eyes are right where they were before. On me. I keep the lights off until I'm out of their driveway, not daring to look back again.

Liar. Liar liar liar liar liar.

Damien lied. Straight to my fucking face. The stupid letter he got, the way he made it seem like no big deal. He didn't even give me a warning. I've told him everything; my irrational fear of sock puppets, that when I was younger Mom and I would make soap because that was the only thing we never seemed to burn, that I don't know what I'm going to do in college because there's only one real thing I'm good at and you can't get a degree for skinwalking. I *gave* him everything; my favorite copy of *A Clockwork Orange,* my virginity. *My* virginity.

He couldn't have mentioned that he ran around with some rogues while he was gone?

And Lark—Lark knew me. Knew how I came to be here. He considers me one of *them.* Why would Damien talk about me to strangers, especially since we didn't even know each other before he left? Why bring them here? We're alone in the mountains for a reason. How could he do that to the clan? He must've known how scared everyone would be. No wonder Ray evicted the Volkswagen rogue so harshly.

But why does Ray give these rogues such a vote of confidence not to massacre the whole town? Because Damien asked them not to? Because the Big Bad can do no wrong? Ray—everyone—must've felt them the way I did, there's no way I'm the only one with the reaction to run. Or fight.

The closer I get to home the more my skin prickles and the hotter my face gets.

The way Lark talked to Damien. No one has ever talked to him like that, talked to me like that. And Damien just let him. I let him, I couldn't even speak. What's wrong with me?

I can't get inside the house fast enough. My skin is already moving, even though I haven't got my hand around a soul yet. I barge into my room, kick off my shoes and pull open the closet.

Stacks of clothes fall on me as I search for my oak box. Ignoring the persistent whispers, I draw out the hawk. She's almost always too intense for me, determined to hunt and strike fast, but tonight I feel like I could kill something.

My shirt feels too tight and the hawk reaches out to me, beckoning. I tie her to my wrist. There's not enough time to get to my spot in the woods; the change is coming, now.

The front door opens.

The bloodlust subsides long enough to call out. "Mom?"

Footsteps on the stairs, too heavy for hers. Little tendrils of fear slither up my spine.

Damien appears in the doorway, presence setting the tendrils on fire. He's shirtless already, body flushed and eyes bright, even though the dark circles. He spots the hawk around my wrist. "Came back to get a skin? I would've driven you."

"How'd you know I was here?"

"You're a creature of habit, Char. Come on, everybody's on a run in the woods. Let's get your cougar."

"No."

"No?" He laughs, tugging a pelt out of his pocket.

"What the fuck, Damien?" I might strangle him.

The smile slides. He feels the blood coursing through my veins, too fast. Can he feel the betrayal, too? "What?"

I point in the general direction of outside. "Why didn't you say anything?"

It takes him a second, like he needs to remember about the rogues. "It was a surprise."

328

Yes, I'll strangle him. "I got that."

"Thought you'd like it. I wanted you to meet them." He comes into the room.

I step back. "Why would I want to?"

He halts at my retreat and rubs the back of his head, trying to come off his high. "I don't know—because you can relate to them?"

"Relate to Lark." My voice is flat.

"I thought you'd get something from meeting them. Closure, understanding. Why Sam and Jule decided life on the road wasn't for them."

I falter.

He watches my fists unclench and steps forward again. "Met the guys on the road, somewhere on the east coast. They almost ate me alive."

"Why didn't they?"

"I tried eating them back."

I study his face. It's set, humor replaced with worry. "You never said anything."

"I wasn't sure I'd ever see them again."

"The letter?"

He takes a step closer. "I reached out to them a few weeks after I got home to see how they were doing, and didn't reply after they answered. They were down south for some derby, in a town in Georgia they hole up in sometimes. After you found that note, and told me you wanted to know more about where you came from, I wrote back. I wasn't even sure they'd still be there."

"Why didn't you tell me then? Why'd you hide it?" I stifle the crack in my voice. The hurt.

"I didn't want to get your hopes up." He has a pained expression. "I wanted it to be a surprise, really. I was going to talk to everybody tonight. It's been so long since they've seen another skinwalker, Char, so long since they listened to any voice besides Ray's. I wanted you to meet them later, first, alone, make it all about you."

"You told them about me."

He slides his hands around my hips and I don't back away. "Just what everyone else already knows, that you came here with your family because you needed a clan."

"I wish you told me." He doesn't feel the threat like I do, maybe no one does. Maybe it's just in my head. The little voice that likes to set me on edge. Today's been too stressful, my brain's overworked. With Ellie's freaky warning and talking to Dad; actually accusing a dead man of hiding something from me. With the stress that Lark's heartbeat puts in my muscles and Damien's too-easy smile for him.

He backs me up slowly against my dresser, pressing his body to mine. "It didn't happen the way I wanted. I'm sorry."

I let him kiss my neck. He moves my hands so they're on his chest, to feel his heartbeat. His sincerity.

"I know they're not the type you bring home to mom, and I'll remind them not to be so creepy in the future, okay?"

I know I should push it further. I want to. But then his tongue finds my collarbone. His fingers press into the hawk pelt, making her purr. His body hums against mine and his heartbeat feels like my own. "Okay," I whisper.

I feel him smile against my cheek, and then his lips are on mine, coaxing them apart.

Twenty-Eight

It's weird being around skinwalkers who aren't in the clan. Unsettling to see them at the bar, crowded into one of the big booths that I've shared so many times with Mom and Freddie on our binges.

Damien didn't waste any time. After he left my house last night, he was out with them. I tried not to text him during the day, but when I did, the reply came late that he was out with "the boys" (his new ones, I assumed) and that I should meet them at Ralph's.

I tried to talk with Mom, get her to tell me more about rogues, but she brushed me off, saying, "They'll be gone in a couple days, so we're not going to worry about it." And then she scurried off to her room like that answered that.

I also tried not to freak out when I pushed into the bar to find it more crowded than usual with half the noise. The back of my head tingled before I even saw them, like a warning bell in my ears: find the anomaly as quickly as possible. It was Lark who shouted my name across the room, and I nearly shed my skin right there. Dozens of heads jerked at the sound of his voice. It might be okay for Damien to be making new friends, but I don't think I can get off as easy.

As I made my way over to them, slowly, I kept thinking about Damien telling me I needed to fit in more, to do things the way the clan expected. Does that extend to inviting shirtless outsiders out for a beer?

I squeezed in on the end next to Damien, and still, two hours later, they're talking about the wilderness loud enough for everyone to hear. Hunting through forests, runs through towns in the open, run-ins with the police and fights in clubs. Every once in a while, one of them will say something that makes Lark shoot them a warning glare, but I can't catch the difference in their stories.

And then Damien will say something like "Remember that time..." or "How about when..." and it makes me wonder how much time he really spent with them. Did he ever talk about Ro or Bass or Ellie and get excited the way he is now when he thought of old times? I didn't know him before, but his excitement now, the way his hands fly and how he drinks his beer like it's the best thing he's ever had because he's sharing it with friends, makes me wonder if reminiscing about the clan riled him up like these rogues do.

I try to relate to them, to find something about their lifestyle that's appealing, but it's hard. They seem to just pick up and move along whenever they feel like it or get in trouble, which is an acceptable reoccurrence. The misfits dress it up real nice: Redwoods with trees so wide you could hollow out a house and live in one. Caves so deep you could spelunk to the center of the earth. Mountains so high you could kiss God. And people so unique, so amazing, so breathtaking, that a look from them could turn you into a virgin again.

But what exactly does complete freedom cost? Never having enough money? No place to call home? Having to sleep with one eye open and one hand on your skins?

Mom passes by our table almost like clockwork, her face locked down. I can't see into her eyes. Somehow I feel like a traitor. Freddie's at the bar, constantly glaring, Ro and Bass beside him ready to pounce.

"So where'd you hole your little self up, Charlotte?" Lark says, making me jump. It's the first time all night anyone's asked me a question.

"What do you mean?"

I'm prey under his eyes. "Before you were here."

I shrug, not particularly wanting reminisce over my happy childhood with someone whose opinion alone could taint it. "Just with Mom and Dad. In a house."

They laugh as if I insinuated they don't know what a house is.

Lark leans on the table towards me and drops his voice. "You ever rough it?"

I assume he means if we ever lived like they do, homeless, but I'm not about to ask to make sure. My mouth is dry and I resist the urge to look at Damien, who's leaned out of my peripheral. "No, just camping trips."

"Bet you hated being dragged here."

Even though he's finally lowered his voice, the room stiffens. Maybe it's more like a pause as those listening take a second to realize Lark's words. No one ever asked me how I felt about moving, or pointed out that maybe I never wanted to. They never let it cross their minds that I didn't have a say in it.

The bar waits for an answer.

Lark scans my face, trying to pry back my skin to take a look inside. There's this urgency about him that he masks with curiosity, but when his eyes lock with mine they twitch. He parts his lips to swallow me and his fingers curl and uncurl. Past the fear, I wish it were enough to make me do something about it.

"It grows on you."

He throws his head back and laughs, startling people nearby back into their conversations.

When Ray comes over to buy Damien's rogues a round, I take it as a cue for me to get the fuck out of here. Normally it's easy for me to sneak out the front door, show up late or not at all for that matter, but tonight everyone's watching. I head to the back, towards the restroom, nearly tripping over the stage and cracking my skull open on a blue and silver jukebox. But Ralph's already in the narrow, wooden hallway, holding the fire-door open for me. His favorite threat is that if anyone tries going through the door it'll set the alarm and sprinklers off, and anyone responsible will pay for damages. Right up until this second I believed him.

"Thanks," I say, sliding past.

He clasps my shoulder. "Jule wants you to wait for her, she's grabbing her purse and she'll be right out. Hang in there, Char."

It's a warm summer night and the crickets are loud. My fingertips itch and my eyes hurt. I just want to grab Damien and go home. I want him to not look at Lark like he's his best friend.

The heavy metal door swings open behind me, and Freddie storms out, followed by Ro and Bass. Still no alarm.

"What's up?" I ask, hoping Ray poisoned Lark's drink. Put an end to this miserable dream.

"They've gotta go." Ro spits onto the gravel.

"What's their deal?" Freddie says, coming to a stop in front of me. His eyes shine in the parking lot flood lights Ralph had installed after my run-in with Joey.

"They want something." I'm not about to feed them Damien's excuse that they're here for me—they're not, even if they've led Damien to believe they are. They couldn't care about anyone who isn't one of them, that's clear. Even if Lark is oddly interested in my life before the clan. Even if he wants me to believe we're sorts of brothers-in-arms. I'm nothing like them.

"What?" Ro asks, cracking his knuckles like a hired goon.

I shrug at them. They're looking to me for answers I don't have. Maybe I should know more. Maybe I should've pressed Damien harder, but why would he keep something from me? From everyone?

"They want Damien?" Bass asks. His voice is almost soft, almost hurt. It makes me want to give him a hug, but I'm not sure the last time he showered.

"Of course they want Damien," comes a voice from the darkness. Ellie appears out of the alleyway. She wasn't in the bar tonight, but by her faded makeup and one shoeless foot, it looks like her party's already started and ended. "Who doesn't?"

"I don't," Freddie says.

"Well that makes you the only one, youngblood." She's a little wobbly on her one heel.

"Do they want him to go with them, out there, again?" Ro says sharply.

"He's not leaving," I say. "He wants us, he wants to stay. He won't abandon us."

"Why—because he has you?" Ellie hiccups. "Who could leave you?"

"You're fucked up, El, go home," Freddie says.

"Stop it, Freddie." Bass steps between them. "She wouldn't even be like this if you hadn't given her that shit."

"Oh, you mean the X she begged me for? I don't see you helping her, brave fucking knight—"

337

Ro plants himself in front of his brother. "You swore to Mom you were done with the drugs."

"Well, golly, guess I lied again. But you're not surprised, are you?"

"What the fuck is wrong with you?"

Freddie jabs a finger into Ro's chest. "What's always fucking wrong with me? If you'd get out of my ass for two goddamn seconds and let me figure my own shit out—"

"This is not the time!" I say over them.

They freeze, and even Freddie closes his mouth.

I take a slow breath and calm my voice. "They don't want Damien or to be part of the clan, they're just passing through." I keep talking, even though I don't know the actual extent of my words. But these guys can't lose it on me, not now, not when we have to keep ourselves level. "They know they're not wanted and they know what'll happen if they step out of line. Everyone is watching them, waiting, especially Ray, Rogue-Hater Número Uno. No matter if they're Damien's friends or not, the clan comes first."

"What if they ever come back?" Freddie questions. "If Damien doesn't mind them dropping in once he's Leader?"

I set my face, bring my tone low. "We've made it clear. I don't care who the Clan Leader is in the future, they're not setting foot in this town again."

Twenty-Nine

It's been three days, and the rogues are still here. I want to strangle them all, starting with Lark and ending with Damien. I've called and left messages, but Damien's responses come hours later (if at all), and when he does reply it's always an invitation to go hunting.

The clan is restless, every night filling up the bar and making rounds through the town as if they're going to catch the rogues running rampant through the streets. I keep to the house, waiting for word that they're gone, for Damien to pop up in his jeep and take me for a ride, but apparently if I held my breath for that I'd be dead.

I can't believe I let Damien talk me out of asking him about what he and Dad might be keeping from me. He distracted me with the rogues, and I lost my nerve. With him, and Lark.

Why am I so weak?

"What's Freddie up to?" Mom calls from the living room.

I slap my book—some contemporary romance—down on the kitchen table. "He's ignoring me, too." When I need him most, he's out on a bender.

The TV mutes. "Come here, hun," she says.

I slink into the living room and collapse on the couch next to her.

Her hair's sticking out all over the place and she's in one of Dad's old shirts. Ralph gave her the day off to look after me. "Boys are dumb."

"It's not about me," I snap. "It's that he's off with *them*."

She sighs, reaching out to pull me into her. "I'm sure this is how Mona felt when Ray first starting spending time with Sam."

"This is completely different. There's six of them, and they're freaks."

"Won't argue there."

"It's just this feeling on my back I can't get rid of." The scar on my shoulder aches.

"They don't belong to a clan. Established tribes grow tighter and tighter with every decade, and new blood upsets things."

I shake my head. "People move clans all the time, you've told me so yourself."

She nods. "And things are super weird for a little while after they do. When we first got here, how do you think everyone felt about us?"

"Not like this."

"Exactly like this. We'd been on our own so long we were practically rogues."

"Then why did Ray let us in?"

"That's a question for another time." She squeezes me.

She's done talking and we watch the silent TV. I know she's trying to put my uneasiness into perspective and comfort me, but I can't take it. The tension weaves into my stomach. It's Lark— the way he looks at me. The way Damien looks at him. They're sharing something deep and maybe if I felt like it didn't involve me I wouldn't care as much, but I do. Out of everyone, he's trusted me with his fears, anxieties, hopes for the future. And I confide in him my resentment, insecurities, how the giant hole in my chest expands and shrinks. He takes it all from me, doesn't hesitate.

So I can't let Lark put something between us. Create something that shouldn't be there.

I stand out of Mom's grasp and go upstairs, for my oak box.

I know Damien won't be home, but he's not answering his phone and I have to do something. Go somewhere. His car isn't in their driveway, but Ray is sitting on the porch, gazing into the trees. He glances at me when I pull up, and we exchange a look.

I get out.

"He's not here," the old man says.

"Do you know where he is, then?"

His eyes tell me he doesn't.

I step forward because I don't know what else to do, and he doesn't object as I climb the steps onto the porch.

"We're losing him again," he says softly, probably more to himself than me considering he already thinks I'm stealing his son.

I watch his old, weathered face. It's like a mask, sunken and fleshy and set in one emotion unless he lets you see otherwise. He gained my respect after our first handshake, and only recently has my allegiance wavered; but he's been a great leader to his clan. Even if he drinks too much and has a bad temper. He cares.

"Damien understands what he's supposed to do," he says, still not looking at me. "He understands who he's supposed to be."

I nod, not that he notices, and lean against the railing.

"I have nothing against you, not personally."

I nod again. I know. I've always known. It's hard to get off to a right start when we've never really had one. Mom and Dad integrated into the society here piece by piece, but I just sort of appeared. And when I did stick my foot in, it was Freddie who grabbed hold.

"And I had *nothing* against your father. He'd cut me down where I stood if he witnessed how I've been treating you these past few months."

I look out into the trees, still hoping Dad might come strolling out of them one day.

"Besides," he says gruffly. "I'd rather Damien running around with you than a bunch of rogues."

That's probably the nicest thing he's ever said to me.

We both turn at the sound of a car coming up the driveway, and my heart flutters when it rounds the bend.

Damien doesn't notice us until he's out of the truck. He looks worse than he did a few days ago; bags under watery eyes and chalky skin. A bruise creeps out of his shirt and he walks like his bones are crumbling.

I force myself not to glance at Ray.

"What's going on?" Damien asks, trying to pull a smile. His eyes are alert, and he doesn't like what he sees.

"I was looking for you," I say.

He stops at the bottom of the steps. "You could've called."

"I tried."

Ray stands. "Why don't we go inside? Mom can make us something to eat."

"My phone died yesterday," Damien says, nearly speaking on top of Ray. "I came to shower and come get you."

I don't like his stare. His heartbeat burns.

"Well, come on in, both of you," Ray says quietly, opening the screen door. "Damien can shower and—"

"No," Damien says, smiling. He holds out a hand. "Let's go, Char."

For a second I have the urge to go inside.

In that second Damien's gaze wavers, something flashing in his eyes. His smile softens and he extends his hand a little more.

"Please."

I take his hand and can't bring myself to look at Ray as Damien leads me to his truck. Can't face him standing with the screen door open, defeated eyes following his son.

When Damien tells me to pick out a CD and I see the duffels in his backseat I know something is wrong. "Are you leaving?"

"You remember the legend of the skinwalkers?" he says like he didn't hear me.

I don't answer, too preoccupied with the way he's gripping the steering wheel.

"Well, do you?"

I hesitate. "Of course."

He looks at me then, and seeing my expression, smiles. "Don't look so scared, little one. I don't bite, remember?" He reaches for me and clasps my balled-up hands.

"You're just freaking me out," I say. He must be on something, or sleep deprived, or dehydrated.

"I'm sorry," he says. "I forgot what it was like with the guys. They're wearing me out."

"You look like shit." I want to calm him down, tell him everything is going to be okay, but my anger won't keep quiet.

He squeezes my hands. "Won't be for much longer."

"They're leaving soon?"

He nods, eyes fixed again.

"Are you going with them?" Out of nowhere, hot tears brim my eyes. My heart thunders. He can't just leave me.

He shakes his head slightly. "I'm not leaving you."

The tears dissipate. I entwine my fingers with his. "You're just so different with them."

The side of his mouth perks. "I'm the same with them as I am with you."

"I don't think so."

He brings one of my hands into his lap. "Remember, in the legend, what happened after the little one turned the hunters into skinwalkers?"

"They couldn't go back to their village," I say. "Why——"

"After that."

I think. "They didn't fit in with the animals in the forest, either."

"After."

I shrug, frustrated. "I don't know. What are you trying to tell me?"

He glances over. "Don't you ever wonder how we incorporated back into society? After we were forced away to fend for ourselves?"

"The Little One took them in, showed them her ways." He's holding onto my hand too tight.

"You think they just crawled back to her after she turned them into monsters?"

I stare at him. We turn off the highway.

"The Little One offered them a way to reconnect to civilization, made them trust her by showing the hunters how to be accepted by the rest of the world."

I try to pull my hand away, but he holds on.

"She gave them an out, a way to hide, move through their old world undetected."

Blood rushes in my ears, the wolf is vibrating, out of the fur and inside me.

"She showed them how to take human skins."

My stomach plummets.

"By showing them how to disguise themselves amongst people, she won their devotion. They didn't just one day decide to thank her for teaching them a lesson. She gave them a gift."

"Gift?" I ask, voice high and empty. "You think the ability to skin people is a gift?"

"It's so much more than that." When he looks at me, his eyes are soft, melting. "It's the ultimate test of our kind. We can all walk as animals, but only the strongest can walk as people. It's a trait that waned as generations wore on."

"Trait?" The word hardly leaves my mouth.

"Lark believes we all have the power to walk as people, buried deep inside us. We just have to practice to unlock it."

My free hand is shaking. Dad's face flickers through my mind, the horrible look he had when he explained what walking as another person can do. "But it's dangerous. And disgusting. Are the rogues putting you up to this?"

"So Sam did talk to you about it?" We're on the dirt driveway.

"Damien, are the rogues skinning people?" They did something to him. My Damien isn't this stupid, this insane.

Instead of answering my question, Damien lifts my hand to kiss my knuckles, too calm. We stop at the tree blockade, and he pulls me out from the driver's side door. He loops his arm around my neck and leads me up the path, through the planted trees that have started dropping their fleshy crabapples onto the ground.

"I know you don't want to, but we need to tell Ray." I push the words out through wavering teeth, getting my trembling fingers to tie the wolf around my arm. She screams at me to run. "I get they're your friends, I really do, but killing human beings is wrong."

He kisses the top of my head and I get goosebumps. Not the good kind.

We round the corner of the looming mansion. Heat rises from the ground, sending the tang of hundreds of flowers ready to die into the air. All the fountains are dried up. Vines tangle across the stone walkway. There's no wind; the only things breaking the stillness are humming insects and birds that take flight as we approach. Nervous sweat breaks on my skin when he releases me and strides a few yards ahead, into the thick of the garden.

"I wanted to do this here," he says. "Somewhere you feel safe."

My brain pumps against my skull and blood floods my ears. "You're scaring me, Damien."

He lifts his shirt above his head and takes something out of his back pocket—a furless band with a wrinkled, flesh-tone to it.

My stomach gurgles and I'm rooted to the spot.

"I won't let you fall," he says, then doubles over in pain.

His skin bubbles, loosens, and melts over muscle as it turns a lighter shade. The color of his hair lifts and some falls out in clumps. His limbs elongate and he drops to his knees, groaning.

Veins burst under his skin and blotches break out over his torso and back. Head dangles while his neck snaps and regrows. He groans and spits out a wad of something black into a patch of roses. Slowly, so slowly, he changes shape. But not into an animal.

When he finally stands to look at me, I scream.

Thirty

He's too tall, features too angular. One shoulder sits higher than the other and his long blond hair is thin and clotted with blood from his scalp. His chest is caved in, cracked open where his heart should be. It's black inside. Damien's jeans hang loose on my father's deformed body.

"Don't be afraid, little one," he says.

I fall. Dad's voice croaks out of Damien's sore throat. Bile rises from my stomach, burns my insides.

Dad—Damien—steps towards me. He shuffles his feet like his limbs won't listen. Blood drips onto the soft earth.

"You killed him." I heave, but nothing comes out. The wolf sets my arm on fire and I can hardly drown out her screeching. She was right. I should've listened. I should've kept running away at camp. Should've pounced on him in North Dakota.

He hobbles towards me, one foot in front of the other. I feel it: Dad's steady thrum mingled with Damien's sad excuse for a heartbeat. "He did fall, I didn't lie about that."

I can't feel my legs. He stops too close, sending the stench of blood and rotting flesh down my throat. It nearly knocks me over, but he catches my arms.

His fingernails are black, bones poking through the skin. Lips move, but I only feel his rancid breath.

"You killed him."

"I pushed him." His eyes aren't the right green. But his nose is just a little crooked like it should be.

"I don't—I don't u-understand."

He drops us to our knees, and his voice is thick and heavy, only a shadow of Dad's reassuring grumble. "One night, before our camping trip, I overheard Ray and Mona talking. About where you came from, why we took you in."

"And?" I want to tear Dad's skin off him, snatch my best friend off his dirty body. "What's so fucking threatening about Virginia?"

He releases me, lets me tumble onto rough stone and weeds. "I couldn't believe it, at first. But then I started watching you, watching Sam. The way you held yourselves, the way you ran. You come from a strong clan, the strongest bloodline. Descendent from the original Little One."

"That doesn't make any sense—She never had kids, there's no way to even trace that back—"

"Sam took you from your family."

"Listen to me, Damien—"

"They're the most powerful clan in the country." He leans in. "Can you guess why?"

"Stop this." Don't tell me. Please don't tell me.

"They practice walking as people. It's tradition, sacred. Sam was the oldest son of the Clan Leader, next in line to take them."

I move but he grabs me tight, pulling me closer to his melting face.

"From what I heard, he was good. The best. And when Jule got pregnant he severed the both of you, because he was weak and scared."

I shake my head, straining against his grip. "Why are you doing this? What do you want?"

The dull reflection of Dad's eyes stare at me as he hauls me to my feet. "Sam has four uncles that share his blood. Eight male cousins, one brother, a dozen nephews. Not a single female has been born in your bloodline, not since the Little One."

"What does that matter? What do you want?"

His mouth is dark and blood trickles out of his ears. "You're the reason it matters, the first girl born out of the Little One. You. You're what I want, a clan is what I want."

"You have a clan." Hot tears stream down my face.

He releases me and my legs hardly keep me up. "It's not enough. There's a reason you were born, reason you're a girl. You're here to change things, just like the Little One did. And there's a reason I found you."

"To kill my father?" A bubble bursts in my chest. Hot, flaming acid spreads through me.

"Sam's still alive." He brings a hand to his heart. "He's in me. He always will be."

This time when I heave, the bile comes out. "Everything you told me was a lie," I choke. "Dad didn't ask you to take care of me, did he?"

"Not exactly." A blood vessel bursts in one of his eyes and hives spread over his body.

"What did he say to you?"

If Damien's feeling the pain, he doesn't show it. He just smiles. "We don't need to talk about that now. Plenty of time for everything, remember?"

My fingers twitch. The wolf's voice is becoming clearer. "I'm not going with you."

"Of course you are. You want out of this town just as much as I do. The boys are ready to go, too. And the others—"

"Others?"

Blood drips out of his nose. "Not just rogues, but people in clans who believe it's time for a change. Your grandad has convinced everyone that walking as people is a gift only for those who are deemed worthy of carrying it."

Looking at the mess in front of me, I believe it. "So what are you gonna do with all these people?"

"I'm not looking for a fight, only a chance."

"And the only way to do that was kill Sam?"

"He severed you out of fear. Fear of the powerful woman you'd become."

"Did you get that out of him while you were digging out his heart?"

He makes a wheezing sound. A chunk of skin falls from his neck when he shakes his head. "Sam actually didn't have much to say when I killed him. He liked to ramble, so I was surprised."

The wolf pants in my ear. "I'm not going with you."

He grins, the faint ghost of Dad's smile shining through. "I know you're mad, and you might never forgive me, but you're not going anywhere, sweetheart. You love me, remember?"

My back breaks. The wolf throws me on the ground and drives herself through my veins. Through my bones. I let her take me. My dress tears to make room for her and I howl with rage. The pain matches my anger and fuels it.

Damien drops to the ground in front of me. Rotten flesh peels away from him and fur replaces it. I see red as the cougar emerges in front of me.

As soon as I take my first real breath I lunge, going for his throat.

He might be stronger, but I have murder flooding my heart.

Before I can get a good grip on his neck he tosses me aside. I roll into one of the flowerbeds, vaguely aware of rose thorns sticking to me.

Damien roars and plunges into the trees.

I keep pace through the cottonwoods and clumps of chokecherries, but with every jab and nip he dances out of my grasp. He's herding me towards the pond. Even though he's weakened from the first shift, his size and weight keeps him grounded and just strong enough to stop from being knocked over. I try to get in front of him, but he barrels forward like a tank.

Instead of going straight to the pond, he turns and starts up the rocky cliff face, towards the waterfall. I follow, scaling up the slick rocks, gusts of wind sending sprays water over us. When I get close enough I lunge, jaws clamping around the back of one of his legs, right on a tendon. He yelps, trying to shake me off. I taste iron, and it makes me hungry for more. I bite down harder while he kicks out at me, struggling to keep his footing.

I don't let go when his blood floods my mouth. The wolf would gladly drown in it. He loses his grip, and I drag him sideways until he falls, crashing down the rocky wall and splashing into the dark water.

I lose sight of him as I scale back down and pace the water's edge, body tense, fur on end.

He resurfaces on the other side with a nasty gash on his head and the skin on his back left leg in shreds. He turns to me on the bank, eyes gleaming. Panting heavily, he weaves around the trees, making his way towards me.

As soon as he's close enough to feel his pumping heart, I charge again.

He catches me, teeth sinking into the back of my neck. He breaks the skin, clamping down on hot muscle. I crackle as he shakes me and sends me tumbling into a tree. My spine hits it hard, and I can't breathe. Vision vibrates, my nerves jump.

He plants himself in the dirt and growls.

I snap my jaws, pushing myself off the ground to come at him again. I can hardly see, but I manage to get a leg in my mouth and yank him forward, sending him off balance.

He catches my shoulder in his mouth. Flesh tears. Blood sprays.

My blood?

He breaks my grip and rams me into the pond.

The icy water shocks my body, and the wolf can't hold on. She's hurt, bad, and I let her go. Dark and cold, I can't find up. My arm is useless where he tore my shoulder and pain splices through my abdomen.

There's no light.

The dark goes darker.

I can't move. This body's done, and it's only my mind still working.

Dad's going to be stuck in Damien forever, linked to him by his skin and blood. His soul will never find peace, his suffering will never end.

And I didn't even know.

I couldn't bother listening to my instincts because a hot guy liked me. I ignored Freddie's intuition, pushed the wolf away, the little voice that keeps me out of danger. I let Dad down, let Mom down, tore apart everything they worked for to get me here. Threw it all away because Damien told me I was special, made me feel like I needed more, made me as happy as I was when Dad was alive.

Has Damien asked you to jump, yet?

Higher and higher and higher.

There's a tug on my hair.

I'm being pulled downward, right to Hell.

Only it's not Hell.

I break the surface, air coming at me from everywhere. Everything is white.

I hack up water after I'm heaved onto solid ground. It takes a few tries to get air into my lungs.

A hand on my back. A naked Damien. My dress hanging in shreds. I twist around, pushing myself up and flinging a fistful of dirt in his face. My bad arm won't cooperate but I force myself to hit him.

He grabs me and pins me to the ground, his blood dripping over my face. "Stop moving, Charlotte, you're hurt." His voice is gravelly and bruised.

"Fuck you."

I strain against his grip, and kick him off me, striking the appendage that's brought so much pleasure. He rolls backwards. "Don't you feel bad at all?" My insides want to leak out through my stomach.

Damien struggles to get to his knees. "I'm doing this for you, trying to give you what *he* should have."

I leap onto him, hands fixing themselves around his neck. I dig my nails into his skin and squeeze. "Well *I'm* going to give you what he should have."

Those beautiful, bright eyes that I know better than my own stare back at me. The mouth I've become so familiar with curls up in the slightest smile to reveal that stupid, hilarious chipped tooth. My favorite messy hair tamed for the first time with blood. Damien's cold body struggles weakly against my grip.

"You had everything," I cry. "You had the clan. The family. Me. *I* gave you everything."

The smile doesn't waver. His pulse slows. I dig deeper.

A grip like iron seizes me around my busted shoulder and yanks me back like a ragdoll. Lark comes into view, bends over Damien as two pairs of arms grapple me. I scream a bloody guttural noise and lash against them. The tear on my shoulder gives some more.

"Calm down there, little lady," Lark says, grinning. He hauls Damien to his feet and hands him a pair of shorts.

"Told you to hang back," Damien says, pulling on the shorts and leaning on him for balance.

Lark scans him. "You said you could handle it."

"She's just hysterical," Damien says.

The wolf whimpers from my forearm.

"Carson, be careful." Damien tries taking a step toward us, but his mangled leg won't let him.

Carson's got his one hand on my shoulder and his other arm looped around mine; his grip doesn't shift. The other one who's got me, Feral, adjusts his hold on my bad arm. His red hair clumps together in dreads, and he hasn't made eye contact with me, or anyone else, in the times I've been around him. I look around us for the others, but we're alone.

"Need to patch you up first. You're losing a lot of blood," Lark says, eyes darting between us, comparing Damien's injuries with mine. "At least we know she's the one."

I spit.

"Let's get back to the truck," Damien says. "Once we're clear of Colorado—"

"I'm not going with you." My voice is low.

The rogues laugh, but Damien doesn't. "You don't have a choice."

My blood turns cold. "You're picking now, after all we've been through, to underestimate me?"

Damien comes at me in an awkward hobble. He slowly, deliberately, unties the wolf skin from my arm. A piece of me falls away. "I think you're underestimating *me*, little one."

I keep my jaw stiff as he pockets my wolf. "Even if you did lock me away, they'd find me." Mom would find me if I was lost at the edge of the earth. She wouldn't stop. Freddie would kill anyone in his path.

He gets in my face. "I took down your father. What makes you think I can't take down your depressed mother? Or—what does he call himself, again?—Baby boy Freddie?"

I slam my forehead against his face, cracking his nose with a satisfying crunch. He stumbles away and Carson kicks the back of my knee in, forcing me to the ground.

"Stop it, Carson," Damien barks, gripping his face.

Lark laughs from behind him. It's a dry, humorless sound.

"We'll need to stop by her house, too," Damien says thickly.

Lark inches closer to me, inspecting the damage like

someone's dented his car. He rolls his eyes. "It's no use, fucking with Sam's skins."

"What do you want with my dad's skins? Haven't you stolen enough?" My mind goes to Dad's little furs, tucked safely under my bed. Right where Damien watched me put them.

"I need them, if I'm going to try," Damien says to Lark.

The scraggly rogue leans to the side, crossing his arms. "It didn't work with his wolf, what makes you think it'll work with any others?"

"What do you want with them?" I feel the mania seeping into my brain but I can't quiet it.

Damien's speaks slow. "The *perk* of stealing the skin of a skinwalker is that you also get their animal souls."

My blood turns to ice.

"If you can take the soul to begin with." Lark winks at me like we're conspiring against Damien, in on something he isn't. "If you have enough control of the soul. If you're doing it right—"

"I can only get better with practice." Damien ignores his challenging tone. "It's all about the mind, not the body. Charlotte said that to me once, isn't that right? Talking about Freddie, weren't we?"

My vision blurs and my rage soars. "You've actually lost your goddamn mind if you think I'd go along with this."

Damien turns on me, spitting blood and taking my face with one hand. "You will never shift again," he says. "I'll make sure you're stuck in your own body for the rest of your life if I have to. You'll skin a human before I'll let you near another animal."

I jump forward, ignoring the tearing and snapping. Slippery blood lets my arms slide out of Carson and Feral's grasps. My hands, pulled with invisible strings, slide into one of the little tears in Damien's flesh. He doesn't blink as I knock him backwards onto the ground. I push deep into his chest, the path to his heart waiting for me.

What I am defines me. My animals define me.

To take that away I'm nothing.

I've never been this close to Damien's soul. Not when we've shifted or made love. Not when I've poured myself into him and not when he chose me over his father. No, the threat of my life pulls me closer than I've ever let myself go. Under his fine layer of confidence and enthusiasm, under the passion of his love and the grit of his determination is something no one else has ever seen.

It's grim towards the center, desolate and crumbling. A monster lives there, curled in the fetal position in a corner. Wild, waiting for its chance.

Desperate, hungry.

Craving loyalty.

Power.

Love.

I stand between the bleak wall he's built and the deranged animal he's groomed. How did it get this far? How did he let it fester to this point?

Damien watches me through blank eyes.

I stop.

A hard blow to my head sends me sideways. Before I can catch myself the back of my skull collides with something hard and my mind slows.

I struggle, unable to move, and as my vision blurs and blood pressure drops into black, figures burst out of the trees.

Thirty-One

It's very bright here. A breeze ripples across my body and grass pokes into my back. I sit up, finding myself in the front yard of our duplex. The elementary school across the street just got out and little kids are laughing and yelling to each other, running down the sidewalk to their bus. I must've stayed home today.

"Hey, kid," Dad calls.

I turn and find him standing at the mouth of our open garage. "I fell asleep."

"Yeah, you did," he says, striding across the lawn. His giant figure almost blocks out the sun. "Good dreams?"

I shake my head. "You died. And then I got hurt."

He squats next to me and falls backward with a thump.

"Doesn't sound good."

I try to reach out to him but I can't. "And then you were gone."

He sighs. "I am gone, Char."

"You're right here."

His hazel eyes find mine, his face basked in light and just how I remember it. How I should remember him. "I left you a while ago."

"It's not fair. He did this to you."

"No," he says sternly. The voice that could cause the whole house to quake, the laugh that you could hear across the street, the whisper that could stick inside your head for hours. "You're not going to give that asshole the credit for taking me down."

I can't help it, I laugh. And then I'm crying. My arms are heavy, useless at my sides.

"You have to look after yourself now, and Mom. You need to be strong for all three of us."

Tears drop from my cheeks, into my lap. "I don't know how. I trusted him. You both lied to me."

He squints into the sun. The faint scar on his neck that runs into his shirt is lighter than I remember. "I know, kid. I know. And you were right, we shouldn't have come here. Not because I died, but because I set you in Damien's path."

I just want to touch him, to hug him, feel his heartbeat against my head when I grip onto his broad chest, but I can't muster the strength.

"I taught you to be strong," he says. "And now you have to be. If you're going to carry this burden, the knowledge of what he did to me, you have to hold it tight, understand? If you decide to do something about it, then you do something about it. And don't worry about me, I'm tougher than you think."

"How could I not have known you were in there?" What kind of daughter am I?

He reaches out as if to hold my face, but his hands stop short of my skin and hover there, sending a wave of sandalwood, grass, pine. "You're not going to blame yourself for this. You don't know how hard he has to fight to keep me from spilling out. I'm screaming inside his head, every time he touches my skin.

"I fed him memories, in the beginning, memories of us." His jaw goes tight. "I tried bringing him back down, lead him to his humanity, give him some compassion for you. I realized too late it was only feeding his infatuation. Now I know how far he's going to go for what he thinks is right."

"Me too," I whisper. My eyelids are heavy.

He steadies himself. "There's no room for feeling sorry for yourself, hear me?"

I nod through the haze and a dull throbbing begins in my stomach.

"Remember, Charlotte. If you're going to do it, do it."

The throbbing turns into a searing pain in my abdomen and shoulder, and the bright world goes black. I'm lying down again, but instead of prickly grass on my back there's an ugly gash ripping my muscles. I move, but something soft and heavy weighs down on me.

A fire crackles to my right, someone moves a little on my left.

Erin's voice cuts through the heavy air with a sharp pang. "I told you not to be so stupid."

I open my eyes, her voice sending my senses flying. The room is dark and made of wood. The fire's coming from a loaded stone fireplace and heavy curtains cover the windows. A thick smoke seeps into every crevice; she's got roots and leaves burning on the table beside me. Her strange frame takes up the space amazingly, like she's part of it.

I'm in the Healer's house.

I blink and move again, expecting an arm or leg missing.

She pats my good shoulder. "You're not dead."

I look up at her. "Mom? Freddie?" My throat is cracked and raw and coated with phlegm.

"They're here. Don't talk."

My heart surges. "Mom?" I call toward the closed door. "Freddie!"

Something crashes, and then the door swings open in one dramatic motion. Freddie stands in the doorway.

"Don't worry, I'll just clean this up!" Sofia roars from behind him.

Freddie's face is unreadable but when Mom sweeps up behind him she's just how I left her, emotion leaking from every pore. She comes at me, throwing herself on the bed. I hug her with my good arm.

"Don't move," Erin commands, in vain.

Mom cups my face in her hands, just where Dad's almost were, tears spilling out of her eyes. "You've been out for so long,

I thought they were too late——"

"I told you she'd be fine," Erin interjects.

Mom engulfs me again. My insides slosh around and the feeling of her arms around me, secure and unbreaking, bring me to tears. I search over her shoulder for Freddie, who's standing at the end of the bed. His face is set, eyes red, lips pressed in a line. I reach out to him.

He stares back at me a moment before gripping my hand in his. He hates me, but I don't care. He's here and okay and that's all that matters.

"Where's Damien?" I croak.

Freddie's grip tightens and Mom pulls away to look me in the face.

"Gone," comes a voice from the doorway.

I bolt upright in the small bed, an almost audible tearing coming from my shoulder and the blaze to go with it. A tall figure fills the doorway. His broad shoulders and thick chest make up his bulk but his dark blond hair and piercing hazel eyes are all I can look at. Dad's eyes, my eyes, stare at me from the shadows.

It wasn't a dream.

"Lie down!" Erin says, coming to my shoulder. There's a faint trickling of warm liquid through the bandage.

The man steps forward.

It's not Dad. A more beaten version of him fills up what's left of the little space, his face gaunter and without the laugh lines. They could be twins.

The man examines my face in turn, sizing me up against Dad,

too. "It's good to finally meet you, kid." His voice is gruff and fitting.

I have an uncle, just like Damien said.

Erin pulls at the bandage on my shoulder.

"This is Kyle," Mom says gently. "He found you. They were following the rogues."

She must have known him from before I was born. Before Dad took us away. For a second I don't even recognize her. She's kept their secret from me my entire life. A wave of nausea hits me when I picture her skinning a person. "Following the rogues?"

Kyle cocks his head at my tone, an almost familiar smirk spreading across his face that makes my heart bleed a little more. He takes a heavy seat on a little stool next to the bed and leans on his knees, eyes never leaving me, like *I'm* the ghost. "We've known about Damien for some time. Since he first passed through our city, looking for trouble. Didn't think we needed to intervene until he called the rogues."

Didn't need to intervene?

He takes in the look on my face and adds, "Of course we had no idea he had his eyes set on you, Charlotte. We didn't even know where you were."

"Did you know my dad is dead?" I blurt.

He flinches like I slapped him in the face, and I wish I could swallow my words.

Mom grasps my arm. "We've been cut off for nineteen years, Char. They didn't know anything back home."

Back home.

Kyle raises his gaze to meet mine again. "We didn't even know you were a girl." He almost smiles. "But apparently, Sam knew. He has a knack for those kinds of things."

I stare into his deep eyes, feel his pulse and try to adjust having another Reed in my presence.

I think it becomes too much for him because he glances to Mom. "Is she the reason you left?"

"Not wholly," Mom whispers.

"He was done skinning people," I say.

Mom's turn to flinch. Erin pauses in the rebandaging of my shoulder and Freddie takes a step back. Only Kyle seems to be unaffected by my statement.

"How much does Damien know?" Kyle asks steadily.

I can't tell them. Even if what just happened in my head was a dream my subconscious made up to make me feel better, I have to believe it's what Dad would've wanted; to make up my mind and live with the consequences. How can I give my mother, my family, the knowledge that a deranged twenty-one-year-old has my dad's soul trapped inside him? I can't destroy them. Can't do that to Mom, can't let them live with the guilt of not seeing it before. Not the kind of guilt burrowing into my stomach, making a home for itself. "He's learned a lot in his travels."

I try not to blink as he stares into my soul. "We never wanted you to go," he says. "Sam was next in line, great at everything he did, strongest skinwalker we've ever known. The best big brother. You would've been a welcome addition to the family."

Not what I need to hear right now.

"Sam was done with it," Mom says softly. "I was done with it. And when we got pregnant we decided our family was done with it."

Kyle opens his mouth, but I reach out and take his hand. It's not as big as Dad's, not as warm, but it feels more like him than anything. "They probably didn't handle it right, just picking up and leaving." I look at Mom. "We know what it's like to have someone we care about just disappear, to vanish without a warning. I'm sorry he did that, but he did it because he thought it was right."

Maybe it's the strong healing smoke in the air, but Kyle's brow softens, taking me in. "You really are your father's kid."

Mom sniffs and Freddie takes a step closer to the bed.

"What about the others?" My voice is fading.

"We managed to catch two of them," Kyle says, frozen under my touch. "But they're not in the best of shape, they won't be talking much here. We'll get them to open up back home."

There it is again: home.

Kyle stands. "Someone has to check in." He looks down at me. "A phone call won't cut it for this one, huh?" He winks a sad wink, like he's trying to convince himself that by finding Mom and me it makes up for losing Dad. "I'll leave a couple guys here, Jule, in case Damien decides to come back. You two should start putting things in order."

"Put what in order?" I say.

"Well we can't just leave you here, can we?" Kyle says, heading for the door. "Time to come home."

Mom squeezes me after he leaves. "Don't worry, everything is going to be okay."

"Okay?" I repeat. "What are we doing? Are we going with them?"

"Hush, hun," she says, gently pushing me back down onto the bed. "No one's going anywhere until you're better."

"You need to stay in bed," Erin says. Her voice is the softest it's ever been.

I blink back tears. We can't leave here, not yet. Not before I find Damien. He's deranged and dangerous. Out there, with Dad's skin. "Mom, we've got to find Damien. He's lost it—"

"Shhh." She nods. "I know, and trust me, we'll find him, and punish him for what he did to you. After you've had some rest you can tell us the whole story and we'll figure out what to do from there, okay?"

I want to keep going, get her to understand, but Erin shoves a cup of hot liquid under my chin. "Drink," she says.

I take a sip and an earthy broth fills my mouth.

"You two can have five minutes," Erin says when I'm done choking. "Then you need to sleep."

Mom gives me a final kiss on my forehead before she and Erin leave, stranding me with Freddie. He sits on the edge of the bed, staring at the floor.

"Just say it," I whisper.

"I told you so."

My lip trembles and I move slowly, so slowly, into a position that doesn't make my insides want to bleed out. "I'm so stupid."

He crawls up the bed. "You're *so* stupid."

I wait until he's lying next to me. "He used me."

He puts a light hand on my shoulder, not enough pressure for me to wince. His touch is cool. "That's all we're good for."

"It happened too fast."

"No, it happened real slow, you just didn't want to see it."

I shake my head. "Those rogues did something to him."

"He did whatever he wanted to do, like almost fucking killing you."

"He wouldn't have."

"You can't know that."

"He never said he wanted to kill me." Only torture me until I wished I would die.

"You're defending him, even now, even after what he did."

"No." I twist to look at his bloodshot eyes. "He doesn't want me dead. I'm no use to him dead."

"You're no use to *me* dead," Freddie says, pushing himself up. "You've shown me you don't give a flying fuck about your life, but you're the only one who's ever cared about mine and you can't just leave me. How could you do that to Jule? You're so selfish." His voice cracks, and all at once he's crying. Freddie doesn't cry.

I try to get into a sitting position but I can't, so I pull him down and wrap my arms around his neck. He buries his face in my hair, letting out a few sobs. His hands grip my wrists.

"Say it," I whisper.

"I love you, you stupid bitch."

Thirty-Two

"But *he* gets to go." I jerked my head in the direction of Ray's truck. Dad and me sat on the front steps of the house, the sun not high enough to warm the chill of the morning.

"Damien is Ray's son," Dad said, tying his shoe.

"I'm your daughter."

"Of course you are, sweetie." He patted me on the arm.

I slapped his hand away. "Don't patronize me."

"I don't know why you keep fighting this," he said, suppressing a laugh. "We went out last weekend."

"Two weekends ago, and we only set up camp at the site. Not in the middle of nowhere."

"The same things get done," he replied, stretching his hands over his head.

I picked at the hem of my shorts. "You said nothing would change when we moved, but it doesn't feel like that."

He looked at me a long time. "You know what you're doing, don't you? Know that we trust you to shift by yourself. You don't need me."

I scowled. Maybe he just didn't get that I *wanted* to spend time with him. I liked having him running alongside me, flying above me. I liked when he threw me out of step, or tucked his wings and made me do the same, so we dropped through the air like missiles. When he heckled me and made me jump out of trees out of pure spite. When we splashed in streams, stayed out late and faced the wrath of Mom together. When we upset bee nests and had to run for our lives, when we wrestled and he let me win, and especially when he didn't.

"You're stronger than you think."

"I'm stronger than *you* think," I retorted. "Strong enough to keep up with you guys."

He laughed and stood up, pulling me with him. I hardly came to his chest. "I can't disagree. But this weekend is about Damien. Ray wants to test him a little."

I glanced at the truck; the back window was down, revealing a brooding Damien. He quickly looked away when I caught his eyes. "Can't you test me?"

Dad grabbed me by the shoulder and pulled me into him. "You don't need testing. I know just how strong you are."

The screen door opened and Mom and Ray came out. Mom

handed Dad his ugly green camping backpack and Ray carried *my* sleeping bag.

"Thanks for letting us borrow this, Jule," he said. "I don't know how that boy forgot his."

As he shuffled to the truck I hissed, "See? Damien doesn't even want to go. He left his *sleeping bag* at home."

Dad clamped a hand over my mouth and kissed Mom. "Love you, see you in a few days."

She hugged him, squishing me in the middle.

As I struggled against their embrace and tried to breathe, Dad rubbed my back with his heavy hand. "Be good, both of you."

This time, I don't leave my bed for two weeks. It took Kyle five days to get to his—our—clan and back to tell them that Dad is gone. That he had a girl. That we're coming home. It's going to be a big deal. Mom's relieved, but it makes me nauseous. What kind of resentment are we going to face? Will Mom's clan be able to look past her and Dad's desertion?

And the fact of Dad's death is bringing a bigger blow. Mom didn't have him cremated because she knew this might happen. Knew we'd go back eventually, or at least didn't give up hope that we would. His second funeral is going to hurt. Mom and I are going to have to relive the pain, this time with people who knew him and loved him. She's going to suffer alongside them, get lost in their ache. And I'm going to suffer alone, knowing a part of Dad is still out there, locked inside Damien.

Heavy feet climb the stairs. Kyle sounds so much like Dad when he moves through our house, like a ghost retracing its steps.

"How many more boxes, kid?" he asks, coming to a stop in my doorway.

I can't bring myself to ask him to stop calling me that. I'm sitting in the middle of my near empty room, Dad's box of skins in my lap, stacked on top of mine. Their whispers are the only things that calm me when my heart beats too fast to stop.

"Just a couple," I say.

"What do you got there?" His voice gets soft.

I look at the Viking brother. He takes up the whole door frame, but as he sets his eyes on Dad's box, he gets really small.

My grip on it tightens.

Enough of an answer for him, he squats, like his knees give out. "Are those Sam's?"

I nod.

He wants to reach for the furs, touch them, listen to them. But he doesn't. "Samuel will want to see those when we get back."

Samuel, my grandfather. Who Dad is named after. I can't picture my father as a junior.

Kyle reads my face, then straightens up. "What about that, then?"

I follow his gaze to the succulent on the windowsill. "It was a present."

"Keep it?"

I shake my head. "No. Let it die."

I help Kyle as best as I can haul down my last couple boxes of books. Mom's in the hallway, staring at our family portrait, the far-off look in her eyes. I know better, but Kyle stops to talk to her, and I continue outside.

"Jule said no more books," Freddie says, leaning against the U-Haul and smoking a joint.

"There's still room left. Might as well make the most of it." I shove the box into his arms, out of breath.

He gives me a dirty look but passes the joint and hoists himself into the truck.

The sun beats down on us in a goodbye-kind of way and I turn to the empty little house. The outside hasn't changed at all since we moved in. The pear tree might be a little bigger. The roof has more green moss covering it. Ivy's claimed most of one side. But the house itself is just the same. Once we leave, it'll be like we never came. The growing knot of fear and guilt tangles in my stomach; the lump that Damien shoved down my throat has made a home in my body.

I drop Freddie's joint and crush it into the grass. He hasn't let a cigarette go unsmoked, pill unswallowed, bottle go unfinished, since the day he said he loved me.

Mom's laugh rings out, and she and Kyle emerge, carrying the portrait.

My eye twitches. "I'll take that with me," I say as they near closer.

"Don't be ridiculous," Mom says. "It'll get ruined for sure in the bed of your truck. We'll cover it and put it in the U-Haul."

She sold the Honda, along with all our big furniture.

A rumbling comes up the driveway and the sight of Ro's truck makes Freddie swear from inside the moving van.

Ro parks haphazardly on the curb and jumps out, shirtless. "Where's the little shit?"

"Hello to you, too, Robert," Mom snaps.

"Oh, sorry, Jule. Hey, *Locklears*."

I flinch. My "real" last name sounds like canon fire every time someone says it; Mom and Dad both changed their last name when they left their clan, but I was born with Reed.

And I'm going to die with it.

"Good to see you," Kyle says smoothly eyes flickering to me for only a second. He likes Ro. Strapping young boy and all.

"Freddie's in the truck," I say, low.

Ro storms the van, and Mom and Kyle exchange glances before going to wrap up the photo.

"Think you could just leave without a goodbye?" he demands.

Freddie jumps down and shrugs at him in an irritated way. "Said bye to Nicole and Liam. You weren't home."

"What the hell, Freddie? I get that you're leaving, fine, but you weren't going to say anything to me, were you?"

"I don't know, alright?"

Ro gestures at the van. "All your shit is packed and it looks like you're ready to pull out."

"Can't you react to anything I do like a normal person for once in your fucking life? It's not a big deal." He looks at me, wanting support, but I just stare hard at him.

"Not a big deal? Did you not think I wanted to say goodbye? I don't know when I'll ever see you again." He glances at me for the briefest second.

Word of our family drama spread too fast. With Damien gone again, disappeared with the rogues, Ray and Mona broke. Proof of his new hobby of skinning people was confirmed with two of the rogues Kyle captured (neither of them Lark). And with Kyle and his men here, our origins no longer became a secret. We've been avoided like the plague; Ralph and Jessica still talk to us, but Ray's made it clear we're not welcome anywhere near the clan. Dad didn't just come upon Ruhn Roads by accident. He counted on the seclusion, Ray's strict ban on outsiders, and the small amount of skinwalkers.

I was beginning to feel like I really belonged. At least as much as I could have. Damien's plan went further than trying to integrate me into the clan—he was conditioning me to the idea in general. The idea of standing next to him as we raised the next generation of murderers. He'd hide behind my name and identity, use who I am to get people to believe in him, to follow him into the wilderness. A leader, through and through.

He gave me a taste of something I never knew I could have, something I don't know if I can ever get again. He ripped it out of me, just like he tore open my belly.

Freddie and Ro are glaring each other down, Ro waiting for a goodbye and Freddie waiting for an apology for not minding his own business.

Out of all the things Damien said to me that day, all his threats and gut wrenching confessions: *You love me, remember?* rings the loudest in my ears. It's the question I've never let myself answer, but the one he assumed.

So, do I love Damien?

Did I ever?

Did he love me?

Will he, as I rip his heart out and steal the life from him?

Wynter Cannatelli currently resides in Virginia with an Associates in Social Science—a practical degree to have when pursuing fiction writing. She loves to travel and knows the East Coast like the back of her hand. *Thick as Blood* is her first novel.

Printed in Germany
by Amazon Distribution
GmbH, Leipzig